Loved by a Dragon
Book II of The Dragon Archives

Linda K. Hopkins

LOVED BY A DRAGON

CHAPTER ONE

It was early winter, but already the weather was cold. Snow lay on the ground, and the rivers and lakes were covered in a thick layer of ice. Keira stood at the edge of the frozen river watching the five wolves on the opposite bank. She and Aaron, her husband of three months, had just been in the village, visiting her parents, but they had stopped in the forest before continuing their journey home to Storbrook. The wolves were huge; big gray beasts, with yellow eyes that stared at her alert and unblinking in the dull light of dusk. They watched her with an intense hunger, but made no move to cross the icy wasteland. At the front of the pack stood the alpha male, his posture tall and erect, while a smaller female stood at his side. They were gaunt, the deprivations of winter obvious in their dull coats. The male growled low, his eyes focused not on Keira, but on the creature that stood behind her. The breeze shifted slightly, blowing away from Keira and towards the wolves, and the ears of the male rose upright as he bared his teeth, his growl becoming louder. The female moved nervously at his side, her gaze intent on Keira, and after a moment she took a tentative step forward. The male's growls grew louder, but the she-wolf ignored him, moving cautiously across the ice.

Keira could feel the hot breath of the wild beast standing behind her, its hulking presence an impenetrable barrier to her escape. It was infinitely more dangerous than the wolves, but Keira felt no fear. Instead, her attention was completely focused on the small pack across the river, and she watched them curiously. The alpha male was watching the beast nervously, but the female, clearly not familiar with the threat, continued to pick her way across the ice. Keira was well aware of her precarious position – if the wolves managed to reach her, she could be ripped to shreds. But she knew that the beast behind her would attack the wolves before they got that close. The she-wolf was growing bolder, her tentative steps becoming more confident as she stood near the middle of the river, where a thin channel of water cut its way through the ice. A low growl rumbled through the air behind Keira, and the female paused, her eyes seeking out the threat as she sniffed the air. She glanced back at her mate, still standing on the riverbank, but before she had a chance to retreat, a burst of flame shot over Keira's head. The blaze caught the wolf's coat, and with a yelp she turned and ran, bounding between the other wolves and disappearing amongst the trees as the rest of the pack bolted after her.

"You set that wolf alight," Keira said, her eyes still on the retreating forms.

"Don't spare it too much pity," the dragon said. "It would have killed you if given a chance. Besides, it will soon seek relief in the cool snow, which will put out the flames."

Keira turned to look at the dragon. "Like other wild beasts, it was just looking to assuage its hunger."

"That is true," the dragon replied, "and if it had set its sights on any other creature in this forest, I would not have interfered. But it was hungering after you, my sweet, and that is quite unacceptable."

Keira smiled as she stretched out a hand to stroke the smooth scales on the dragon's neck. "I love you," she said.

The dragon smiled, revealing a mouth of sharp, pointed teeth. His scales glimmered and shone a pale gold in the dull light, while huge wings lay folded across his broad back. A tail, armed with fierce spikes, curled around his body, the tip stretching beyond where Keira stood and curling around her protectively. He bent his long neck, lowering his massive head with its sharp horns which stood stark against the light, and brought his eyes down to her level. They were blazing as brightly as the fire that had streamed from his mouth, and his breath was hot and musky. "And I love you, my beautiful wife."

CHAPTER TWO

Keira looked down at the list in front of her, tapping the shaft of her quill against the pot of ink. A streak of sunlight fell from the window across her shoulder, highlighting the rich chestnut browns of her hair. She adjusted the quill and added something more to the list, before setting the instrument back in its stand and nodding to herself. It was the season of Advent, and with the Christmas Feast Day fast approaching, Keira wanted to make sure nothing had been overlooked. The menus for the Christmas season had already been planned with Cook, while Thomas had been tasked with finding a troupe that would entertain the residents and guests at Storbrook Castle. It would not be a large gathering – Keira's family would be the only guests for the season – but it was the first time she would be celebrating the feast with Aaron, and she wanted everything to be perfect.

Keira smiled to herself as she leaned back in the chair, then jumped in surprise a moment later when a pair of warm hands descended lightly on her shoulders. She looked up with a smile into Aaron's tawny eyes as he stepped around the chair, his warm lips descending on hers for a quick kiss. When he pulled away a moment later, the color of his eyes had been swallowed up in a blaze of flames, reminding Keira that the man she had married was not like other men, for just beneath the surface of his human guise burned a creature of such strength and power that just the mention of the beast made people hide themselves in fear. The thought excited Keira, and she reached up to pull the beast back to her, opening her mouth to him as he responded hungrily. His hands were tangled in her hair when he pulled himself away with an audible intake of breath. He pushed himself upright and leaned his weight against Keira's desk.

"You seemed very intent in what you were doing."

"Just putting some finishing touches on my plans for Christmas," she said. "Thomas has found a troupe willing to risk their lives and provide entertainment at Storbrook." In fact, most people refused to venture anywhere near Storbrook Castle, where a dragon was rumored to have its lair. What they didn't know was that the dragon could disguise himself in human form, and often walked amongst them.

"Thomas is certainly resourceful," Aaron replied, "and seems to have no qualms about spending gold from the dragon's hoard. I wonder how much this entertainment is going to cost me." In Aaron's tone there was a grudging respect for his steward, one of the few people who knew the true identity of the dragon. Keira stood up and slipped her arms around Aaron's waist.

"Is the dragon really so miserly that he begrudges a few coins spent on the entertainment of his guests?" she asked. The dragon laughed, and pulled his wife hard against his firm body.

"The only thing the dragon truly treasures is you," he said, his eyes glowing as he kissed her. He pulled away a moment later, resting his forehead against hers.

"It looks like we'll have another guest for Christmas," he said, drawing away to look into her eyes.

"We will? Cathryn and Favian?"

"No. Max."

"Max? Who is Max?"

"Do you remember Beatrix and James?" he asked, and Keira nodded. Beatrix was Aaron's aunt, and she and her husband James had been at Keira and Aaron's blood-binding ceremony a few months before. "Do you remember me telling you that James had fathered two children before he met Beatrix?" Again Keira nodded. "Max is James's son. From what I've heard, he is earning quite a reputation in the city as a rake and a cad. It must run in his genes," Aaron added cynically. "Beatrix has asked me to send for him in the hopes I can convince him to give up his foolish ways."

Keira pulled herself out of Aaron's arms. "Can you?"

"I can only try. As Master, it falls to me to bring him into line."

"All right. So tell me about him. How old is he?"

"He's thirty-five, charming and handsome. Women adore him, his friends admire him, and his enemies, which includes most of the husbands in the city, are jealous of him. He treads a fine line between recklessness and caution, and it is amazing he hasn't spilled the secret of what he is over the whole city. Or maybe he has, but his friends have been too drunk to give it any attention," Aaron added dryly.

"So you think that being away from the city will help?"

"I'm not sure, but Beatrix thinks I will be able to influence him where others have failed."

"Why?"

Aaron turned away and stared out the window at the mountains surrounding Storbrook. "Because my own past has been rather checkered," he finally replied.

"Yes, but Aaron, you rejected humanity. You stayed away from people. You didn't drink and carouse with them."

"You are right, but only partly," Aaron said, turning around to face her. "For many years I did shun all humanity. But for a while, after Favian tracked me down and forced me into the human world, I went to the opposite extreme. Part of it was because I could – humans are attracted to dragons without knowing why. And part of it was to prove that I was right all along – that people are selfish and irresponsible, and that love makes you weak. I used people, and they allowed themselves to be used. I took advantage of all that the women had to offer, both giving and taking a momentary pleasure that their married lives did not afford." Aaron smiled grimly. "They loved me for it!"

Keira eyes widened and she drew in a steadying breath as he went on.

"I drank with their husbands, matching drink for drink, and they thought I was a great sport even though I trounced them at cards. And the women could not stay away from me – I could ask for anything and they were happy to give it. So you see, I know what Max is doing – I know how powerful and important it makes him feel, and I know how meaningless it all is." Keira took a step back, holding up her hand when Aaron moved towards her.

"I knew you had been with other women, Aaron, but married woman?" she said. "How many?"

"Keira, they did not mean anything to me. And I certainly didn't mean anything to them either."

"Really? Did you just sleep with them once, or did you have ongoing affairs?"

"Keira, please."

"Tell me, Aaron."

"Sometimes once or twice, other times more. But Keira, that's in the past. They meant nothing to me."

"But you still slept with them. How do I know that I'm not as meaningless to you as they were?"

"The fact that I married you should tell you that!" Aaron said sharply. He took a deep breath, and ran his fingers through his hair. "I love you, Keira," he said, his tone softening. He reached for her hands, grabbing them when she tried to move away, and took a step towards her.

"I cannot take back things I have done, as much as I may

wish to," he said. "But believe me when I say that you hold my heart, and there is no-one else I have ever loved as I love you."

Keira stared up at him, her mind spinning with these revelations, but when Aaron wrapped his arms around her, she let him to pull her close, resting her head against his chest. It stung a little, knowing there had been so many others before her, but she could not doubt the love he had for her. They stood in silence for a few moments until she finally pulled away.

"So you want to invite Max for Christmas?"

Aaron nodded. "But only if you are comfortable with him being here."

"What about Anna?"

Anna. The name hung between them as the memories of what had happened came rushing back. Anna had been abducted the previous autumn by Edmund, who had planned to kill her as revenge against Keira and Aaron. They had found the teenage girl before Edmund could carry out his threat, but ever since the attack she had become even more difficult and self-absorbed than she had been before.

"Anna is far too young and naive to interest a man like Max," Aaron said, "and Max is too worldly wise to allow a rude and distrustful girl like Anna to get under his skin. I would never do anything to place Anna in harm's way. I have failed her and your father once, but I will not do so again. However, I suspect she will ignore Max, and he will do the same."

"You are not responsible for what happened to Anna, Aaron. If it hadn't been for you, we would never have found her in time."

"If it hadn't been for me," Aaron responded wryly, "Edmund would never have turned his sights on her. It was my presence that flamed his jealousy for you, and when he turned his anger on Anna, it was only because you were beyond his reach."

Keira shook her head, knowing the futility of continuing the argument. "Go ahead and invite Max for Christmas," she said. "It will be nice to have more company over the festive season, and if he is as charming as you say, he will be a welcome diversion through the dreary months of winter."

CHAPTER THREE

Anna pulled her cloak tighter around her shoulders as she slipped out the side door and picked her way through the snow towards the distant corner of the gardens. The air was frigid, and she curled her hands into fists within her mittens in an effort to maintain the warmth in her fingers. Before her the gardens were covered in a shimmering blanket of silver-white, while behind her the pristine covering had been marred by the trail of her fur-lined feet pushing through the snow, a record of her passing. The trees had long since lost their leaves, and hoar frost clung to the bare branches, the delicate feathering sparkling in the weak rays of winter sun and presenting a stark contrast against the deep blue of the sky. Silence hung in the air, with just the faintest voice occasionally drifting on a wayward breeze from the direction of the towering heap of stone that formed the walls of Storbrook Castle. To Anna, the walls of Storbrook seemed at times to be more like a prison than a sanctuary, and it was at these times that she felt the need to escape the thick walls, dark passages, and smoky halls. Treading through the snow, she filled her lungs with the cold air, then released it slowly, watching as it hung in a small cloud for a moment before dissipating. Peace flooded her mind with each breath, blowing away the dark, depressing thoughts which so often plagued her.

There was a wooden bench in the far corner of the garden, and it was to this that Anna made her way. The seat of the bench was buried under three inches of snow, smooth and unspoiled until Anna swiped her hand through the thick powder and pushed it onto the ground below. She sat down cautiously – the seat of the bench was cold – before slowly relaxing against the backrest. At her approach, a robin had flown into the branches of a nearby tree, but after a few moments it fluttered back to the ground, foraging around the base of the tree as Anna watched. The winter sun was shining feebly on the glittering landscape, and she lifted her face so she could feel the warming rays on her cheeks. She closed her eyes and allowed the serenity of the moment to filter through her mind.

A shout in the distant courtyard startled her, nudging open the door that held back the memories of her abduction the previous autumn. They no longer had the power to terrify her, as they had at first, but they still managed to bring a mild sense of panic. She had been nothing more than a tool in Edmund's hands – an opportunity for him to exact his revenge against Keira for her rejection, and when Anna had stumbled across his path that fateful day, he had seen in her the means by which he could obtain his retribution. Anna no longer recalled the individual events of that terrible afternoon, at least not in her waking hours. The way he had dragged her, pulling her stumbling through the woods, was now just a blur, but she could not forget the terror of those hours. And although she could not recall the exact moment when Aaron had arrived, pulling Edmund from her, she remembered the flood of relief when she realized she was free from him, and that her persecutor was dead.

It had been Aaron who had saved her that day, but in the deep recesses of her mind Anna could not help blaming him and Keira for all that had happened. After all, it was Keira's rejection of Edmund that had made him focus on Anna. And surely Aaron should have realized her predicament sooner. If he had, she would not have suffered as much. And the blame didn't stop with Aaron and Keira. Perhaps if Father had spoken more forcefully against Edmund, once he realized Edmund's true character, events would have played out differently.

But it was Mother's actions that hurt the most. Long before he set his sights on Anna, Edmund had attacked Keira, but Mother had clung to the belief that the son of her dead friend was a man worth defending, even when it meant denying her own daughter. Perhaps if Mother had stood by Keira, Edmund would not have persisted in his belief that she belonged to him. And Mother still did not know how evil Edmund truly was. Father had chosen to protect her by keeping her in ignorance of the terrible events that had affected Anna so deeply, and so she knew nothing about Edmund's plan to kill her daughter. Father knew Mother would be devastated that the son of her closest friend could have done such terrible things. Edmund's mother had died years earlier, but as she lay on her death bed, Mary had begged Mother to watch over her boys. Anna guessed that if Mother admitted Edmund's true character, she would feel that she had failed her friend. Her thoughts returned to the attack, and she shivered slightly. She had not forgotten the feeling of helplessness she had felt when Edmund had taken her; the surety that she was going to die, and there was nothing she could do about it. She never wanted to feel that helpless again. Never wanted to find herself at the mercy of a man again.

Anna clenched her teeth, grinding them together in annoyance at where her thoughts were leading her. All this reflective thinking was making her miserable once more, and Anna was sick and tired of feeling miserable. She wanted to leave all of this behind her, but where could she go? She knew she could never go back to life in her little village. She had outgrown it, somehow. The girls she had grown up with seemed silly and immature now, thinking only about boys, marriage, and children.

If she was honest with herself, Anna had to admit that in unguarded moments she wondered what it would be like to be in love. To have a man love you the way Aaron loved Keira. But then she would remember how it was the actions of a man that had made her suffer so much, and she would push the thoughts away. There was no point chasing after a rainbow that only promised an illusion of happiness. She would never be able to trust a man enough to spend the rest of her life with him. She would rather remain a spinster forever. When she had told Keira, her sister was horrified.

"But Anna," she had remonstrated, "you cannot measure the behavior of all men against that of Edmund. His actions were not the norm, and he received his just desserts for his behavior."

"Are you so sure?" Anna had retorted. "What about Widower Brown? Some say he murdered his last wife, although I'm not sure how he managed that since he is barely ever sober. And Gwyn's father beats her mother."

"Yes, but look at Father," Keira pointed out. "He has never raised an angry hand to Mother, and Aaron would never hurt me."

"Two, Keira!" Anna had shot back. "You can only name two worthy men! And Aaron doesn't count! So one man. That is hardly a glowing recommendation!"

"There are plenty of others, Anna," Keira had argued, but Anna remained unconvinced.

"Maybe there are, Keira, but I would prefer not to risk my future happiness on that chance."

Anna shivered again as a slight breeze ruffled her hair. Although it was still early afternoon, the sun was already dropping towards the western horizon, giving way in defeat to the long winter night that followed closely on its heels.

Her toes were starting to feel numb through the thick fur-lined boots that wrapped around her feet, and she wiggled them against their confines to get the blood moving once again. Pushing herself up from the bench, she retraced her footsteps, the light glowing in the windows of the castle a beacon that promised a warm fire to chase away the chill.

CHAPTER FOUR

It was a clear winter's day one week later when Keira left the confines of Storbrook, venturing past the castle walls into the snowy landscape beyond. She had convinced Anna to join her as she went in search of boughs of greenery to decorate the castle for the coming season of Christmastide. They were accompanied by Garrick, Cook's nephew, who lived at Storbrook, helping around in the yard or stable as needed. At sixteen he was a tall lad, but the lack of weight on his gangly frame reminded Keira of an ungainly colt. His sandy hair was cropped short, while his nose and cheeks were scattered with freckles. He didn't say much, but he had a quick and easy smile that crinkled his blue eyes at the corners.

Garrick walked apace with the two women, guiding the large, bad-tempered mule that pulled a small sleigh behind it. Keira noticed that Garrick often glanced their way, his eyes falling on Anna as she trudged through the snow which reached almost to their knees, sometimes spilling over the tops of their boots as they hitched up their skirts.

They had entered the forest when a flash of red caught Keira's eye, and she pushed aside some branches to see crimson berries, their color bright against the virgin snow on the ground. Waxy leaves of green protected the berries with sharp thorns, and edging closer through the deep drifts, Keira leaned forward to grab the branch. A tall tree stood sentinel over the holly, its thick branches laden with snow, and as she pushed past a branch that stood between her and her goal, the snow slipped off the needles and landed on Keira's head, covering her neck and shoulders as it slid beneath the neckline of her gown. She shrieked, jerking around in sudden shock, causing more snow to dislodge and fall over her, where it settled around her legs. Anna let out a whoop of laughter, stumbling backwards when Keira narrowed her eyes. Garrick turned away, his shoulders shaking with silent laughter, as Keira gathered a handful of snow, and pressing it into a ball, threw it at her sister.

The snow splatted against Anna's chest as Keira lobbed another snowball, this time hitting the unsuspecting Garrick squarely between the shoulders. Keira laughed and he spun around, staring at her in shock; but when another scoop of snow from Keira splattered over his face, he gathered a handful of the white powder, bent on revenge. Laughter rang through the forest as snow sparkled in the air like fairy dust, covering the three players in a fine sprinkling of white that quickly melted into small droplets of water against their hair and cheeks, until finally Keira held her hands up in surrender.

"Stop," she gasped, "enough." Another ball of snow thumped her on the shoulder, and she sank to the ground, laughing, and the other two quickly followed suit. A shadow passed overhead, and Keira glanced up to see the form of a dragon high in the sky. As it circled around them, Keira squinted into the sunlight to try and make out the color, but the creature was silhouetted against the light, and she finally gave up the attempt. Her attention was called back to her companions when Anna's voice broke the silence.

"Careful, you fool! You're going to do me an injury!"

Keira looked up to see Garrick glaring at Anna, a pair of shears in his hand.

"You shouldn't have moved," he said.

"And you should have been more careful!" she retorted.

"Children, please," Keira said, holding up her hands, grinning when they both turned to glare at her. Garrick quickly dropped his gaze with a mumbled apology, but Anna continued to glare at her sister for another moment, finally turning away in a half-hearted huff.

"Garrick, can you cut that pine branch?" Keira said, pointing to the once snow laden bough. "And also some branches of holly." She directed Garrick to the branches and stems she deemed suitable for her purposes, with Anna soon joining in as she added her own opinion on which specimens were the best, and by the time they were done, the sleigh was a jumble of greenery, with crimson berries breaking the sea of green.

"Perfect!" Keira said, surveying Garrick's handiwork, before turning to her sister. Anna's cheeks were red from cold and laughter, and strands of hair that had worked loose from her braids framed her face. Her eyes were sparkling, and it occurred to Keira that she had not seen her young sister so happy in a long time. She linked her arm into Anna's, and turned in the direction of Storbrook.

"Are you going to help me decorate?" she asked.

"Definitely not!" Anna replied. "I'm going to go find a warm fire and thaw out my toes."

"Come on," Keira coaxed, "it will be fun. You'll start to feel warmer as soon as we're back inside."

"In that heap of stone? The only place that is warm is directly before a fire!"

"I'll send for a nice, warm cup of mulled wine," Keira promised.

Anna sighed. "Fine," she said, "but it better be warm. And one cup might not be enough!"

The three were shivering by the time they reached the gates of Storbrook, their clothes stiff with cold.

"Go change into something warmer," Keira said to Anna, "and I'll meet you in the solar."

Anna nodded as Keira turned to Garrick, instructing him to carry the branches to the hall.

"Yes, Mistress." Garrick turned away, leading the mule across the courtyard.

Keira pulled her cloak closer around her as she headed for the doors that opened into the low hall, quickly crossing the floor and mounting the stairs that led to the top of the castle and the chambers she shared with her husband. She could hear voices as she passed the second landing, and remembering the dragon she had seen flying overhead, she hurried on, anxious to remove her damp clothes and make herself presentable. She had just finished twisting her hair into a neat braid when a knock sounded on the door, with a message from Aaron to join him in the solar.

When Keira pushed open the door to the private sitting room a short while later, she was not surprised to see a second person in the room with Aaron. The newcomer looked to be in his early twenties, although Keira knew he was at least a dozen years older. Thick, brown hair curled loosely around his face, while dark gray eyes regarded her curiously. Aaron rose to his feet and crossed over to her.

"You're cold," he said, rubbing her hands between his heated ones.

"Anna and I were collecting greenery in the woods," she explained. "If you think my hands are cold, you should feel my feet."

Aaron grinned and leaned towards her, his mouth close to her ear as he whispered huskily. "I look forward to warming not just your feet, my sweet, but we will have to wait until later. Right now we have a visitor."

At his words the color sprang into Keira's cheeks, and she threw a quick glance at their guest – then hurriedly looked away, her heart sinking. The amused grin that he wore confirmed her suspicions that he had heard their exchange.

"Keira, this is Max," Aaron said, and the man rose to his feet. Gaining mastery over her emotions, Keira turned and met his amused gaze steadily.

"Madame Drake," Max said, executing a neat bow. "I am glad to make your acquaintance. Please accept my humblest apologies for not attending the celebration of your blood binding, but unfortunately I was detained by, um, unforeseeable events." Keira glanced at Aaron during this speech, to see him looking at Max with a quizzical expression.

"Very nice, Max," Aaron said. "Do I dare enquire what, or who, took precedence over your Master?"

Max flashed Aaron a grin. "That would be telling, Master," he said as Aaron snorted in response. Max turned back to Keira.

"Thank you for inviting me to celebrate the feast of Christmastide with you. I look forward to the pleasure of your company. And," he threw Aaron a sly look, "Aaron's too, of course."

"You are most welcome to Storbrook," Keira said with a smile, turning to seat herself near the fire. "Was that you I saw earlier on?" she asked as Max took the seat opposite the door.

"When you were playing in the snow?" Max said with a laugh. "Yes, that was me. Who were your companions?"

"My sister Anna and Cook's nephew, Garrick. We were collecting greenery to decorate the castle."

"Ah! And your sister is also visiting for the feast?"

"No, she lives here at Storbrook."

"Oh?" Max threw a surprised look at Aaron.

"Yes, she knows what I am," Aaron said. "It doesn't matter how she came by this knowledge, but since then she has been cruelly mistreated by a young man who wanted to harm her. She has lived with us since that time. She is young, just seventeen," he added, his gaze intent on Max, "so I know you won't show her the slightest attention beyond that which you would show any young relative."

"Of course not," said Max, returning Aaron's look with a cynical smile. The two men gazed at each for a moment, until Aaron finally nodded.

"Good. Keira, my sweet, will you please pour us some wine?"

CHAPTER FIVE

Anna walked quickly along the cold passages of the stone castle, eager to reach her chambers where a fire would be blazing. But despite the cold, she felt more invigorated and alive than she had in a long time. For a moment, all her cares had been forgotten as she rolled clumps of snow in gloved hands and threw them at Keira and Garrick. She had seen the shock in Garrick's face when Keira threw the first snowball, but it had only taken a moment for him to lose his inhibitions around his Lady, returning as many volleys as he received. Anna had noticed Garrick watching her, and she knew that he liked her. It amused her to think that she had an admirer, although Garrick was just a boy, even younger than herself. Certainly not someone to be mistrustful around, with his boyish looks and ungainly limbs.

Anna pushed open the door to her chambers, grateful to feel the warmth that had spread from the blazing hearth. A fur pelt lay on the floor beside her bed, and pulling off her damp boots and stockings, Anna sunk her toes into the thick pile with a sigh of pleasure. Plucking the ties of her gown free, she slid the wet garment off her shoulders, allowing it to fall in a heap around her ankles. The damp had also soaked through her chemise, and she went to stand in front of the fire, turning slowly in an effort to dry the thin garment. Her hair had started coming loose from her braid, and tugging the ribbons free, she used her fingers as a comb to separate the damp strands, reluctant to leave the warmth of the fire to fetch the hairbrush beside her bed.

She had warmed up slightly when she finally moved away from the flames and headed over to the large chest that stood in the corner of the room, in which her gowns were neatly folded. A pink gown of fine wool lay near the top of the chest, and she pulled it out quickly, before hurrying back to the fire and pulling the garment over her head. The cloth was cold after being in the chest, and she shivered as it settled over her frame. A pair of slippers had been placed near the fire, and she pulled these onto her bare feet, grateful that they were a little warmer than the gown had been. With deft movements she twisted her hair into a braid and secured it once more with a ribbon, before leaving the room and heading in the direction of the solar.

As she neared the room, she could hear Aaron and Keira's voices through the door, but a third voice made her pause. It belonged to a man, but not Thomas. A visitor, maybe? The door was slightly ajar, and pushing it open, she entered the room, pausing once more when she saw the stranger sitting in a chair directly across from the doorway. She barely heard Aaron speaking as she stared at the man slowly rising to his feet, his gaze locked on hers. A slight smile played around his mouth, while his eyes held a challenge that Anna could not decipher. Perhaps it was the bold stare, or the challenging smile, or the graceful way he pulled himself up to his full height, but whatever it was, a wave of dislike for this stranger swept over her. She stared back at him, her eyes narrowing as his smile grew wider, taunting her, as though he were fully aware of the immediate, intense and irrational reaction towards him. The smile was meant just for her, she knew that straight away, a silent communication between them, and she disliked him even more for it. And she knew, with unerring instinct, that despite his appearance of youth, this was no inexperienced boy who could easily be dismissed. This person standing before her was the fulfillment of her deepest fears. A man who could easily gain mastery and control over any woman he chose. This knowledge was based on intuition, rather than rational thought – all she knew in that moment was that she hated him.

As though speaking from far away, Aaron's voice addressed her.

"Anna, this is Max."

"Max?" With an effort Anna pulled her gaze away from the man standing before her, but not before she saw his lips twist with arrogant humor.

"Yes. Max Brant. He will be staying at Storbrook as our guest."

"I see." Anna nodded as she turned back to the guest. "Max."

"Anna." He was still staring at her, and she dragged her eyes away, biting her lip. Her name rolled off his tongue with an air of familiarity which she immediately resented, but before she could think of an adequate retort, he was speaking again. "I saw you playing in the snow earlier today," he said. His words made her glance back at him. Was he laughing at her?

"Yes," she said. She sat down near Keira, who was watching their exchange in silence.

"You looked like you were having fun." This time she met his gaze with narrowed eyes. He was definitely taunting her.

"Tell me," she said, "how long will you be visiting Storbrook?"

Once again Max grinned at her, but it was Aaron who answered.

"As long as he wishes."

"I see." Anna turned to Keira. "When do you wish to start

decorating?" she asked. But before Keira could respond, Max was speaking again.

"Why do I get the feeling you wish me gone, Anna?" he asked. Out the corner of her eye, Anna could see both Keira and Aaron look at Max in surprise.

"I have no idea," she said. "Just stay well away from me, and I'm sure we will get along famously!"

Beside her Keira gasped softly.

Max's smile widened. "Well, that shouldn't be a problem. I have no desire to keep company with a shrew!"

Flushing with indignation, Anna leaped to her feet. "And I don't fancy being burned by a dragon!"

With one swift step, Max closed the distance between them. "Perhaps, darling," he said, "a little burning is exactly what you need! You might even enjoy it!"

There was a resounding slap as Anna's hand connected with Max's cheek. He didn't move, but his expression turned mocking.

"Is that all you've got?"

Anna gasped, and spinning on her heel, stomped away. She had only gone a few steps when she paused, then stalking back to Max, poked her finger into his chest.

"Don't ever call me 'darling' again," she ground out, before turning once more and marching out of the room. Her legs were trembling as she walked, while her hands shook with rage. The arrogance! The insolence!

Aaron's voice rang from the room, his words making Anna stop in the passage to listen. "Max! Just what game do you think you're playing?"

"Do you always allow your guests to be treated with such rudeness?" she heard Max respond.

"She's a young girl, and you certainly played your part in provoking her," Aaron said.

"That is no young girl," Max said. "That is a young woman who needs to grow up."

Anna turned away with a scowl and stalked down the

passage in the direction of her room.

She hastened her flight when she heard footsteps behind her, and the sound of Keira calling her name. She was already at her chambers when Keira caught up.

"Anna! Just what do you think you are doing? How can you be so rude?"

"Me, rude? Did you hear how he was talking to me? That is the most arrogant, conceited man I have ever met!"

"Max is here as our guest and is a member of Aaron's clan. No matter how he provokes you, you need to treat him with courtesy. You cannot allow him to goad you into unwomanly behavior, Anna."

"Fine," Anna snapped, before closing the door in Keira's face. After a few moments, she heard Keira's footsteps fade away, and she sunk down on her bed. There was no excuse for her behavior, and she was completely mortified. It was no wonder that Aaron considered her a child when she could not even control her reaction to a stranger. But just the remembrance of his cool arrogance and mocking smile had her grinding her teeth in annoyance. Somehow, she had to remain civil to this rude stranger, but for the life of her, she had no idea how.

CHAPTER SIX

Keira made her way slowly back to the solar, wondering at Anna's response to Max. Anna could be hot-headed and immature at times, but this had been ridiculous. As she approached the room, Keira could hear Aaron and Max talking, but the conversation ceased as she crossed the threshold. Max rose and walked over to where she stood.

"My apologies, Mistress Keira," he said with an abashed look. "It was my provocation that caused your sister to act as she did."

"Thank you," Keira said, "but Anna's behavior was inexcusable. I trust she will behave with more decorum in future."

"Oh, I don't know," Max replied with a grin. "Decorum might be rather dull after that spirited performance."

"Max," Aaron said warningly, and Max threw him an amused grin.

"But I know my boundaries."

Supper was served soon after, with Anna seated at the opposite end of the table to Max. The main table, where the master of the estate sat with his wife and guests, was placed on a raised dais at the end of the great hall, overlooking the benches where the servants ate their meal. An occasional laugh or shout rang through the hall over the friendly babble of conversation, but at the main table, Anna sat stiff and silent. After a few attempts at conversation, Keira turned away, ignoring her sister as she leaned forward to talk to Thomas and Max.

A fiddle was produced by one of the servants when the meal was done, and the benches were pushed to the walls as the diners rose, eager for an impromptu dance, each grabbing the hand of a partner as a circle was formed. Aaron pulled Keira to her feet and led her into the dance, his hand warm around hers. As they swung around the room, Keira saw Garrick approach Anna, and a moment later, she was being led into the circle, laughing and smiling. Max was left alone at the table, but he did not seem perturbed, and after throwing back the contents of his cup, he rose and interposed himself between two serving maids, who giggled, blushing, as he took their hands.

A few dances later the fiddle was put away, and the servants laughingly cleared the halls of the remnants of supper and turned to their last duties of the evening. Anna had already slipped from the room, and Keira wished Max a goodnight before leaving the hall, Aaron close on her heels.

"Do you think Max will behave himself?" Keira asked as they entered their chambers.

Aaron shrugged. "He knows he will earn my displeasure if he doesn't."

"I wish your displeasure meant as much to Anna," Keira said with a sigh. "I cannot believe how rude she was!"

"She's young. But Max is right – she's no longer a child, but a young woman. Perhaps Max being around will help her grow up."

"You're not suggesting that Max –"

"Of course not. But unless she wants to remain in her chambers every day, she will have to learn some restraint and manners in Max's presence."

"Well I hope Max can show some restraint as well," Keira retorted. "He should not have provoked her the way he did."

"No, he shouldn't have. But he knows that, and I believe he will be more cautious in her presence."

"My parents arrive tomorrow. Maybe that will help."

"Tomorrow? Then we had better make good use of these few remaining hours before they arrive." Aaron took a step towards her, his tawny eyes starting to glow slightly. "Of course, there are plenty of places in this pile of stone where we can hide away from prying eyes. A dragon always manages to find a place where he can devour his beautiful victims."

"Victims?" Keira said, meeting his gaze in amusement. "And just how many victims do dragons usually hide away?" Aaron bent his head closer to hers.

"It depends on the dragon, my sweet, but in this case the answer is only one!"

Keira and Anna spent the following morning decorating the castle with the greenery they had collected the previous day, filling the halls and chambers with the fresh scent of pine as they waited for their parents, Richard and Jenny, to arrive. It was a thirty-mile journey on horseback through the mountains, and the light was already failing by the time they reached Storbrook.

A light meal soon revived them, and they sat with Keira and Aaron in the solar, where the light of a roaring fire flickered against the stone walls. Anna had also joined the little party, but of Max there was no sign.

"How are your wounds, Father?" Keira asked. Richard had been accidentally injured a few months earlier when a group of villagers attempted to draw out and kill the dragon. The wounds had been the inadvertent result of a villager, not the dragon, and although the injuries were near-fatal, dragon blood had worked wonders in healing the wounded man.

"Completely recovered!" Richard replied. "I owe the dragon my life, and will forever remain in his debt." He glanced at Aaron as he said the words, but Aaron was already shaking his head.

"You owe the dragon nothing," he said, his voice low. "If anything, the dragon failed you by failing to protect your daughter!"

Richard leaned forward, his reply just as low as he met Aaron's gaze. "A dragon is not omniscient, son. You did what you could, and for that I am grateful!"

"How is the reeve?" Keira asked, her voice pulling the two men from their low intercourse. The door of the solar opened, admitting a maid from the kitchen, a tray of sweetmeats weighing down her arms, which she carefully placed on the table before leaving the room.

"He's recovering slowly," Richard replied, "but the nature of his injuries means he will no longer be able to serve as reeve. Lord Warren will appoint someone else in the coming months. In the meantime, Edmund is still missing, and the reeve fears his son is dead." Keira swapped a quick glance with Aaron as she remembered Edmund's last few moments on earth. He had been killed by the dragon after kidnapping Anna and threatening her life, and the dragon had ensured that there were no remains to be found.

"It's very sad," Jenny said from the cushioned bench where she sat. "You know, his mother, Mary, and I were best friends when she was alive. I'm sure Edmund would have turned out to be quite a fine young man. After all, his mother was such a wonderful woman. So gentle and sweet. Edmund may have made some mistakes, but he was his mother's son." Keira and Anna both stared at Jenny in disbelief as she made this speech. Although she had no knowledge of what Edmund had done to Anna the night he died, all indications were that he had taken after his father, who was cruel and proud, rather than his mother. Keira opened her mouth to protest, but Aaron grabbed her hand as both he and Richard shook their heads to silence her. Keira slid a glance over to her sister, but Anna seemed intent on examining her feet, her brows drawn together in a scowl.

"Did you hear that some in the village want your father to become the new reeve?" Jenny continued, oblivious to the heightened tension in the room.

"No," Aaron said, glancing at Richard. "I think you would make a splendid reeve. Do you have the favor of Warren?" Although the reeve served the people in the village, it was as the representative of the lord, and it was he who made the appointment.

"The freemen of the village sent a delegation to His Lordship advocating my appointment, and I believe he will give their proposal due consideration," Richard said.

"Excellent."

Jenny turned her attention to her daughter. "Keira, I understand that you have a visitor here at Storbrook."

"Yes," Keira replied. "Where did you hear that?"

"Jane Tanner told me. She met him at market."

Next to her Anna harrumphed. "Probably strutting through the village, making sure everyone takes notice," she mumbled beneath her breath.

"What's that, dear?" Jenny asked, but Keira quickly responded before Anna could say anymore.

"Yes, Mother. Max is a distant relative of Aaron's, and he is staying at Storbrook for the present time."

"Really? And how old is he?" she asked, casting a quick glance in Anna's direction.

"Oh, um … Aaron?" Keira turned to look at him.

"I believe he will be joining us any moment, so you can ask him yourself," Aaron said with a grin. Sure enough, the door to the solar opened as the man in question entered the room, and all eyes turned to look at him. Scooting forward in her chair, Anna straightened her back and lifted her chin, refusing to meet his gaze, which traveled around the room to take in the other occupants.

"Aaron, Keira, I see you have guests," Max said.

"Max, these are my parents, Master and Madame Carver.

They will be staying at Storbrook during Christmastide."

"I am very pleased to make your acquaintance, Madame Carver," he said with a smile at Jenny. He turned to Richard. "Master Carver, I believe I saw some of your wares when I stopped at the village market yesterday on my way to Storbrook. I'm sure we will share a very merry Christmas season together. I understand that Keira has organized some wonderful entertainments for her guests. I'm sure," he added, turning to Anna, "you will enjoy that, Anna. You seem like someone who enjoys entertainments."

"Certainly," Anna said, "when in the midst of genteel company." Max bowed his head with a mocking smile as Jenny interjected.

"What could be more genteel than the company of family, Anna? And being the only child in our midst, you are bound to enjoy all the distractions that Keira has to offer."

Anna's lips thinned, but she remained silent as she glared at her hands.

Max helped himself to a sweetmeat on the tray, before taking a seat across from Keira. "What entertainment do you have planned for us, tonight, Keira?"

"Since my parents are weary from their travels, I thought we could pursue a more sedate activity." Reaching down, Keira produced a book from beneath her seat. "How about a story?" she said, carefully holding up the precious volume.

"What story?" Anna asked, leaning forward to see the leather-bound manuscript.

"*Guy of Warwick*," Keira said with a grin in Aaron's direction as he raised his eyebrows at her.

"I've heard of it," Jenny said. "What is it about?"

"Guy of Warwick has to prove his worth in order to marry the woman he loves," she explained. "To do this, he battles all kinds of horrible and fantastic creatures, like huge boars, giants, and dragons."

"He kills dragons?" Anna said with a glance at Max. "It sounds like a fantastic story! Who is going to read for us?"

"Max," Keira said, holding the book in his direction, "would you do us the honors? I am quite convinced you would be an excellent reader." With a grimace in Aaron's direction, Max took the proffered volume, and opening it to the first page, started to read.

Anna watched Max closely as he read. He had only delivered a few sentences when he stopped, demanding a drink before continuing. Anna tucked her legs beneath her as she waited, curling her toes to keep them warm. She cradled a goblet of wine in her hand as she listened to the flow of Max's voice.

> *Valiant he was, sooth to say*
> *And earned great prizes in every play*
> *As a knight of great valor.*
> *Out of this land he went his way*
> *Through many diverse country*
> *Beyond the sea.*

Max's voice was soft and lyrical, and she found herself falling under the spell woven by his voice and the adventures of Guy of Warwick. She rejoiced when he returned home to marry the woman he loved, and mourned when he left her to live life as a hermit, unable to carry the weight of his violent past. By the time the story was finished, the fire was low, and the mood had become reflective. Max gently closed the book and laid it down on a small table, his eyes catching Anna's as he glanced around the room. She looked away, allowing her gaze to rest on Keira, curled up in Aaron's arms. Keira turned to Max with a smile.

"That was wonderful. Thank you, Max. And I was right, you do have a wonderful reading voice." She glanced around the room. "I believe I am ready to retire, so if you will excuse me —"

"We will retire as well," Richard said. "It has been a long day, and I think we are both ready to sleep." He glanced at

Jenny as he spoke, and she nodded, rising to her feet.

"Yes, goodnight," she said.

As the couples exited the room, Anna hastily rose.

"Afraid to be alone with me?" Max said as she placed her cup on the table.

"Certainly not," she retorted. "However, I prefer my own company to that of rogues such as yourself."

"Rogue, am I?" He laughed. "I give you leave to retire so you can think of all the nasty names to call me. Of course, it will just reinforce my opinion that you are not only a shrew, but a spoiled brat as well." Anna glared at him for a moment before lifting her chin in the air.

"I do not need your leave to retire, Master Brant. And I will not wish you a good night. I hope you have a dreadful night, with horrible dreams and rats running over your toes." And with as much dignity as she could muster, she turned and swept out of the room, Max's soft laugh following her down the passage.

CHAPTER SEVEN

Keira shivered. It was the first day of Christmastide, and the bed was cold. She reached out to find her usual source of heat, but Aaron was not there. Eyes springing open she glanced around the room, then smiled when she saw Aaron standing at the huge, open window, gazing out at the surrounding mountain ranges.

"Morning," she said sleepily. Aaron turned and walked over to the bed, sliding down next to her and pulling her close. She snuggled against his chest, immediately feeling far warmer.

"Good morning, my sweet."

"What were you doing?"

"Just watching the sunrise. The light was catching the snow, and it looked beautiful." He smiled. "Not as beautiful as you, but lovely nonetheless. Let's go for a flight before we join the rest of the household."

Keira nodded. "Give me a moment to dress in something warmer," she said as she rose from the bed and headed towards the small antechamber.

A few moments later she was on Aaron's broad, scaly back as he launched himself out the window. His hard scales were warm, and Keira leaned forward and wrapped her arms around his neck as her hair and cloak streamed out behind her. The sun had not completely risen over the mountains, and the early morning light stained the white snow of the mountain peaks a delicate shade of pink. She turned to look at Aaron's wings, spread wide behind her, and blinked when the sun glanced across their golden surface, sending bright rays scattering into the surrounding air. The wings were massive, stretching at least twelve feet on either side of him, while behind him streamed his tail, sharp spikes standing at attention along the thick, scaly length. She turned back to his neck as a stream of flame curled from his mouth, quickly dissipating in the cold air. He was starting to lose height, and Keira glanced down to see the river curling below them. Where the river curved in a sharp bend, the ground beside it was bare of snow, and it was here that Aaron gracefully landed. He waited for Keira to slide off his back before transforming to his human form in a flash of light that flared for a moment before collapsing back into solid form. His arms wrapped around her, pulling her against his chest.

"I love you, Keira," he whispered.

His body was bare against hers, but she knew that he did not feel the cold. She pulled away slightly and turned to look at the river. The ice stretched across the surface, cold fingers gripping the edges of rocks and limp reeds. In the summer, this place where the river changed its course was a deep pool of calm water, just beyond the reach of the raging river. She had been here with Aaron before the cold had come, and knew that the water was deep.

"The one thing I miss most about summer," Keira said slowly, "is being able to go swimming."

"In a few short months it will be summer again," he said, with the infuriating practicality of a man who had seen many, many summers. "We can go swimming together," he added softly, his warm breath brushing against her cheek.

"But I don't want to wait," she said, looking up and

meeting his gaze. "In fact, I want to go swimming right now."

Aaron frowned at her in confusion. "I'm sure you do, but you cannot survive the cold, my sweet."

"Hmm," said Keira, stepping away from him. "The cold. That is a problem." She pulled on the tie of her cloak, releasing the knot, and it fell to her feet.

"Keira. What are you doing?" Aaron's voice was sharper, but she laughed, taking another step back.

"I'm going for a swim, Aaron. Are you going to join me?"

"You cannot go swimming," he repeated. She could hear the worry in his voice, and she sighed.

"I won't get cold, Aaron. You will keep me warm."

"But the water –" Aaron began, before stopping and staring at her. "That is an insane idea," he said, a grin started to tug at his mouth. She dropped her gown to her feet and stared at him as she shivered in her chemise.

"Better hurry, Aaron. I'm starting to get cold."

Keira smiled as a flash of light filled the air, and the huge dragon stepped cautiously onto the ice.

"Are you sure you want to do this?" he asked as Keira pulled off her chemise and held it against her chest. Already the ice was starting to melt around him, pooling at his claws. He opened his wings as it grew thinner, spreading them as he breathed flame onto the melting surface. A small hole appeared where he breathed, growing larger as he applied more flames to the spot. All around him the water was starting to steam, and then, with a sudden groan, the rest of the ice gave way beneath Aaron's weight, and he launched himself into the air. He transformed into human form midair, and landed next to Keira, his wings still spread behind him.

"Take off your boots," he said. Gingerly, she pulled off one boot, and then standing on her toes, quickly removed the other, hopping on the ice as she did so. As soon as her footwear was off he grabbed her against his chest, lifting them into the air then dropping them both into the icy water. She gasped, then grinned as his body heat quickly warmed the water around them, creating a cloud of steam. Holding his hand, she pushed herself away, moving unhurriedly through the water. It was colder the further away she moved, and she turned, pulling herself slowly back to his heat. Wrapping her legs around him, she pulled him close as his hands wound into her steam-damp hair. His mouth found hers and he kissed her leisurely. His legs supported her as his hands brushed over her skin, slow and languorous. She clung to him, feeling his bare skin press against hers, and when he claimed her, he covered her mouth with his, swallowing her gasp.

The sun had climbed high above the mountains when Aaron lifted Keira from the water. She shivered as the cold air touched her skin, but he held her close, running his hands over her body, the steam rising from her skin where he touched her. He held her chemise in his hands, warming the fabric, before gently tugging it over her head, and then did the same with her gown. His feet were too big to warm her boots, but he wiggled his fingers to the bottom before pulling them onto her feet, while she steadied herself against his shoulder.

He wrapped his arms around her and ran his hands through her wet hair. She stared into his burning eyes, and when he bent down and brushed his lips against hers, she knew that she would never be happier, more content, than she was at that moment. She loved him and he loved her, and there was nothing else.

CHAPTER EIGHT

Anna lay in her bed, the quilts pulled up to her chin. The sun was already well above the horizon, and weak rays of light were finding their way through the slats of the shutters. It had been long past midnight when she retired to bed, following the midnight mass in the small chapel at the edge of the courtyard. The troupe would be arriving today, and Anna smiled as she thought of the entertainments they would offer. The smile quickly turned to a frown, however, as she remembered the mortification of Mother calling her a child in front of Max. If only he wasn't here, then everything would be perfect.

Pushing away the quilts, Anna rose from the bed, and flinging a cloak around her shoulders, crossed to the window and opened the shutters to allow the light into the room. Her chamber was on the floor below the master chambers, and was situated at the end of the eastern wing. Windows on adjacent walls gave her panoramic views of the mountains to the east, south and west, filling the chamber with light throughout the day. The sun spilled in as she opened the shutters, and she leaned out to breathe in the bracing air. In the distance she could see a shape moving through the sky, but it was too far away to tell whether it was a bird or a dragon. She watched it for a moment before turning to open the shutters on the adjacent walls. The creature was circling in the distance, and she could see it from the south-facing window as well. It had drawn closer, and she knew it was a dragon, but it was not gold like Aaron. This dragon was darker, and she realized that it must be Max. She had not seen him in his dragon form before, and her eyes followed him as he lazily circled through the air. The sun glittered against his wings, and he blew out a stream of flame which curled around his head like a smoke ring. He was quite spectacular to watch, she thought, but only as a dragon.

A gust of cold air rushed through the room, ruffling her hair, and she saw him lift his head and then turn in her direction. She pulled herself away from the window, pushing herself against the wall, but when she peeked around the corner, she saw that he was flying straight towards her window. She pulled back again, not daring to breathe, her heart sinking when she heard his voice.

"It's a lovely morning, Anna. Why don't you come to the window and enjoy it?"

"Go away," she said.

"Are you scared of me?" he asked.

"Of course not!" She drew in a deep breath and turned towards the window, stifling the gasp that almost escaped when she saw the massive dragon hovering only a few feet away. His wings moved slowly through the air, while his scales glittered in the sunlight, throwing reflections against the walls. "What are you doing?" she demanded.

"Stretching my wings," he said. "Do you want to go for a ride with me?"

"Most certainly not!"

He laughed. "That is exactly what I expected you to say. Like a sullen child. It matters not to me whether you come," he said.

"I most certainly am not a child," she said, stung into a

retort. "I just have no desire to go with you."

"Now *that* I don't believe," he said, drawing closer. "I think you are trying to spite me." She could feel the heat rising from his body as he looked at her with blazing eyes.

"Fine! I'll come!" She glanced down at the cloak that hid her chemise. "But I need to get dressed first."

"I'll take another turn around Storbrook," he said, "and come back for you." Before she could say another word he was gone, his tail the last thing she saw as he disappeared around the corner. She leaned back against the wall. Why did he always manage to provoke her? she wondered. She was already regretting her hasty agreement. She glanced at the chest that held her gowns, and then reluctantly pulled it open.

When Max returned a few minutes later she was standing at the window dressed in a dark green gown, the fur cloak laying on the bed.

"I've changed my mind," she said, as he drew close to her window.

"Why? Are you suddenly scared of me?"

"No," she replied. "I just decided that I have no desire to go anywhere with you."

"Anna," he said with a splutter of sparks that made her step back, "don't think of this as a ride with me. Just think of me as a dragon, like Aaron. I won't even talk to you, if you don't want me to." She chewed her lip as she looked past him to the mountains beyond. In the light of the wintery sun they glistened and gleamed, white against a dark blue sky.

"Very well," she said. "I'll come, but no talking." Grabbing the cloak, she swung it around her shoulders and tied it at her neck. "How do I get on your back?"

"Sit down on the window ledge," he said. She did as directed, gasping in shock when he wrapped his tail around her waist and pulled her onto his back. She breathed in relief when she felt his solid weight beneath her.

"You could have warned me," she grumbled.

"No talking, remember," he said with a snort of humor.

He spread his wings wide and plunged through the air, quickly leaving the castle behind him.

"Where are we going?" she asked.

"Not far. We'll head to one of the peaks where the snow lies completely untouched." Anna leaned down against his neck as the cold wind rushed past them, getting herself closer to the heat that rose from his body. Her cloak streamed out behind her, whipping in the wind. The ties were coming loose, and she lifted her hand to pull them tight again, but Max banked at that moment, and the cloak went flying into the wind.

"Oh, no," she gasped.

"What?" Max asked, twisting his long neck to look back at her. The movement brought the cloak into his line of sight, and before she answered he was circling around in a tight loop. "Hold on," he said, increasing his speed as he chased down the cloak. He quickly gained the distance and snagged the garment with his talon.

"I'll hold onto it until we land," he said. He directed himself towards a peak in the distance. Crystal flakes of snow glittered in the sunlight, making the whole peak shimmer and sparkle. He slowed down as he reached the crest, plowing into the soft snow, his body cutting a wide swath through the pristine perfection.

"You ruined it," Anna said, but her voice was teasing. She slid off the dragon's back, and looked around. On all sides the mountain fell away in steep slopes, blanketed in thick snow. "It's so beautiful," she said softly.

"Glad you came?" he asked. She blushed, but remained silent. "Here is your cloak," he said, holding the item out with his talon. She gently lifted it off the sharp claw, and throwing it around her shoulders, tied it around her neck once more. Turning in a small circle, she looked at the snow-covered landscape that surrounded them all sides, then bending down, picked up a handful of snow. She had left her mittens behind and the cold stung her fingers, but she ignored the tingle of pain as she rolled the wet snow around in her hand. She turned to look at the massive dragon, his dark bronze scales contrasting with the bright white snow, and smiled as she flung the icy clump at his chest. It melted against his heated skin, running in streams down his body, and Max looked down in surprise. He glanced back at her, but another snowball, this one aimed much higher, was already heading in his direction. He ducked, and it glanced against his neck, once more melting as soon as it made contact.

"That," he said menacingly, "was uncalled for, especially since I cannot exact a similar revenge."

"Oh?" she said, "Can't you make snowballs with claws?"

"No," he said, "but I can do this." He swung his tail around his body in one quick motion, shoving the snow in its path into a deluge that landed on her in a dump.

"Why you … you … monster!" she yelled, grabbing handfuls of snow and flinging them at him.

"Never start a war you cannot win," he laughed, shaking the droplets from his scales. Swinging his tail in the opposite direction, he cleared the snow in its path with a quick sweep, burying her up to her waist in the white powder.

"Hah!" she shouted. "Now I have all the snow!" Scooping her hands through the thick pile, she compressed the powder and flung it at him repeatedly, laughing when he hopped back, placing himself beyond her reach. His hide was steaming as the snow melted against his scales, heating the air around them. Her laughter rang out, and despite the cold stinging her hands, the heat rose in her cheeks as she fell on her knees into the snow.

He leaned forward, bending his head down to where she knelt. "Are you ready to surrender?" She opened her mouth to deliver a sharp retort, but the blazing intensity of his gaze caught her off-guard, and she could only stare up at him as the words flew from her mind. She pushed herself to her feet and took a step back. Looking at the huge dragon, who was also so human, she suddenly felt very confused.

"I'm all wet," she whispered. "Please take me back." She pulled her eyes away and dropped her gaze. He swept his tail around her, raising her onto his back. Pulling herself forward she settled against his neck, wrapping her arms around it as he lifted them into the air. She was silent as Max flew towards the castle, and when he lifted her into her window, she refused to meet his gaze.

"I'll see you at dinner," he said, turning away when she didn't respond. She lifted her eyes to watch him fly away, then turned with a sigh to find dry garments to replace those wet from the snow.

CHAPTER NINE

Storbrook was a place of gaiety and laughter in the days that followed. Christmas Day was celebrated with feasting and dancing, while the troupe of entertainers that arrived later that afternoon filled the rest of the season with plays, songs, and story-telling. The entertainments chased away all thought of the cold and snow that blustered around the castle. Roaring fires were lit in every room, and hundreds of finely-made wax candles reached flickering fingers into the shadows, burning low in their sconces through the long evenings. Keira noticed that Anna danced often with Garrick, but she avoided all contact with Max, exchanging only a few polite words. And he seemed just as reluctant to engage her, too, although he often watched as she danced with Garrick, frowning slightly as he followed their movements. And Max was not the only one took notice – when his back was turned, Anna would also cast furtive glances his way.

Evenings were mostly spent enjoying the entertainments of the mummers, but there were some nights when the family withdrew to the solar, seeking more sedate pursuits. The eve of the feast of Epiphany was one of these.

Keira sat in the solar watching Aaron and her father as they battled over a game of chess. Anna had remained in the hall where the musicians were plying their instruments for the dancers, but Max had joined them in the solar, and was engaged in conversation with Jenny. She had been charmed by Max's pleasant smile and easy laugh, and had just finished telling him how much she enjoyed the play performed by the mummers at supper. The conversation had lapsed when she turned to Aaron.

"The dragon has not been much in evidence while we have been staying at Storbrook," she said.

"Dragon?" Max said. "There is a dragon around Storbrook, Aaron?"

"Yes," Jenny said, not waiting for Aaron's reply. "We saw the creature in the autumn. It even carried us on its back after Richard was injured."

"Really?" Max said. Richard had just moved his bishop forward to check Aaron's king, and Aaron was deep in thought as he contemplated the board before him.

"Do you know dragon's blood can heal someone's injuries?" Jenny said. "Richard was mortally wounded, but the dragon allowed Keira to stab it with a knife and spill its blood over the wound. It saved Richard's life, but even so, I would not like to be near that monster again."

"What an interesting story." Max watched Aaron intently as he moved his queen forward, before leaning back and meeting Max's gaze. "The dragon allowed its blood to be spilt, in order to save a human?"

"That is the story as I understand it," Aaron said. "Unfortunately, I was not present at the time."

"Unfortunate," Max agreed.

"Since it was my life that was saved," Richard said, "I can attest to the fact that the dragon did indeed spill his blood to save my life. I will forever be in its debt."

"No," Aaron said, dragging his gaze from Max to look at Richard. "A dragon does not hold a human in its debt."

"Even when the dragon has spilt its blood on the human?" Max asked softly.

"Yes," Aaron said. "Enough talk about dragons."

"The reason I mentioned the dragon," Jenny continued, "is that I am worried about Anna. I don't think she is safe living so close to the dragon's lair. I want her to come home."

Max laughed. "Storbrook Castle is probably the safest place for Anna to be. Aaron will ensure that this dragon, or any others that may venture into the area, will never harm your daughter."

"Others?" Jenny said. "There are others?"

"Jenny," Richard said, "Max is right. Anna is probably safer here at Storbrook than anywhere else."

"But she's my little girl. She's already stayed here too long. She should be at home with her parents."

"Mother," Keira said, "Anna is not a child any longer."

"She's only seventeen."

"Anna is old enough to make her own decision in this regard," Keira said firmly.

"No, she needs to come home with us when we leave after the Feast of Epiphany."

"Madame Carver," Max interjected, "I understand that you would like Anna to return home with you, but as an outsider, let me say that I don't see a child when I look at Anna. She is a young woman, a very beautiful young woman, just blooming into full maturity. I understand that she experienced some very distressing circumstances, and you wish to protect her, but Aaron can protect her better than anyone."

"Distressing circumstances?"

"Max," Aaron warned, but Max gave Aaron no heed.

"Yes," he continued, "when that boy kidnapped Anna and threatened to kill her."

"Threatened to kill Anna? What boy? What are you talking about?"

"Max. Enough!" Aaron said, but Max wasn't paying

attention to his Master.

"Wasn't his name Edmund?" Max paused. "You do know about this, don't you?"

"Max!" Aaron pushed himself to his feet, his face furious. "I said *enough!*" As Max looked up and met Aaron's gaze, Keira saw the blood drain from his face. He stared at Aaron for a long moment, before lifting his right hand and touching it briefly over his heart in a fist.

"Master," he said, his voice very low. Aaron flicked his head towards the door, and Max turned towards it as Richard knelt down on the floor next to Jenny.

"It's not true. Tell me it's not true," she whispered, clasping Richard's outstretched hands. "There must be some mistake. Max must be mistaken." She turned to look at Aaron. "This is your fault! You never liked Edmund. You have been telling Max lies about him."

"Jenny," Richard said softly. "What Max said is true."

"No, it can't be. Edmund wouldn't do that." Her expression was pleading. "Would he?"

"Jenny, I'm sorry. I should have told you. Edmund kidnapped Anna with the intention of killing her."

"But...why?"

"Who knows why anyone chooses a particular path."

"Where is he now?"

"I'm sorry, Jenny," Richard said gently.

"Where is he?"

"He's ... Jenny, Edmund is dead."

"No!" Jenny stared at Richard in horror for a moment, before dropping her head into her hands. "Oh Mary," she moaned, "I'm so sorry." She looked up at Aaron with a snarl. "This is all your fault. If you hadn't come to Storbrook —"

"I still wouldn't have married Edmund, Mother," Keira said. Dropping down to Jenny's side, she took her hand. "Mother, Edmund was a terrible person long before Aaron came to our village. You just didn't see it. It's not your fault. I know you were trying to be loyal to your friend. But it is time you understood what Edmund was really like. He hurt me. He hurt Anna. And if it wasn't for Aaron, one of us might now be dead because of him."

"No," Jenny whispered again, but Keira could see that the denial was her last defense. Already the truth was in Jenny's eyes as she looked at her daughter. Slowly she turned to Richard, her hands fumbling for his. "Please, take me home," she said.

"Yes," he said, gently pulling her to her feet. "Soon, my love. But first you need to rest." His eyes fell on Keira for a moment, and then he turned to Aaron with a nod as he led his wife out of the room.

CHAPTER TEN

Keira lay on the bed later that evening, watching as Aaron stripped off his clothes before going over to the window and staring out at the night sky.

"Aaron?"

"There is something I need to do." Aaron turned to face her. "I'm sorry to leave you, but I will probably be gone all night."

"Does this have something to do with Max?" she asked.

"Yes." Jumping onto the window ledge Aaron launched himself out the casement, his transformation sending shards of light in all directions before it disappeared, swallowed by the darkness. A moment later Keira saw a second flash of light, and a large form followed in the direction taken by Aaron. She curled herself into a ball beneath the quilts and pulled them up around her ears. She shivered, cold despite the fire blazing in the hearth near the window.

It was a long night. Keira dozed fitfully, waking repeatedly. At one point she heard a roaring that rolled through the night sky from some point far away, and when she turned towards the large open window, she could see fire blazing in the distance.

Aaron returned shortly before the encroaching dawn touched the sky, when the night is at its darkest and coldest.

49

He landed on the floor of the chamber on feet as light as feathers, and quietly moved towards the bed. Keira rolled towards him as he sank into the down mattress, her eyes watching him blearily.

"Why are you awake?" Aaron asked softly.

"I couldn't sleep," Keira said, snuggling herself against his warm body as he lay down. He wrapped his arms around her and pulled her closer against his bare skin. "I heard roaring," she said. "Was that you?"

"Mmm," he said, kissing her forehead.

"What were you doing? What was happening?"

"Nothing much," he said, running his lips over her cheeks.

"Aaron," she said, pushing him away. "Tell me."

Aaron looked down at her, then rolled onto his back and stared at the ceiling.

"Max needed a reminder in submission," he said. "He had forgotten that he has sworn me an oath of fealty, and owes me his obedience."

"What did you do?"

"I drank his blood."

"Drank his blood? Why?" Keira was fully awake now as Aaron rolled onto his side and looked at her.

"When a dragon gives an oath of submission, he offers his blood to his Master in a symbolic gesture that shows that his life belongs to his Master. And Max also drank my blood, renewing the bond that ties him to me."

"But how does a dragon drink another dragon's blood? Did you cut him like you did me?"

"No. Apart from the oath ceremony, the only way a dragon can draw another dragon's blood is to fight him."

"So you had to fight Max?"

"No, Max had to fight me."

"I don't understand."

"Just as humans have certain rites and traditions, so do dragons. By not obeying me, Max was challenging me as his

Master. Only a weak Master would ignore such a challenge. And once it is made, a challenge cannot be withdrawn, even if it was given unintentionally. Max knew when he left the room last night that he would have to fight me, but his heart was not in it, so it was quickly over. I drank his blood as soon as it was drawn, and in allowing me to do so, Max resubmitted himself to me. He then drank some of mine, renewing the bond."

"He *allowed* you to drink his blood? Hadn't you just beaten him in a fight?"

"Yes, but if Max did not want me to drink his blood, he would have fought to the death – either his or mine."

"Oh." Keira looked at the lightening sky through the window for a moment, then turned back to Aaron again.

"So when I offered you my blood, was I taking an oath of submission?"

"You were submitting to me as a wife submits to her husband. But I offered you my blood, so in the same way, I submitted myself to you."

"But drinking your blood means I'm bonded to you."

"It does. And when I drank yours, I chose to bond with you as well."

"So Max can choose to bond with you?"

"No. He can choose to submit or fight to the death, but when a less powerful dragon drinks the blood of a more powerful dragon, a bond is always created, binding the weaker dragon to the stronger. But if the more powerful dragon drinks the blood of a weaker dragon, or a human, the bond becomes a choice. It is not a choice usually made by a stronger dragon, unless he is choosing a bond with his mate, as I did with you." Aaron lifted his hand and ran his fingers down her cheek. His eyes were turning to flames and Keira drew in her breath before dragging her gaze away.

"What about my father? He's had your blood, although he didn't drink it."

"The tie is stronger with humans, and even though your

father didn't drink my blood, enough was spilt that it now runs through his veins."

"So my father has to submit to you now?" Keira lifted her eyes back to Aaron's.

"He does not have to submit. I demand no fealty from him. But he chooses to. He feels a bond with me that was not there before, and he welcomes it. It is why he feels such a deep debt of gratitude, and why he offers me his allegiance."

"You knew that would happen when you gave him your blood?"

"Yes, I knew. Should I have let him die instead?"

Keira looked away again, her face troubled. "No, you should not have allowed him to die."

Aaron watched her closely for a moment, before turning her face and looking her in the eye. "Keira, I would never demand anything from your father. But is it so dreadful that he surrenders himself to me? By taking you as my wife, I have also taken your family under my protection, which means that he too is part of the clan of which I am Master." Keira stared at him for a long moment.

"No," she said, "it is not a dreadful thing. And I am glad that my father loves you." She paused. "What about Max? Where is he now?"

"Max will spend the rest of the day recovering from his wounds and reflecting on his lesson," Aaron said. "However, Max is the least of my concerns. And I am done talking." He lowered his mouth to hers, his kiss unyielding as he demanded her submission once again. It was capitulation she was quite willing to make, and she pulled him closer.

CHAPTER ELEVEN

It was a gray and miserable day, the air icy fingers that reached into every crevice. Standing at the open window, Anna pulled her cloak tighter around her shoulders, trying to create a barrier to the frigid air. Far in the distance she saw a figure gliding through the clouds, oblivious to the cold. It was Max, and she watched as he soared through the clouds, sometimes disappearing in the mass of gray. Occasionally a flame would light the air around him, a glimmer that dispersed the gloominess for a second before descending once more.

Her parents had left Storbrook a few days earlier, and Anna found herself once again thinking about their departure, going over her mother's strange behavior. Never a woman of affection, she had held Anna close as she wrapped her arms around her. Tears had spilled down her cheeks as she stroked Anna's hair. When she finally pulled away, she stared into her daughter's eyes for a long time.

"I am so sorry for failing you," she had said before turning away and quickly mounting her horse, urging it into motion without a backwards glance.

Anna returned her attention to the clouds that hung over

the mountains, obscuring the peaks. The gloomy weather seemed to match the atmosphere that hung around Storbrook, making it seem even more dismal. The mummers had left the castle the same day as Anna's parents, taking the laughter and gaiety with them. As the cold had grown more intense, the residents became withdrawn and sullen. Max and Aaron were the only ones unaffected by the cold, a fact which Anna found incredibly annoying. She trained her eyes on the figure moving through the clouds once more. It didn't matter how cold it was, he took to the skies every morning. And if he knew she was watching, he never acknowledged it. Ever since that day in the snow, they had ignored each other, as if by some tacit agreement. He had even ignored her when she danced night after night with Garrick. It was as if he had completely forgotten her existence. She turned away from the window, suddenly restless. She needed to get away from the confines of the castle.

A few minutes later Anna opened the heavy wooden door that led into the courtyard. It was much colder outside the castle than it had been within the stone walls, and she had added a second cloak over the first. The courtyard was empty as she crossed the cobblestones to the other side, looking for the path that had disappeared under a blanket of white. It remained hidden, so she lifted her skirts and placed a booted foot in the snow. It came just above her ankles, and dropping her skirts slightly, she continued walking toward the portcullis that hung over the entrance to the castle. She had not ventured beyond Storbrook since that fateful day when Edmund had captured her, but there seemed little chance of anyone being out there in the cold. Besides, she reasoned, she would not go far – just to the edge of the woods. The sound of her voice being called made her spin around in surprise, but she smiled at the caller.

"Garrick, what are you doing out in the cold?"

"I'm just fetching more wood from the shed," he replied. "But you should be inside keeping warm beside a fire."

"I was going crazy, cooped up within those walls," Anna said with a laugh. "I shan't go far, just far enough to clear my thoughts."

"Then I'll come with you," Garrick said.

"No! I just need to be alone for a while."

"But you could catch your death of cold. At least stay in the gardens."

"I promise I won't go far. If I'm not back in half an hour, let Master Drake know." Garrick stared at her for a moment before nodding reluctantly.

"Half an hour then."

With a sigh, Anna turned towards the gate. She knew Garrick was right about the dangers of the cold, but his concern had felt confining, chafing at her, and she was even more eager to get away.

Anna paused as she passed under the portcullis and stepped beyond the castle walls. The mountains stretched out in every direction, a sea of snow-covered peaks as far as the eye could see. She drew in a deep breath, letting the crisp air fill her lungs which she held for a moment before slowly exhaling. The lonely cry of an eagle could be heard in the distance, while the wind whistled softly around the stone walls, making the few sparse trees creak and groan. She hunched her shoulders against the cold and carefully placed her feet on the path.

Ice clung to the ground in patches, while loose stones bounced and tumbled down the steep slope of the mountain as she walked. There was very little vegetation at this high elevation, but one or two stunted pines stubbornly held to the rocky slopes of the mountain, and she clung to these as she cautiously placed one foot in front of another. A single tiny bird flew around the trees, foraging between the needles, and Anna watched it for a moment as it hopped from branch to branch before finally flying away, oblivious to the chill.

As she moved further down the path, all was silent except for the crunch of her feet against the loose gravel. Away from the castle walls the air seemed colder, and she raised mitted hands to her stinging cheeks, trying to rub some warmth into them. Her eyes watered, too, and she squeezed them shut.

A stone slipped beneath her foot and she gasped, throwing out her hands to break her fall as she tumbled to the ground. The earth was freezing beneath her skirts, and she pushed herself back to her feet with a shiver. Turning around, she looked back up the slope she had just come down. From below it looked more treacherous, and for a brief moment she regretted not taking Garrick's advice to stay in the gardens. But she had come this far, and wasn't quite ready to return. She was almost at the edge of the forest, and already the trees were beginning to grow thicker. Once she was between the trees the wind would not be as cutting, nor the air as cold.

She turned and continued along the path, carefully testing the ground as she walked. The cold made the pine smell sharper, and she breathed it in deeply. As she neared the trees, the snow thinned out, until it barely covered the ground. But the needles, which lay thick on the ground, made the path slippery, and she reached out a hand to steady herself. A breeze stirred the boughs above her, and the needles rustled together as the branches creaked. Apart from that, it was silent. Even the little bird she'd seen earlier had disappeared. She closed her eyes for a moment, enjoying the peace and serenity, before turning back towards Storbrook and looking up the steep slope. She hadn't realized how far down the mountain she had come.

Reaching from tree to tree, she started retracing her steps. Her leather boots slipped slightly on the needles, and she turned her feet sideways to get a better grip. She gained the edge of the forest and paused to look up the slope. She certainly would not make it back within the half hour she had given Garrick. In fact, the time had probably already passed, and Garrick might even now be sounding an alarm. She glanced up at the sky, wondering if Aaron was already looking for her, and high overhead she saw the familiar shape of a dragon. As it grew closer, however, she ground her teeth in annoyance. It was not the dragon she was hoping to see.

"Max," she ground out as he dropped towards her, "What are you doing here?"

"I think the question is, what are *you* doing here?" he said. "I may be mistaken, but it seems you are in need of assistance."

"I'm surprised you even noticed."

Max laughed. "Are you upset at my lack of attention, darling? It hasn't escaped my notice that you have been ignoring me too."

"Urgh, you are so … so …"

"Insolent?" he supplied. "Rude? Impudent?"

"Yes, all those things. Now just help me get back to Storbrook, then you can go back to ignoring me."

"I may ignore you, Anna, but I always notice you. And dancing with that boy was like waving a red flag."

"I happen to like Garrick," she said. "Not that it has anything to do with you."

"Really? Well, I am sure he has his uses, doesn't he?" Anna blushed, but he continued relentlessly. "And it has everything to do with me, since you were only dancing with him to get my attention."

"You are so arrogant!"

"A rather childish ploy, I might add," he continued. "If you wanted my attention you only had to tell me, and I would gladly have given it to you."

"You know, I think I can manage my way back to Storbrook on my own," she said, turning to face the path. Gripping the spindly branch of a pine, she cautiously placed a foot on the loose stone. The hold was good and she took another step, still clinging to the stunted tree. She could feel the weight of Max's stare on her back, while the air around her warmed with the heat emanating from his body, but she still gasped when her arms were caught up in sharp talons that curled around her, holding her fast.

"Let me go," she shouted, kicking her feet in an effort to loosen his hold on her. It was a useless gesture, and Max laughed.

"And send you tumbling down the mountain? Aaron would have my hide if I did that."

"If you're so concerned about your hide, you should have left me alone," she yelled.

"Where would the fun be in that? I rather enjoy having a helpless woman hanging from my claws." A thousand words rushed to Anna's tongue, but she clamped her teeth together, determined to remain silent. It only took a minute for them to reach the gate once more, and opening his talons, Max dropped her unceremoniously to the ground just in front of them. She glared up at him before turning her attention to her garments, which hung askew as a result of her unrefined mode of transport.

"No need to thank me, darling," Max said, a stream of flame flowing from his mouth as he turned towards the clouds. She jumped back as sparks reached to the ground, before glaring at the retreating figure.

Garrick was standing in the courtyard watching the gate when she passed under the portcullis.

"Oh, good, you've returned," he said in obvious relief. "Did I just see a dragon?"

"You did. The most rude, arrogant, conceited, horrible dragon that the world has ever seen," she said, her voice rising until it was a yell. High above a stream of flame lit the sky, and Garrick looked at it nervously.

"You shouldn't antagonize a dragon like that," he said. "You never know when they might turn on you."

"That dragon wouldn't dare hurt me," Anna said with a toss of her head. Crossing the courtyard, she dragged the heavy door open and made her way through the depths of the shadowy castle towards her chambers. As she passed the solar, she saw Keira curled up in front of the fire, her fingers deftly embroidering threads through a canvas, while on a bench to her side lay a book.

"What are you reading?" Anna asked, changing direction and walking into the room, where she picked up the small volume.

"*Tristan and Isolde*," Keira said. "I've reached the point where Tristan has gone to claim Isolde for his uncle, King Mark, and is trying to discover a way of approaching her. But the words are so small and the light so dim, I needed to give my eyes a break."

"I can read to you if you like," Anna said, sitting down on a chair. She opened the book to a page marked with a piece of thread, and started reading.

"Now it chanced once upon the break of day that he heard a cry so terrible that one would have called it a demon's cry; nor had he ever heard a brute bellow in such wise, so awful and strange it seemed. He called a woman who passed by the harbor and said: 'Tell me, lady, whence comes that voice I have heard, and hide me nothing.'

"'My lord,' said she, 'I will tell you truly. It is the roar of a dragon the most terrible and dauntless upon earth. Daily it leaves its den and stands at one of the gates of the city: Nor can any come out or go in till a maiden has been given up to it; and when it has her in its claws it devours her.'

"'Lady,' said Tristan, 'make no mock of me, but tell me straight: Can a man born of a woman kill this thing?'

"What a marvelous story," Anna said, settling herself more comfortably in her seat. She picked up the book again and continued reading, the only other sound the fire which crackled and sparked in the grate. Keira looked up every now and then as she followed the story, groaning when Tristan killed the dragon and won Isolde's hand for King Mark, and sighing at the wretchedness of the queen, knowing that her love was for Tristan and not for her husband, the king.

Anna had just finished reading when Max entered the

room, dressed in a thin, light brown tunic over tan leather breeches, with no further protection against the cold. She looked up at him.

"Enjoy your flight?" she asked.

"It was most enjoyable, thank you. In fact, I had more entertainment today than I've had since Keira's mummers left Storbrook." He looked at Anna, returning her glowering look with a shameless grin.

"Excuse me, Keira," she said. "I think I will retire to my chambers. And if you don't mind, I will borrow your book. I would like to reread some of Tristan's heroic victories against his, uh, foes."

CHAPTER TWELVE

Aaron looked up as Keira let herself into his study. He had been locked away with Thomas all morning, going over matters of business with his steward. Apart from Keira, Anna, and the priest, Thomas was the only human at Storbrook who knew Aaron's true identity. He had spent many years with Aaron, and was not only a trusted advisor and dependable manager, but also a good friend. Aaron gave Keira a smile.

"Almost done, my sweet." Keira headed over to a high-backed chair near the window, pausing to pour herself a cup of wine from the flagon on the table. She watched Aaron as he turned his attention back to Thomas, finishing up some instructions as he signed a pile of papers. A moment later Thomas was gathering up the loose sheets, nodding to Keira as he headed out the door.

Pushing himself away from the table, Aaron crossed the room and sat down in the chair opposite his wife.

"Anna and Max are at each other's throats again," she said.

"They've been on their best behavior lately, but with Storbrook so quiet, they were clearly in need of some entertainment."

"Entertainment?"

"Don't fool yourself, my sweet," Aaron said. "Anna may glower and scowl at Max, but the sparring thrills her, and as for Max, he thoroughly enjoys playing the game." Aaron grinned at her skepticism before changing the subject. "How would you like to visit the city?"

"I would love to," Keira said. "You know I have never been beyond the village, except to Storbrook, of course."

"Well, I received a letter today from His Royal Highness Prince Alfred," Aaron said. "He has requested that I come to the city to lend him my aid."

"Why?"

"Prince Alfred and I are well acquainted," Aaron explained. "And although he is unaware of my true identity, he knows I have some influence over dragons."

"How does he know that?"

"I first made the prince's acquaintance about ten years ago when I saved him from a dragon." Aaron rose and poured himself a cup of wine. "I had heard rumors of a rogue dragon causing problems near the city, so I set out to find him," he continued, settling back into his chair and crossing one leg over the other.

"What's a rogue dragon?"

"A rogue dragon is one that has been banished from his clan," Aaron explained. "This dragon had traveled a long distance to reach our lands, and I had been tracking him all day when I heard the sound of a small band of people traveling along the road, so I changed into human form and met them along the way. It was the prince, returning from a day of hunting with a group of friends. Since I was standing in their path, they were forced to come to a halt, but as they were deciding whether to shoot me or greet me, the dragon I had been tracking flew overhead. Of course, the prince and his men were terrified, but they stood their ground, drawing their swords to defend themselves from the beast, who they were sure was about to kill them. And he probably would have if I hadn't been there. I told the prince I could talk to the dragon, and although it was clear he did not believe me, he did not try to stop me. And since the dragon already knew that I was a Master —"

Keira raised her hand to stop him. "How?"

"Well — a dragon can see how powerful another dragon is by his inner hue." Keira looked at Aaron in confusion as he continued. "You know that dragons are created from fire. If you have ever watched Smithy at work, you will know that the color of a fire changes, depending on how hot it is burning." Keira nodded. "It is the same with dragons. The more powerful a dragon, the hotter he burns. The most powerful dragons burn white. And although *you* cannot see what color I am, another dragon can measure my strength at any distance with just a glance. So the dragon knew straight away that I was far more powerful than him."

"How powerful are you?"

"More powerful than most."

"And when a dragon looks at you, what color does he see?"

"A pale shade of yellow."

Keira nodded, considering this. "So the dragon could see your power even though you were in human form?"

"Yes. It is not as bright, but still visible. That's why he did not attack. He knew how easily he would be defeated." Keira nodded and Aaron continued. "Once I was beyond the reach of the prince's hearing, I spoke to the rogue. Dragons do not suffer from the same hearing inadequacies as humans," Aaron said with a grin.

Keira poked him with her boot. "What did you say?"

"I told him that if he did not leave the area immediately, I would hunt him down and kill him."

"Oh." Keira blinked.

"Then I returned to the prince, and assured him that the dragon would not return. I could tell that he did not believe me, but when all the attacks suddenly ceased, he summoned me to court, eager to show his thanks."

"And now he requests your aid once more?"

"Yes. It seems that the city has been plagued with attacks from another rogue dragon."

"Another dragon? Do you know who it is?"

"I don't know for sure, but I suspect it is Jack."

"Jack?" Keira leaned back in her chair in surprise. Jack had been banished by Aaron a few months earlier after forcing his attentions on Keira – the last in a long line of defiant acts. "Why would he be attacking people in the city?"

"I suspect he is trying to get my attention. He knows the prince will call on me for aid, and he knows I will not refuse to come. I believe he intends to challenge me for Mastership of the clan."

"Is he strong enough to do that?"

"No. But he might just be wily enough." Rising to his feet, Aaron refilled his cup and leaning back against the table, looked at Keira. "So, how about a trip to the city?"

CHAPTER THIRTEEN

Anna stared at Aaron in horror. "You want me to travel with Max?"

Aaron had just finished explaining to Anna that he and Keira needed to travel to the city, and that she could either accompany them or return home to her parents. Since Anna was only seventeen, staying at Storbrook was out of the question. It was far too remote, Aaron explained, for her to remain there without protection. But if she chose to go to the city, she would have to travel with Max and Thomas, traversing the countryside on horseback.

"Why can't I go with you and Keira?"

"No!" Of course, Anna knew he would refuse, since he would fly no one but Kiera unless it was absolutely necessary. Still, it had been worth a try.

"Anna," Keira said, frowning at Aaron, "it is not practical for you to travel with Aaron and me."

"Very well," she said. "I suppose I will travel with Thomas and Max."

"Come, Anna," Max said with a grin, "it won't be that bad."

"It will be dreadful," she replied tartly, frowning when he

laughed.

Aaron had decided that Anna and Max would leave Storbrook a few days before them, since, traveling by horseback, their journey would take far longer than it would for a dragon flying over the mountains. They would rendezvous at Drake Manor, the home of Aaron's cousin, Favian, before continuing to the city.

The day before Anna and Max were to leave, the four of them traveled into the village to bid farewell to Master and Madame Carver. The two women were carried by the dragons, the quickest way to travel. Anna hated the idea of being carried by Max again, but as the alternative was to stay behind, she had allowed him to sweep her onto his back and settle her between his wings for the trip down the mountain. Thankfully, it did not take long for them to reach the outskirts of the village, and within a few minutes Anna was walking next to Keira as they approached their old home.

As they drew near, Anna could see her father through the open door of his workshop, bent over a long table, craft knife in hand. He glanced up as they approached, before quickly rising to his feet.

"Anna, Keira, how wonderful to see you, daughters." He embraced them each in turn before turning to Aaron. "This is an unexpected surprise, Aaron," he said. "Is the visit prompted by filial duty or is there another reason?"

"We have come to inform you that we'll be leaving Storbrook for a while," Aaron said. "There is a matter I need to attend to in the city. Anna will be coming with us, and Max has agreed to accompany the party as well." Anna darted a quick look at Max, who was watching Aaron closely.

"The city?" Richard said. "How long will you be gone?"

"I cannot say," Aaron replied, "but we will be back before too long, God willing."

"And this matter you need to attend to, does it carry an element of danger?"

"You know what I am, Richard," Aaron said. "What

could possibly present a danger to me?" Richard frowned as his gaze wandered over to Max, who was listening in silence. He stared at Max for a moment, then turned back to Aaron.

"Another dragon, perhaps?"

"Ah." Aaron turned to look at the mountains, his eyes distant.

"I'm right, am I not? There is another dragon, one that could be a threat to you and my daughters," Richard continued. He dropped his voice. "My life belongs to you, Aaron, and I would bid you use it in any way necessary." Flames flared in Aaron's eyes as he turned back to Richard, and Anna started in surprise at the vehemence in Aaron's words.

"Your life is your own, man," he said. "You owe me nothing, and I do not demand your allegiance."

"You do not demand it," Richard said, "but I offer it freely regardless. I may not be a dragon, but you are still my Master."

"No!" Aaron gripped Richard's forearm, leaning closer. "I refuse the gift. Your place belongs right here, with your wife, serving the people of this village." He paused, dropping Richard's arm. "Thank you for the offer, Richard, but your gift is more than I can accept."

Richard nodded slowly. "At least accept my offer of friendship, then."

Aaron smiled. "That I accept most readily, along with the expectation that you love me like a son." Anna glanced at Max again, and saw his eyebrows raise at Aaron's words.

"I do already," Richard said as Jenny came out the door.

"Why are you all standing in the cold?" she demanded. "Come inside next to the fire."

It was already warm inside the parlor, but the temperature rose perceptibly as they entered the room, the heat from the dragon men adding to the warmth of the fire. Anna caught Keira's eye and mimicked a fan over her face, and Keira smiled in response as she stripped off her cloak.

"Any news about the reeve position?" Aaron asked as he accepted a cup of wine from Jenny.

"I've been asked to attend his lordship next week," Richard replied.

"Richard is the best possible person to be the next reeve," Jenny said proudly.

"Anyone would be better than the last one," Richard retorted.

When Jenny heard that her daughters would be leaving for the city, she tried to convince Anna to stay at home and not return to Storbrook. Her pleas were in vain, however, and Anna was adamant in her refusal.

"Please, Mother," she said, "You must understand that I have outgrown the village. Storbrook is my home now."

"What do you mean? This is your home."

"I'm sorry, Mother."

"Fine." Jenny flung her hands into the air, but before she could turn away, Richard put his arm around her.

"We both know Anna is right," he said gently. "Let her go with our blessing, knowing Aaron will keep both our daughters safe." He looked at Aaron, who nodded briefly before Richard looked away.

CHAPTER FOURTEEN

Keira stood in the courtyard, watching as Thomas helped Anna mount her horse before turning to check the straps on a pair of packhorses, tethered to his own mount. Satisfied that they were secure, he swung himself onto his horse's back and lifting the reins, turned to look at Aaron and Max, who were standing a short distance away.

"Don't let them out of your sight," Aaron said to Max. Max nodded, locking his gaze with Aaron's. Raising his right hand, he clenched his hand into a fist and placed it against his chest over his heart with a thump. Aaron nodded, then placed his own hand over the clenched fist. "I have your fealty, but you have my friendship," he said. "I know you will keep her safe." Keira saw Aaron's eyes flicker with a small flame. "I will wait for you at Drake Manor," he said. The flickering flame was mirrored in Max's gaze, and each man held the other's eye for a moment, until Aaron pulled his hand away. Max's fist fell to his side, and he dropped his head in salute before turning away.

"Lead the way, Thomas," Max said, following when Thomas turned his horse towards the gates. Although Thomas had offered Max a horse, he had quickly declined the offer.

"I can travel just as fast on foot," he declared, "but if my feet grow weary, I will take to the sky."

Keira sighed as the trio disappeared from sight beyond the castle walls. Aaron had moved to stand behind her, and he lifted his hands to her shoulders.

"Max will take care of her," he said. Keira turned to him with a wry smile.

"It's not Anna I'm worried about." Aaron laughed.

"Oh, I think Max can take care of himself." He bent down to her ear. "This is the first time we have been alone in months, my sweet." A shiver ran through Keira as his breath tickled her neck. She turned around to face him as footsteps sounded on the cobbled stones. The courtyard was busy as servants went about their duties, rushing from one building to another. Aaron pulled back and met Keira's amused expression before glancing at the mountains beyond Storbrook. "There's a cave in the mountains where we could be truly alone," he said. "Will you come with me? We could spend the night there."

"In a cave?"

"Mmm, yes," Aaron reached for her hands and pulled her closer. "I'll build a fire, and we can take along a quilt to make the ground more comfortable for you." He paused and looked into her eyes. "And while we are there, there is something I've been wanting to show you."

"Oh?"

"But I can only show you there." He grinned down at her as Keira rolled her eyes.

"A dragon wants to show me something in a cave in the mountains. Should I be scared?"

"Should a lovely woman be scared when trapped with a dragon in a cave? Absolutely," he said. "Now let's go find some provisions and be on our way."

The sun had already passed its zenith by the time they set out, and as Aaron flew, it slowly dipped lower in the sky, until it eventually dropped below the horizon, turning the sky from pink to gray to black. The air rushing past Keira was cold, and she shivered as it flowed around her.

"Not much further," Aaron said, glancing back at her.

Stars were beginning to appear in the sky above them, small pinpoints of light in a sea of darkness, when Aaron started to descend. Keira craned her neck to see where they were going, but the night sky swallowed everything around them, leaving only a looming shadow even darker than the black sky. Unhesitatingly, Aaron headed towards the shadow, slowing as they approached an oppressive wall of rock. As they got closer, Keira could make out a hole in the dark surface, high in the sheer rock face, and it was to this that Aaron headed. Small trees, stunted and twisted, clung tenaciously to the rock around the entrance to the cave, and as he flew by, Aaron grabbed one in his claws, ripping out the shallow roots with ease before landing at the edge of the cave. The darkness within was so complete that as Keira slid off Aaron's back, she was unable to see her hand in front of her face, and she breathed a sigh of relief when Aaron blew bright, glowing flames onto the branch in his claw, creating a torch that sent the nearby shadows scattering. The cold air struck Keira as she moved from Aaron's warmth, and she shivered as she looked around the cave, peering into the shadows that the flickering torchlight failed to penetrate.

"What is this place?" she asked in a whisper, half afraid of monsters lurking in the shadows. There was a flash of light, too brief to do more than dazzle, and Aaron came up behind her, wrapping his warm arms around her shivering shoulders.

"This, my sweet, is the dragon's lair," he said.

"Oh, so this is where you hide with your grisly meals?" she replied with a laugh, turning within his embrace to look up at him.

"Exactly so!" he agreed, before dropping his arms and taking her hand. "Come, I'll show you around." Tugging her gently, he led her deeper into the darkness. The burning branches were still in his hand, and they cast an eerie glow against the smooth, uneven surfaces. The cavern was vast, widening beyond the entrance and stretching more than a hundred feet into the mountain. Towards the back of the cave columns stretched from floor to ceiling, too high for the light to penetrate. A large ring of stone lay on the floor towards the back of the cave, within which were half-burned logs and a pile of ash. Letting go of her hand, Aaron threw the flaming tree within the stone circle before sending a cascade of flames onto the logs. They sprang to life, chasing away more of the shadows, and Keira stepped closer to capture some of the warmth. This deep into the cave the air was warmer, although slightly stale, and the flickering fire scattered away the last of Keira's shivers. She tugged open the small satchel that hung over her shoulder, drawing out a quilt which she laid on the ground. A small clay jar followed it, filled with wine, and a loaf of freshly baked bread. She smiled at Aaron as he knelt down on the quilt in front of her. The light of the fire danced across his chest, mimicking the flames Keira knew were burning inside him. She lifted her hand and gently traced her hand over his skin as his heat warmed her fingers.

"I can feel the pulse of your heart," she said.

"You are the only one it beats for," he said.

The fire crackled and sparked as Keira reached for the loaf of bread, and she looked at it thoughtfully.

"Aaron," she said, tearing off a chunk of bread and passing it to him, "what makes the fire within you burn?"

"You," he said, biting off a piece of the bread. She smacked him playfully.

"No, really. All fires need fuel, so what fuels the flames within you?"

"Blood."

"Blood?"

"And flesh."

"You mean when you go hunting?"

"Yes. The human food we eat is not enough to feed the flames, which is why we need to hunt as well. The fresh flesh of an animal just slain is needed to keep the fire burning."

"And humans."

"On occasion, yes. The essence of humanity is captured within human flesh, which is why we need it to sustain ourselves."

Keira nodded and reached for the wine, taking a sip before passing it to him. He took the jar and drank, handing it back to her when he was done. Taking her hands in his, he massaged them with his fingers as he looked down at them.

"Keira," he said, "I told you I want to show you something." He waited a moment before continuing. "You already know me as a man and as a dragon, but there is something else about me that I want you to know." He paused as she watched him questioningly. "It may seem strange, but please don't be afraid. Remember that I would never, ever, do anything that could harm you in any way!"

Keira nodded slowly. "I'm feeling afraid already." Aaron pushed himself to his feet and held his hand out to her.

"I don't want to burn the quilt," he said as he pulled her to her feet. She stepped onto the stone as he swept it away with his hand.

"Burn the quilt? What are you going to do?"

His fingers plucked at the ties of her gown, and it fell to the floor, followed by the chemise a moment later. "You will understand in a minute. Now stay here, and don't be afraid!" He took a few steps back, placing a short distance between them.

As she watched, light began to glow beneath the surface of his skin, rippling and shimmering. Keira sucked in her breath as his features grew hazy and indistinct, while his skin stretched thin, turning translucent. She could see the flames just below the surface, rippling through his form. She held her breath when she saw his skin dissolving, disappearing;

and when his form lost its shape, leaving only flickering flames in their wake, she gasped. The flames stretched into the vague shape of a dragon, but without any frame, twisting and wavering through the heights of the cave, before pulling suddenly back into themselves, shrinking down to resemble an indistinct, burning image of a man. A wisp of flame reached out towards her and she shrunk back, but threading through her mind she heard a whisper, carried through the fire: "*Don't be afraid, I won't hurt you. I love you.*"

She paused as the words wrapped through her thoughts, unspoken yet clear, and watched as the wisp of flame drew nearer. It brushed her cheek, a touch soft and gentle as a warm summer breeze. Her eyes widened in surprise, and the flames before her moved closer, another fiery wisp cupping her other cheek gently. More wisps broke away, scattering the flame into hundreds of glowing tendrils which wound around her, gently brushing against her skin, twisting around her arms and legs, caressing her. Her mouth opened slightly as a light touch brushed against her lips, and she drew in a breath when the flame filled her mouth, warm air swirling against her tongue. Her thighs clenched as the flames swept over her, stroking every part of her body, the intensity of the touch so strong she could barely stand. She could feel the gentle caress of tendrils against her face, and she leaned into them as they brushed over her neck, sweeping down her shoulders, caressing her back and stroking against her breasts to her stomach. The swirling flames seemed to completely surround her, encasing her in a swirling, fiery eddy, brushing and caressing her skin.

She closed her eyes as her senses erupted, a moan escaping her mouth as the intensity threatened to overwhelm her. A growl threaded through her mind a moment before the flames suddenly withdrew, pulling away from her and leaving in their wake an astounding sense of desolation. She opened her eyes to see the flames coalesce before her, pulling back into one large blaze before shaping into a human frame.

The flames pulled inward, as sinew and skin materialized around the inferno. Even as Aaron's form returned, his entire being seemed alight, flames held at bay by the physical elements of his body. Wings of burning flame swept the air behind him, churning the air into swirling eddies around the cave. His eyes were pure white, his hair like spun gold, while beneath the layer of skin, flames rippled and swirled. He stepped towards Keira, pulling her into his arms, his touch light and feathery, but when his lips descended onto hers, his kiss was all-consuming, born of a passion that was wild and savage, and she responded with equal fervor, clinging to him as though drowning. Her knees finally gave way, but he caught her in his arms, lowering her to the ground beneath him as they grasped each other, their desire demanding immediate fulfillment. It was fast, intense and explosive, leaving them both gasping in each other's arms, their hearts racing in unison. Aaron rolled onto his side, pulling Keira with him, his hand caressing her face as they gazed at each other in wonder. His eyes were no longer white, but glowing flames, while beneath his skin slight ripples showed that he had not fully returned to his human form.

"How?" she breathed.

"I'm born of fire," he said. She lay in his arms silently for another few moments.

"Can all dragons do that?" she finally asked.

"No," he said. "At least, I don't think so."

"But —"

"Shh," he said. "I'll tell you later. Right now I just want to hold you." They lay silently for another few moments, until Keira spoke again.

"I could hear you. In my mind," she said.

"Mmm. That's because we are connected. Not just because we have shared each other's blood, but because you are a part of me."

"I felt like I was being consumed. I didn't know where I ended and you began."

"Being like that, one with the flame, I can feel everything so much more than usual. Things are smoother, or rougher. Softer, or harder. But being with you was the most intense thing I have ever felt. Every part of you seemed to become me. I could feel everything about you – every hair, the soft skin of your eyelids, the warmth of your tongue." Keira blushed. "Your lips were so soft, and you looked so beautiful. I wanted to wrap myself around you and never let go, but then – I wanted even more. I wanted to feel you holding me too, a man of substance, not wisps of flame. And when I held you, it was the most incredible feeling in the world." They lay in silence for another few minutes.

"How is it that you didn't burn me?" Keira asked. She could feel Aaron smile into her hair.

"The first time it happened, I burned everything in sight. But after a few times I discovered I could control the heat – I could make myself burn warmer or cooler. It took a long time, but eventually I was able to burn no hotter than a stone heated by the sun."

"But the quilt?"

Aaron laughed. "There's a limit to my self-control, my sweet. I knew I would be focused on you, and thought I shouldn't add any further risk."

Keira lay in silence for another few moments. "When did it first happen?"

"So many questions! I will tell you everything, but right now I need to hunt. Changing like that leaves me completely empty, in desperate need of –"

"Fuel?"

"Yes." He paused. "Will you be all right if I leave you alone for a short while? I won't go too far, but I do need to eat, or I may not have the strength to stand in the morning."

"I'll be fine," she said. "As long as you get that fire going again."

"That I can manage," said Aaron, getting to his feet and heading over to the ring of stones, where a few embers still glowed. Keira sat up as he threw a stream of flames from his fingers, making the fire roar back to life. He picked up the quilt and wrapped it around himself for a moment, then headed over to Keira and draped it over her shoulders. It was warm from his skin, and she snuggled herself deeper into its folds.

"I won't be long," he promised. She nodded, and a moment later he flung himself off the ledge, transforming in midair. It was immediately colder in the cave, and Keira scooted over to the fire, resting her back against one of the stone pillars. Her gown and chemise were lying on the ground and she pulled them on. Her eyes were starting to grow heavy when the dragon returned a short while later, a hunk of meat clasped in his claw as he towered over her.

"What is that?" Keira asked, eyeing it suspiciously.

"Supper."

"And what exactly is it?"

Aaron blew out a flame-lit sigh. "It's venison. Do you really think I would bring you something else?" Ripping off a small piece of meat, Aaron seared it with his breath, then held it out to her. "Come, eat!" She took the meat from his claw and took a small bite. It actually tasted pretty good, and her stomach rumbled in response, making her realize just how hungry she was. Aaron pulled off more pieces for her, searing each one before handing them over. By the time she had had enough, there was none left, and when she licked the juices off her fingers, Aaron raised his bony eyebrows in amusement. He settled himself down on the cave floor, his legs tucked beneath him as he stretched out his long neck along the ground. Keira watched him for a moment before picking up the quilt and settling herself down next to him, leaning her weight against his side. He pulled his tail up around her as he turned to look at her.

"Do you mind sleeping with a dragon, my sweet? If I make another change, even to my human form, I will need to hunt again, and I would rather be here with you."

Keira nodded. "Tell me about the time you first changed into flame," she said.

"The first time was right here, in this cave, after my parents were killed. I think it was my rage that first sparked the change, but after that I could make it happen at will."

"Can other dragons do this?"

"I've heard tales of dragons being able to become one with the flame, but until it happened to me, I thought they were just stories. I don't know of any other dragons with the ability."

"Did you live in this cave?" she asked, glancing around the shadows.

"Yes. After my parents died. I lived here for a few decades, always the dragon. And I never returned to the village."

"Never?"

"Not until that first time you saw me."

Keira smiled. The first time she had seen Aaron was as a dragon. The villagers had been terrified, but she had been fascinated by the beautiful beast that had sailed through the sky, wings outspread. But she knew Aaron was referring to the first time she had seen him in his human form, strolling through the village market where she tended her father's stall of wooden tableware. She closed her eyes and leaned her head back against the solid form behind her.

"I'm glad you came into the village," she said.

He pulled his tail tighter around her. "So am I," he said.

CHAPTER FIFTEEN

The sun was starting to rise when Keira awoke. Long fingers of light were reaching into the cave, slowly probing the dark depths. She was lying on the quilt, her back pressed against the hard, warm scales of her husband. He had wrapped his long body around her in a protective circle, his head close to hers and his tail stretching around her to his neck. His clothes had been folded beneath her head to serve as a pillow, and her hand was intertwined with his claws. She could feel them pressing against her skin as she awoke. Hard and strong. She opened her eyes slowly to see him watching her, his golden eyes meeting hers and holding them. Sparks flew from his nostrils as she reached out her hand to stroke his face, running her fingers over the hard, scaly ridges of his eyebrows and across the top of his skull, gently stroking the smooth horns that rose from the top of his head.

"I love you," she said. He lifted a claw and ran it carefully down the length of her cheek, his eyes glowing as he watched her.

"And I love you," he said softly. His warm breath washed over her, and she shivered, remembering how she had been wrapped in flames the night before. She gazed at him for a long moment before placing a kiss at the corner of his mouth. His forked dragon tongue flicked out briefly, caressing her fingers, and she drew in her breath, before slowly pushing herself away and turning to look out of the cave.

Rising to her feet, Keira walked over to the entrance to look at the snow-covered peaks that lay below them. For as far as she could see, mountains rose from a sea of cloud, the bare rock purple in the morning light, while the faint blush of dawn stained the peaks in oranges and pinks. Aaron rose up behind her and moved to where she stood at the cave edge, his long neck stretching out from the entrance of the cave. As she turned to look at him, she saw his body freeze, suddenly alert. His eyes blazed slightly as he sniffed the air, and when he looked down, she followed his glance to see the trees far below rustling with movement.

In silence, Aaron dropped from the ledge, directing himself downward towards the trees. A stream of flame flowed from his mouth, and when the rustling amongst the trees grew more frenzied, she knew that whatever it was had been alerted to the hunter plunging through the air. Aaron soared silently above the trees, his tail streaming out behind him as he followed his prey. A stag broke into a small glade as Aaron's roar broke the silence, sending a shiver down Keira's back. His huge body slammed into the animal, flames curling from his mouth as his jaws clamped over the neck of the majestic creature. Its body turned limp, and Keira watched as the dragon ripped the flesh open with his wicked talons, lapping up the hot blood that poured from the body before tearing off huge hunks of blackened meat. All other sounds fell quiet as his growls rumbled through the air, every other creature having hidden itself away from the dangerous predator. Once, he looked up, his gaze resting on her for a moment as she stared back in awe, before he turned back to his meal with a loud growl that reverberated around the mountains.

His snout was red with blood when he had finished, and

he launched himself into the air, turning towards the river that ran through the trees. The water was frozen, but he brought his tail down on the surface with a mighty whack, causing the ice to shatter. He drank deeply as she watched, and it was only then that he turned and faced her direction once more. Even though she was too far to make out more than his shape, she knew his eyes were intently trained on her. His golden scales glittered and glowed in the early morning sunlight, throwing a thousand rainbows into the air, and she stared back as a slow burn started in the pit of her stomach. The most powerful creature in all the world yearned for her, and he was the only thing she wanted. He was the most dangerous hunter the world had seen, but for her he was the most sensual lover. He could hold her gently, whisper to her tenderly, or love her with more passion than she had believed was possible, losing himself in her as she lost herself in him.

He did not stop looking at her as he rose silently into the air on golden wings, and a tremor ran through her at the sight of him. He flew towards her slowly, and as he drew near she could see his flaming eyes. He transformed in midair, turning from a dangerous beast into a beautiful angel that angled towards her with intent. The angel seemed no less dangerous, and she shivered again as excitement spread through her, making her stomach clench. She took a step back as he landed on the ledge, wings outstretched behind his glowing body, his eyes piercing. His body was hard against hers as he roughly pushed his hands into her hair and pressed her against the stone wall of the cave. He was savage and wild, and his kiss took her breath away as he claimed her as his own. There was no escape from him as his body pressed around hers, dominating her, but she wanted no escape, and claimed him like for like. Her hands wrapped around his neck, pulling him closer, and she opened her mouth to his kiss. She moved against him, demanding her own satisfaction, knowing that he needed her just as much when she heard him groan.

He started changing as he pressed against her, becoming a curling flame that wound around her body, hotter than before. She moaned when the flames swept up her legs and swirled around her thighs. He stroked her neck with burning fingers and pushed fiery tendrils through her hair. She opened her mouth and he filled her, immersing himself in her. He was consuming her, and she no longer knew where she ended and he began. Flames moved along her shoulders, brushing over the edge of her gown as she heard a growl run through her mind.

"*Take it off.*" She shrugged her arms, and the gown fell in a heap at her feet. She cried his name when wisps of flame brushed from her neck to her legs, filling her and consuming her. She opened her eyes to see herself surrounded in a fiery, flaming blaze that twisted around her. She reached for him, but her fingers moved unchecked through the insubstantial wisps. The flames started pulling together, taking shape and form as she watched. His eyes, blazing white, stared into hers as fingers still rippling with flame trailed over her cheeks.

"I love you," she whispered. She saw his lips move, but his voice was in her mind.

"*I love you more than life,*" he said. "*This beast is completely at your mercy. I could not survive without you.*" His mouth closed over hers, even as his voice sounded again, so soft she wondered whether she imagined it. "*I wish I didn't love you so much.*"

His lips claimed hers and she pushed the words from her mind as she wrapped her arms around him, pulling him closer as he led her to height after height, until they finally lay panting in each other's arms, their legs tangled together as he stroked her thigh. Keira ran her fingers over his chest as they lay in silence. There were no words to describe the depth of what she felt, and she didn't even try. A long time had passed when Aaron gently pushed her away and rose to his feet.

"There is much still to be done before we leave Storbrook," he said. "We should get going." He reached for

Keira's gown and tossed it over to her, turning as she pulled it over her head. She folded the quilt as he stood at the entrance to the cave, and when she had slung the satchel over her head and shoulder, he transformed.

He said little on the flight back to Storbrook, grunting at Keira's attempt to make conversation, until finally she, too, lapsed into silence. Once, when a small deer broke through the bush, he stopped, waiting for Keira to slide off his back before he ripped it apart and seared it for her. They were on their way again soon after, and as Aaron glided through the cold air, Keira's mind wandered over the events of the last few days. She was overwhelmed by what Aaron had shown her, and a little in awe of her inhuman husband. That he had chosen her, and that he loved her, still astonished her, and there were times when she wondered when she was going to awaken from this incredible dream. For how was it possible that the most powerful creature walking the earth could really love such a simple, weak and unsophisticated woman? A sense of foreboding passed over her, like a shadow passing over the sun, but then it was gone, and she shook her head at her foolishness.

CHAPTER SIXTEEN

Anna shifted on her saddle, trying to find a more comfortable position. They had been traveling for two days, and she was saddle sore and weary. The road was a morass of melting snow and mud, and already the hem of her gown was stiff with dirt; if she descended into the mire it would soon stretch all the way to her knees. It would be another five days before they reached Drake Manor, the home of Aaron's cousin, and she shuddered to think of the condition she would be arriving in. She glanced up at the sky, looking for Max. He was up there somewhere, but when she could not see him, she returned her attention to the road. Ahead of her rode Thomas, the two packhorses close behind carrying provisions for the trip. Thankfully they had not had to use many of these, being able to find room at an inn for the last two nights. As the time dragged on, Anna felt herself being lulled by the motion of the horse, rise and fall, rise and fall. The light was beginning to fade when a voice in her ear made her start.

"Don't fall asleep, Anna," Max said, "unless, of course, you would like to go bathing in the mud." Anna pulled herself upright and shot him a glare. "That was a positively evil look for someone bringing you good news," he said. She raised her eyebrows, waiting for him to continue, but he met her stare in silence.

"Very well," she snapped, "what is the good news?"

"For such a beautiful young woman," he said, "you can be quite insolent."

"And you –" she started, pausing when he quirked his eyebrows. Straightening her back, she turned her head away and stared into the distance in silence as he laughed.

"The good news, darling Anna," he said, "is that there is an inn only a few hundred yards up the road. We will be stopping shortly for the night."

"At long last," Anna said, relief making her turn towards him with a smile – before she hurriedly looked away again when she saw his amused grin.

The inn was timber-framed, built around a courtyard that was open on one end. The hall was smoky and reeked of unwashed bodies, as well as the tallow and dung that had been trampled into the floor, but the room was warm and Anna entered gratefully. It appeared that Max had already attended to their affairs, as the innkeeper nodded in recognition and gestured for them to sit at the table. Thomas joined them a few minutes later, reporting that the stables were clean and the hay was fresh; a sign of a well-kept inn, he assured her. Cups of ale and plates of stew soon appeared before them, and Anna dug in with enthusiasm, the smell of the food making her suddenly hungry. She glanced around the room as she ate, watching the patrons of the inn. At the table behind them sat a small party, eating in silence. The group included a middle-aged man, dressed simply but in clothes cut from quality cloth, and a prim and stern-looking woman that Anna took to be his wife, dressed in somber brown. A young man sat next to the woman in sullen silence, his brightly contrasting tunic and hose making the woman's gown seem drab and dull. He wore shoes that stretched into a long point, and Anna looked at them with interest. She had never seen shoes such as these, which seemed very impractical for a winter journey through the countryside, and she found herself searching the young man's face, wondering what kind of person he must be. A friar completed the company, his tonsured scalp gleaming in the candlelight. His gaze wandered between his travel companions with a frown, but he kept his silence.

There was another table pushed into the corner of the room. The light of the tallow candles did not reach into the shadows, but even so, Anna could see two men sitting hunched over the wooden surface, facing in their direction. She felt a shudder of fear pass through her as she looked away.

"What is it, Anna?" Max asked. He was seated across the table from her, his back to the two men.

"It's ... nothing. I just don't like the look of the men at that table." She paused. "I think they're watching us."

"Describe them to me," Max said, dropping his voice.

"I can't really see them," she said. "It's too dark."

"Ignore them," he instructed her. "Don't make them aware that you've noticed them." Anna nodded. "And smile," he whispered. "Don't look so tense."

Anna glared at him, and he laughed out aloud. He stood and walked around to where she sat, glancing in the direction of the two men before taking her by the hand and hauling her to her feet. "Come, my darling," he said, loud enough for the others in the room to hear, "let's to bed." She opened her mouth to protest, but he quickly covered her lips with his own, startling her. The kiss was light, but when he moved his lips to her ear, his tone was hard. "Don't say anything," he said. "If the men have ill-intent, then it's better that they believe you're not alone. If they are just innocent travelers," he shrugged, "you will never see them again. And who's to say I am not your husband."

She pulled back to look at him with narrowed eyes, unable to refute his logic. He cocked his eyebrow at her with a grin, and she bit her lip in annoyance. Taking her hand, he led her from the room and up the stairs, where he stopped outside a wooden door. Lifting the latch, he pushed it open, and stood back to allow her to enter; following on her heels, he closed the door behind him.

"Don't worry," he said, seeing her look anxiously at the closed door, "I don't intend to stay. I will make my escape out the window as soon as those rogues are no longer about."

"Did you see them?" Anna asked.

"I did. They reek from a mixture of fear and excitement, which makes me think they are up to no good. Do not leave this room until I fetch you in the morning. Understand?"

Anna nodded, and Max sat down on the woven leather chair in the corner.

"What are you doing?" Anna asked. "I thought you were leaving."

"And so I shall. But it would not do you any good if I left now and ran into our friends. If they know you are alone, it may give them some ideas."

"Fine! But make sure you stay on that seat. I'm not sure I trust you."

"Anna. Do you think I created a ruse just to get you alone? I am wounded at your lack of confidence in me." The thought had crossed Anna's mind and she blushed, turning away as he gave a dry laugh. "I can have my pick of women, Anna. Do you really think I would want to bed a shrew?"

"You are so –"

"Yes, I know," he said wearily. "Arrogant. Rude. Insolent. Anything else?"

Anna stared at him before turning around and flinging herself onto the bed. Tears pricked the corners of her eyes, and she turned her face into the thin covering that lay over the straw mattress, hiding them. She tensed when she heard Max rise, then relaxed when a log was tossed into the fire that burned in the grate. She continued to lie on her stomach, refusing to turn and see his derisive look.

The inn started to grow quiet, and after a while she heard Max rise again and move over to the window. There was a rustling sound as he pulled his tunic over his head, and she resisted the urge to look at the man in her room. She heard a creak as the shutters opened, and then a few moments later they were pushed closed from the outside. Anna rolled over on the bed and looked around the room, her eyes falling on the chair where Max had been sitting. Suddenly the tears were spilling from her eyes again, and she scrubbed at them furiously. What did she care what Max thought of her, she thought angrily. She pushed herself up from the bed and walked to the window, opening the shutters slightly to look outside. There was nothing there, of course, and she was suddenly angry at herself for even looking. Removing her gown, she lay back down on the bed in her chemise, pulling the quilt up to her chin and closing her eyes. Sleep was a long time in coming, though, and when she finally did fall into a fitful sleep, it gave her no rest.

CHAPTER SEVENTEEN

It took a few minutes for the knocking to penetrate Anna's sleep, and when she finally opened her eyes, she closed them again immediately. The thumping on the door seemed to mirror the timing of the pounding in her head.

"Anna," she heard Max calling. "It's time to wake up, darling."

With a groan Anna pushed herself from the bed and stumbled towards the door, lifting the bar and pulling up the latch. She barely had time to step aside before Max was entering the room.

"Anna, what took so long?" He ran his eyes over her. "You look terrible," he said, taking her by the hand and leading her back to the bed. "Couldn't you sleep?"

"No," Anna said. She lay down and placed her hand over her eyes. "My head," she moaned.

"What you need is a good meal and fresh air," Max said. He picked up Anna's gown and threw it in her direction. "Get this on. I will wait for you outside." When Anna didn't move, Max stepped over to her. "Come on," he said, dragging her to her feet, "let's get you dressed." He pulled the gown over her head and deftly did up the laces, then gently pushed her back to the bed. A pile of linens sat on a table next to a jug of water, and wetting a cloth, he sat down beside her and carefully wiped it over her face. The touch was gentle and tender, and Anna opened her eyes to stare at him. He returned her gaze for a moment, before glancing around the room. Her leather satchel lay on the floor beside the bed, and he leaned down and pulled a hairbrush from within its depths. Carefully, working a few strands at a time, he pulled the brush through her hair, laying the silky tresses over her shoulder once they were smooth. She could feel his fingers teasing out the knots and tangles, gentle and soothing, and she closed her eyes, enjoying the sensation. She opened them when he was done, pulling in a breath when she saw him gazing down at her intently. There was a faint flicker of light at the back of his eyes, and she stared back, held by the glow. He blinked, and the glow was gone.

"Come along," he said, "no time for loafing. Let's find you some nourishment and be on our way." He was out the door before she had time to respond, his footsteps echoing on the wooden stairs. She stared at the door in confusion. His soothing touch had helped to ease her headache a little, but she could not understand what had prompted him to act so tenderly.

She rose and followed his path down the stairs, pausing to glance around the hall to see who else was about as she entered, but it was already empty, the other travelers having started their day's journey at the break of day.

Max was right, she reluctantly thought to herself a short time later. A hearty meal and fresh air had done much to relieve her headache. Soon after leaving the small village, Max had disappeared behind the trees, reappearing in the sky moments later, a huge fire-breathing dragon. He soared through the air, disappearing into the clouds for a moment, as if relieved to be free from the bonds of his human form. Flying as high as he did, it was difficult to tell that he was not some bird of prey, unless he breathed fire, which he seldom did. Anna knew that if she hadn't been looking for him, she would not even have known that a dragon was there.

The temperatures had dropped overnight, and the path they followed was covered in a layer of ice, making the going slow. The sky was clear, however, and Anna knew that the conditions would be less treacherous once the sun had a chance to thaw the ground. They were about an hour beyond the inn when Thomas held up his hand to bring them to a halt.

"What is it?" she called, but he placed his fingers to his mouth to silence her.

He glanced around, and then Anna heard it as well, the sound of feet crunching through the snow. She looked in the direction of the sound, drawing in a breath as the two men she had seen at the inn the night before stepped from behind the trees, followed by two more. Her eyes opened wide as the man in front turned to her, quickly covering the ground between them, his mouth pulled into a leer.

"Well, look what we have here," he said, reaching out to run a finger up her leg. She kicked her feet against the side of her mount, but the path was blocked by the two pack horses that trailed Thomas. Before she could turn the horse, the man had his hand on her shoulder and she was tumbling from the saddle. She had a moment to scream before big, rough, dirty hands were covering her mouth. The bodice of her gown ripped as one of the man's hands covered her breast, and she struggled, trying to break free from his grasp. His fingers twisted into her arm, grabbing her painfully, and she stopped her struggle, aware that he could quickly overpower her.

"That's better," he sneered, sliding his hand from her mouth and holding her chin as he brought his lips down to kiss her. She yanked her head away, but he jerked her back with a growl. His teeth were cracked and broken, and the few remaining in his mouth were black. His breath stank of rotting food and stale ale, and she felt herself gagging. Her hands were free, and she rained them down against his chest, but in a quick movement, he dropped her arm and grabbed her hands, holding both of hers in one of his. Desperate now, she pulled back a foot and kicked with all her might, connecting with his shin.

"Why, you little …" He yanked back her head as she started screaming. "Shut up," he growled into her ear. She was unable to turn, but she lifted her foot for another kick. The foot still on the ground slipped in the mud and she flew up into the air, her knee connecting with a soft part of his body before she landed on her backside on the muddy ground. He yelled, releasing her, and dropped to his knees, but at that moment a dragon swooped down from the sky, catching him in his talons. In another swoop a second man who had been grappling with Thomas was in the dragon's claws, screaming and struggling to free himself as flames poured from the dragon's mouth, a roar ripping through the air.

Anna pushed herself back to her feet as the dragon flew straight up, his form growing smaller as he climbed towards the clouds, until high above them he slowed down, and turning in a circle, flung both men into the air around him. Twisting around, he headed straight down again as the two men fell, their yells growing louder, before they disappeared behind the trees and their screams abruptly stopped. She glanced around to see the other two thieves backing away as the dragon headed straight towards them. Turning on their heels, they ran into the trees, but the forest did not prove to be a hindrance to the dragon, and with outstretched claws, he plowed into the retreating men, knocking over any trees that stood in his path. She heard the men screaming, and then all was silent. Dropping to the ground, Anna buried her head in her hands as the tears began to flow.

Max returned to the clearing a few moments later, his voice low as he asked Thomas a question, then he dropped down on his haunches before her.

"Anna." The concern in his voice made the tears flow faster, and then she was in his arms, his hard chest against her face as he rocked her gently.

"It's all right," he whispered. "You're safe. The men are gone and will not be returning." She nodded, allowing herself to lean against his steady frame. He pulled her to her feet and led her to a fallen log, where he made her sit once more.

As he stepped away she called his name, her voice panicky, but he was back in a moment.

"I'm right here," he said. "I was just finding some wine. Here." He pressed a flask into her hand. "Drink a little. It will help you feel better." Lifting the canteen to her lips she took a long swallow, handing it back to Max when she was done. He was watching her closely, and she gave a weak smile.

"He reminded me of Edmund," she said. Max nodded.

"Edmund is gone, and so are those men."

"Did you kill them?" she asked.

"Yes."

"When Aaron killed Edmund, he ate him."

"What?" Max pulled back in surprise. "How do you know?"

"I was there. I didn't watch," she added. "I think Keira did, though." Max stared at her, then dropped his head with a wry laugh.

"What?" she demanded.

"Anna, I'm not going to eat those men."

"Why not?" she said. "Don't you eat human flesh?"

"I do," he said, watching her carefully, "but only when absolutely necessary."

"Well, no point letting a good meal go to waste."

"Anna," he said in exasperation, "we need to get going." He pulled her to her feet, then glanced down at her gown. "Should I burn that for you?"

"What?" she said, following his gaze. She blushed when

she saw how much the ripped gown revealed, and quickly pulled it closed.

"Go away, you, you ..."

"Yes?" he said, lifting his eyebrows.

"Urgh! You are so annoying. Go away." She turned her back to him, gritting her teeth when she heard his soft laugh. She pulled another gown from her saddle bag and stomped off into the woods. Her chemise had also suffered some damage, but she would change that in the evening, in the privacy of an inn. For now, the gown would cover all that needed to be covered. A few moments later she stomped back out again, ignoring the two men as they watched her in amusement. Leading her horse to the log she had been sitting on, she pulled herself onto her saddle and waited for Thomas to lead the way.

CHAPTER EIGHTEEN

Keira and Aaron left Storbrook Castle at dawn two days later. Aaron flew all of the first day, his strong wings carrying them over the mountains with ease. Keira carried her satchel across her back, with some food and a change of clothes for both of them.

She had barely seen Aaron since their return from the cave. He spent much of the time in his study, finishing some business, he explained, staying there long after she retired to bed.

As the long day of flying dragged on, Keira felt herself growing more and more weary. The sun was starting to drop low in the sky, the pastel hues mesmerizing her as she gripped Aaron's neck. Her bones ached and her limbs were numb from holding onto him, and she leaned forward, slipping down Aaron's back, wedging herself against one of the upward-pointed spines. If she just closed her eyes for a moment ...

The weight of the satchel swinging forward and hitting her knee startled Keira awake, making her jump. She could feel herself slipping against the smooth scales down Aaron's side, and she gasped when he banked slightly, forcing her back up again.

"We need to stop and rest. You're exhausted!" he said, concern coloring his voice.

"No, I'm fine! All I'm doing is sitting here."

"Sitting there, hanging on," he said, turning towards an open field and landing smoothly. Keira slid off his back as he turned towards her.

"Lie down next to me. We'll rest for a few hours and then be on our way again." Keira opened her mouth to protest, but instead found herself stifling a yawn. Realizing the good sense of Aaron's suggestion, she nodded and slid down onto the ground next to him. Aaron curled his legs beneath his huge frame and sank down, pulling his tail tight around her. She could feel his heat warming the ground beneath her as her eyes drifted closed.

"Psst!"

Aaron was hissing at Keira as she clung to his back. No, that wasn't right. She was dreaming. Slowly Keira came to wakefulness, as the hissing came again.

"Psst! Over here!"

Forcing her eyes open, Keira peered through the darkness surrounding them as they lay in the field. There was movement ahead of her, and after watching it for a few moments, she realized it was an arm, waving her over.

"Quickly! The dragon's asleep. You can get away."

Keira screwed up her eyes to peer through the dark at the man standing about six feet away. Was he trying to rescue her?

"Quickly! But be quiet. You don't want to wake the dragon."

Keira glanced back at the huge body behind her. He looked to be asleep, but his eyelids flickered slightly, a thin ray of gold seeping out from his eyes. She turned back to the figure as he edged closer. Keira sighed, realizing he was determined to save her from the monstrous beast at her back. Pushing herself up to her feet, she tiptoed forwards. As she drew closer, Keira could see that her rescuer was only a few inches taller than her, but with broad shoulders and thick arms. He wore a felt cap on his head, folded up at the temple, and when he lifted his hand to push it back slightly, she could see that he had an open, friendly face. He kept an eye on the dragon as she moved towards him, and he reached out a hand to grab her.

"Come! If we move quietly we can get away before the dragon even realizes you're gone!"

Keira allowed him to pull her forward a few feet, before freeing herself from his grasp.

"Thank you for rescuing me," she said, glancing back at Aaron, "but I'm not here against my will. I don't need saving."

"It's all right," he said gently. "You don't need to be frightened. I promise I won't allow the dragon to hurt you." He grabbed her around the waist and pulled her another few steps. Wriggling beneath his hand, she tugged herself free from his grasp once more.

"Please," she said, her voice growing urgent, "I don't need rescuing. The dragon is not going to hurt me. I appreciate your concern, but it isn't necessary." The words were barely out of her mouth when he lifted his head, the flames above him illuminating his expression of horror. He pushed her behind his back as another stream of flame lit the air.

"Stay away," the man shouted. "I will not let you have this maid." Above him, the dragon roared as the man turned, took her by the arm, and started running with her.

"No," shouted Keira, trying to pull free, but the man paused only a moment to throw her over his shoulder, strong arms wrapping around her legs and holding them to his chest. "No! Let me down!" she shouted, pounding him on his back as he ran. The weight of her blows threw him off balance, and he stumbled, tumbling them both to the ground. Keira pushed herself onto her knees and looked up to see Aaron swooping down towards them. The man stood and tugged at her arm, but she shrugged him off, waving at the dragon bearing down on them.

"Stop!" she yelled.

Changing course, Aaron started circling around them, and for a moment Keira felt a wave of relief, until she saw that he was setting the ground alight, catching herself and the man in a trap that could only be escaped from above.

"Run," shouted Keira, pushing the man ahead of her, but the man was slow to realize what was happening, and before he took a step, Aaron had completed the circle, landing within its perimeter. He looked at Keira for a moment, his bony eyebrows pulling together as he cocked his head, then turned his attention to the man. The man returned Aaron's gaze, but he was shaking.

"He won't hurt you," Keira said. "Or at least, I don't think so," she added with a frown in Aaron's direction.

"I'm not worried about me," the man said. "Dragons prefer maidens."

Keira laughed. "He hasn't eaten me yet," she said.

"That could always change," the man said. "How long has it kept you prisoner?"

"I'm not a prisoner," Keira said. She turned as Aaron blew out a sigh of frustration.

"Enough, Keira." Aaron's voice was hard. "Let's go."

"No."

"No?" He dropped his head to her eye level, glaring at her as the man stumbled back a step.

"Not until you lift this man out of this little prison you've created," she said.

"No," he said.

"He was trying to help me. He only had my best interests at heart."

Aaron snorted. "This man had his own interests at heart, my sweet. I could smell his lust for you from the moment he first saw you."

Keira drew in a deep breath and turned back to the man, who was watching them in bewilderment.

"Why are you talking to this creature? And how is it that he can talk to you?" he said.

Aaron's head swung towards the man. "She talks to me because I am her husband," he said. "And you will be fortunate if I leave you alive."

"Her husband?" The man looked at Keira in horror. "You are married to this ... this beast?"

"Yes," she said.

"But, I don't understand. How can a pretty maid like you be married to a monster such as this?"

Aaron's eyes flamed and he brought his head within inches of the man's. "That is no maid, that is my wife," he said with a growl. "And she is well satisfied with the monster." He turned to look at Keira, who was glaring at him. "Let's go. Now."

"No," she said. She crossed her arms over her chest. "Not until you have lifted this man to safety."

"I will not," he said.

"He will die."

"Yes."

Keira turned towards the man. "Come," she said, "I will run with you through the fire."

"But we'll get burned," he protested.

"You will most definitely succumb to the flames if you stay here. But you will just get a little burned if you run." She grabbed him by the arm and pulled him towards the flames. "We will get burned together."

With a glance at Aaron, the man nodded, and together they ran towards the blaze. Behind her, Keira heard Aaron growl, and then she was lifted into the air, her hand slipping from the man's arm as Aaron grabbed her with his talons. Her first thought was that Aaron had taken only her, but a glance to the side showed Aaron carried the man as well. It was clear that Aaron was not being too gentle with him, but better a few scratches than burns, she reasoned.

A moment later they were both back on the ground, the ring of fire behind them. The man stared at Keira, then turning on his heel, started to run. Keira watched him for a few moments, before grabbing her satchel and walking in the same direction.

"Keira." Aaron's voice was cool, but when she turned around to face him, his eyes were blazing.

"How dare you," she said.

"I said nothing but the truth."

"You shamed me. And you would have killed that man."

"I saw how he looked at you. Damsel in distress. Gallant hero. He would have quickly offered himself as a shoulder to lean on after your traumatic experience at the hands of a monster."

"He was trying to help me!" she yelled.

"He wanted to have you," Aaron growled.

"You were just going to let him die!"

"Yes."

Spinning around, Keira marched away. She felt a wave of hot air roll over her as Aaron passed over her head, his tail mere inches from her face. He swooped into the sky, pushing higher and higher, then disappeared altogether against the lightening sky.

The field Keira was standing in was fallow, a scattering of snow creating a pattern of light and dark over the brown earth. A few crows gathered in the field, picking over some fallen animal, while in the distance Keira could make out the shadowy outline of a rock. She started towards it, pulling her cloak around her shoulders; once there, she sat down and rummaged in the bag, finding some bread and cheese to eat which she chased down with a sip of wine.

The sky was already light, the sun well above the horizon when a blur of shadow in the sky caught her eye. She watched as Aaron dropped towards the ground, his body in human form. His wings, stretched out on either side of him, glowed in the morning light, again making Keira think of an angel. A beautiful, dangerous, avenging angel. She watched him cautiously as he reached the ground, his wings still outstretched as he walked toward her, stopping a few feet away.

"Did you kill him?" she said.

"No." He glanced back at where the man had discovered them. "I probably should have, though."

"Why?"

"Because I revealed more than was wise."

"That's not his fault. He was trying to help me."

"He was," Aaron said, "but only so he could have you himself. Still, given what he believes about dragons, his concern for you was valid." Aaron paused. "Keira," he said, "I should never have spoken about you in such a way. I'm sorry."

"You should never have tried to burn that man," she said, looking up at him. He towered over her, his golden wings stretched to their fullest extent, his eyes blazing. He stared at her for a moment, then dropped down to his knees before her.

"I was jealous," he said. "Instead of telling him that you belonged to me, you were defending his actions. He wanted you, Keira, but you saw him as a hero."

"Of course I belong to you," she said, but then his lips were on hers, stopping all further argument. His arms slipped around her, and she leaned into him. She was still annoyed, but she knew that had the situation been reversed, she probably would have been jealous, too. Besides, they had each other – what did a nameless stranger matter?

CHAPTER NINETEEN

Aaron flew with Keira until dusk began to fall, then landed once again so that Keira could get a few hours' rest. Instead of landing in the open, he found a small cave at the base of a hill that had long since been abandoned by some animal. It was too small for Aaron to crawl into, but rather than change his form, he lay his huge body across the entrance, while Keira slept within, pressed up against his side. He wrapped his tail into the cave, however, circling it around her as she slept.

They left the cave early the next morning, before the sun had even risen, and continued their journey. As they traveled, Keira noticed that the snow was thinner on the ground, the temperatures not quite so cold. It was mid-afternoon when Aaron finally pointed to a cluster of buildings in the distance.

"That's Drake Manor," he said. As they drew closer, Keira could see that the house had been built in a horseshoe shape around a central courtyard, but the off-center plan suggested that there had been additions to the original building. High chimneys rose at regular intervals around the walls, smoke trailing from each of them. There were people in the courtyard, and as they neared, they looked up at the dragon, their hands shading their eyes. Keira saw a boy disappear into the building then run out the front door a few moments later, tugging a small girl behind him. He was shouting over his shoulder, and soon a small group of adults joined the pair outside. Drake Manor was the home of Aaron's family, and as Keira looked down from Aaron's back, she could make out the people standing below. Owain, Aaron's uncle, stood next to his wife Margaret, while Favian stood behind Cathryn, his hands on her shoulders as he looked up at his cousin circling above. Even from a distance it was clear that the men were father and son, with their tall, broad figures and red coloring. Dancing excitedly around were the two children, Bronwyn and Will.

"Look, we have a welcoming committee," Aaron said with a laugh. He dropped lower as he neared Drake Manor, landing on the ground before the assembled company. Keira slid down from Aaron's back, her gaze meeting Cathryn's. The two women smiled as Aaron's uncle stepped forward, lowering his head as he sank to his knee.

"Master," he said, "welcome to Drake Manor." He thumped a clenched fist over his heart before looking up to meet Aaron's gaze.

"Owain Drake," Aaron said. "Thank you for your welcome. Power and might to you, and strength be over your home." The two dragons, one in human form, stared at each other, flames seeping from both their mouths, before Owain rose to his feet.

"Aaron," he said, "it is good to have you back."

"It is good to be back," Aaron replied. He turned to look at the others standing at the doorway, his eyes quickly landing on his cousin, who was staring at him intently. Favian's face relaxed into a smile as he met Aaron's gaze. "Favian," Aaron said. Favian grinned in response, but before he could reply, the two children were running towards Aaron.

"Uncle Aaron." The dragon looked down at the children, then lowered his head as they collided with his chest.

Bronwyn wrapped her arms around his snout as Will came to a flying halt and placed his fist over his heart.

"Master," he said solemnly.

"William Drake," responded Aaron with the same air of solemnity. "Thank you for your welcome." Will nodded, and then broke out in a smile. "Take me for a ride, Uncle Aaron," he said.

"A ride?" said Aaron. "Does your father not take you flying? Or your grandfather?"

"They do," said Will, "but you are much more fun!"

"Me too, me too," shouted the little girl.

"I will definitely take you for a ride sometime, but not right now. Why, I haven't even had a chance to greet your mother and grandmother yet." He lifted his head and looked over the children to the two women smiling in amusement.

"My apologies Margaret, Cathryn," he said. "I have been very delinquent in my manners, but as you can see, it was quite beyond my control."

"Quite," agreed the older woman with a smile. "It is good to see you again, Aaron. You know that Drake Manor is as much your home as it is ours."

"Thank you," Aaron said, "but my home is wherever Keira is." He turned to look at his wife, and she smiled at him.

"Of course it is," said Margaret, "and Keira is welcome here not as a guest, but as family." She turned to Keira with a smile. "We are very happy to have you here, Keira, and hope you will indeed feel at home."

"Yes," said Cathryn, stepping up next to Margaret, "welcome to Drake Manor. I am so glad to see you again." Keira returned the smile as Aaron turned to his cousin.

"Favian," he said, "I need to hunt. Come with me."

Favian nodded, then turned to the others. "I will bring him back soon," he assured them. He pulled off his tunic and handed it to Cathryn. Huge red wings unfurled from his back, stretching out on either side of his body. He winked at his wife, then quickly dropped a kiss on her lips before shooting straight up into the air. Aaron looked at Keira, catching her gaze, then followed Favian heavenward. As she watched, Keira could see Favian contorting himself high above the ground before a bright flash indicated his transformation. A pair of trousers drifted down to the earth as Cathryn groaned. There was a laugh high above them, and then the two dragons were gone.

Owain shook his head as he stared at the two retreating figures, before turning towards Keira with a smile. "Welcome, Keira. We are so pleased that Aaron has brought you to Drake Manor so soon after your wedding, even if it is for reasons other than pleasure. You are as much a part of our family as Aaron is." Walking over to her, he pulled Keira into an enveloping embrace that startled her, but she relaxed a moment later, remembering her first introduction to Owain at Storbrook Castle, when he had done the same.

"Thank you," Keira said.

As a dragon elder, Owain had been the one to perform the blood-binding ceremony that had tied Keira and Aaron together as mates. It was a ceremony usually performed by the Master, but since Aaron was the one being bound, the task had fallen to one of the elders, and as Aaron's closest living relative, and the brother of his father, Owain had been the one chosen.

"Come," said Margaret, taking her by the arm, "Cathryn will show you to your chambers soon, but before she does, I'm sure you are in need of refreshments. How long did it take you to get here?"

In no time at all, Keira was seated in a small parlor before a blazing fire, a cup of wine in her hand and a tray of sweetmeats on a table near her elbow. Owain had excused himself and shooed the children out as well, leaving the three woman together as Keira described the wearying journey, omitting any mention of the man who had been determined to rescue her. After refreshments, Cathryn led Keira to the guest chambers. As they walked, Cathryn explained how she and Favian occupied one wing of Drake Manor, while Owain and Margaret occupied the other. Favian had enlarged their wing, adding additional rooms for the children plus two more guest chambers. Unlike Storbrook, which had rooms that could accommodate dragons in their natural form, Drake Manor had been built to human dimensions. When Keira commented, Cathryn explained that Favian and Owain were content to leave it that way.

"There are private stairways built from each wing that lead to the roof," Cathryn said. "They use that as an entry or exit point, transforming on the roof."

"But what about the servants? Do they know what Owain and Favian are?"

"The roof has been built in such a way that a person on the ground cannot see what is happening above, but if the residents here have an inkling of what happens, they do not voice their opinions beyond the walls of Drake Manor. They have lived here for many generations, and the Drakes have always treated their people very well, never giving cause for complaint." Cathryn paused outside a heavy wooden door. "These are your chambers," she said, pushing the door open and gesturing Keira inside. The chamber was much smaller than the one Keira and Aaron shared at Storbrook, but still larger than the bedchambers of most houses. A huge four-poster bed stood in the center of the room, while beyond was a large window that looked out over open fields. Leading from the room was a small antechamber in which stood a wooden chest.

"There is a small forest that lies on the other side of the house," said Cathryn, joining Keira as she walked over to the window. "I always love leaving the city and coming home to Drake Manor."

"Aaron told me you have a house in the city," Keira said.

"Yes. My father moved to the city a few years ago, so we decided to buy a townhouse as well. We often stay there so I can help my father with his business."

"His business?" said Keira, turning to face her friend. "What kind of business?"

"He's a wool merchant. I disappointed him greatly when I married for love instead of using marriage as a way to extend his business alliances. Although I must confess, I was not easily won over to the idea of marriage for love myself. I was incredibly hard-headed and stubborn, and almost lost Favian." She shook her head with a wry smile. "But that's all in the past. When Father realized that Favian was quite accommodating to the idea of me still working in the business, he came around, deciding Favian wasn't quite as terrible as he first imagined!"

Keira laughed. "Does he know what Favian is?" she asked.

"Oh, no, Favian would never reveal that to anyone." Cathryn sounded shocked at the idea. "Surely your parents don't know?"

"Just my father. Aaron saved his life by giving him his blood."

"Aaron gave your father blood?"

"Yes." Keira said in surprise. "He was dying."

"But giving a human blood creates a bond with the dragon."

"Yes, I know." Keira looked back at the open fields. "But Father would most certainly have died." Next to her Cathryn turned and gazed out the window as well.

"Well, I'm sure Aaron knew what he was doing," she said finally. "And no-one is going to question the Master." Turning back into the room, she pointed at the chest in the antechamber. "I know you traveled light," she said, "so I arranged some gowns for your use until your own arrive. I understand Max travels with Thomas and the luggage?"

"Yes. And my sister Anna travels with him."

"Anna. I've heard about her. Aaron saved her life, too, didn't he?"

"Yes," Keira said, meeting Cathryn's gaze.

"Well, I have a chamber arranged for her, and Max will be staying in the other wing. Now come, let me show you around some more."

The supper hour had come and gone before Aaron and Favian returned to Drake Manor, laughing as they made their way down the passage to the parlor.

"You must have had a good time hunting," Keira commented later as they were preparing for bed.

Aaron smiled. "We did. Two deer and three sheep."

"Sheep?"

"Favian has a flock of two thousand. But I wouldn't recommend eating sheep unless they are sheared – their wool gets stuck in your throat."

"I will keep that in mind," Keira promised with a laugh.

CHAPTER TWENTY

Anna was more shaken by the attack than she was willing to admit, especially to Max. She knew that she had not been in any real danger, since the thieves would never have stood a chance against a dragon, but the memory of the thief's thick, dirty hands touching her, and his foul-smelling breath against her face still made her feel ill. Max had stayed close by for the rest of the day, electing to walk near her horse instead of taking to the air again.

"I don't mind if you want to fly, you know," she told him.

"You will let me carry you?" he asked.

"Definitely not!"

"Then I will walk," he said decisively. And although Anna shrugged her disinterest, she had been relieved. He did take a quick flight late in the afternoon, soon returning with the news that there was an inn not too far ahead. It was smaller than the one they had stayed in the previous night, and the light shining brightly through the windows made it appear homely and snug.

Max pushed open the door ahead of Anna, and by the time she had stepped over the threshold, the innkeeper was making his way over to them with a welcoming smile.

"Come in, come in," he said. "There is a warm fire and good food in the hall. Make yourselves comfortable."

"Go ahead," Max said. "I will just secure us some rooms." Anna nodded and crossed over to the hall, glancing around as she did so. Two men sat at a table in one corner of the room, leaning towards each other in animated discussion. They ignored the other people in the room, but when one of them pulled back with a good-natured laugh that rang through the room, she felt herself relax slightly.

"Ah, those two," said a voice behind Anna, and she turned to see a stout woman of middle age smile at the two men indulgently as she wiped damp hands against the apron tied around her waist. "They come here every night and argue about everything under the sun. Some nights we have to drag them away from the other's throat, but they are back again the next day, friends once more." The woman gestured towards a table near the fire.

"Come sit down, and I will bring you a nice, hearty bowl of broth." A moment later she returned as promised with three bowls, their contents sloshing slightly as she walked. Her cheeks glowed in the fire-light, a result of exertion and heat.

"Your husband should be along soon. My man loves to talk, and he has been keeping him standing at the door." She sat down across from Anna. "Handsome man, your husband. Been married long?"

Before Anna had a chance to reply, a commotion sounded at the door, and the party that Anna had seen the previous night at the other inn stumbled into the room, the innkeeper following close behind with Max a slight distance back. The innkeeper's wife was on her feet with an alacrity that belied her stoutness.

"What is it, John? What has happened?"

"These people were attacked on the road, and all their possessions stolen by a band of thieves."

Anna's eyes flew to Max's, who crossed over the floor to

where she stood.

"Do you think they were attacked by the same people?" Anna asked softly.

"It sounds like it," Max replied.

"Did you tell the innkeeper we were attacked too?"

"No. It would have been too difficult to explain our escape. At least the thieves are no longer around to inflict harm on others."

"Why didn't we see these travelers on the road?"

"They were taking a different route and had already left the main road when they were attacked. It appears there was a whole gang of thieves, patrolling all the roads in the area. Our two friends from the inn must have passed on news of the travelers to others in the gang." Max gestured to the group, who huddled miserably together. "They returned to the main road afterwards."

"Did they hurt the woman?" Anna asked, her voice dropping even lower. Max turned to look at Anna, his gaze catching and holding hers, before he turned back in silence to observe the small group. They looked disheveled and dispirited, and Anna could see the woman had been crying. The innkeeper's wife was rubbing her hands between her own, speaking in soft and soothing tones. As they watched, Thomas came into the room and joined them. Anna turned away, her appetite vanishing as she faced the bowl of soup before her. Max settled himself across the table, and she looked up to see him watching her. She gave a tentative smile before lifting her spoon and slowly pushing it around her bowl.

"You must eat, Anna," he said. She nodded, and brought the spoon to her lips, swallowing the now tasteless broth. The stress of the day had suddenly caught up with her, and she felt incredibly weary. She managed a few more mouthfuls before she pushed the bowl away and rose to her feet. Max immediately followed suit, and placing a hand at the small of her back, leaned down to whisper in her ear.

"I told the innkeeper we are married," he said.

"Why?"

"So that no one questions your propriety when I go with you to your room," he replied.

"To my room?" she said, her voice rising in volume.

"Sshh," he said, glancing around the hall as he propelled her towards the stairs. "I'm not leaving you alone. I don't intend to share your bed, of course."

"Of course. But as much as I appreciate your concern for my safety, I really don't think this is necessary."

"Well, I do. Furthermore, I've discussed it with Thomas, and he agrees that this is the best course of action."

"He does?"

"Mmm. I suppose he trusts that I am not going to force my attentions on you." The passage at the top of the stairs was dark, and the wooden floorboards creaked as they made their way to the room.

"Hmph! He is far too trusting."

"And," Max continued, "he seems quite confident you won't be giving yourself willingly."

"Most certainly not!"

Max laughed softly. "Once again, you have cut me to the quick, darling."

As they entered the room Max glanced down the passage, then bolted the latch and secured the door. He dropped into a seat as Anna eyed him warily.

"I will stay right here," he assured her. She watched him for a moment, then moved towards the bed, dropping her satchel onto the floor.

"Close your eyes," she said. He raised his eyebrows questioningly, then turned away when she tugged at her gown. Pulling it over her head, she dropped it to the floor, then quickly jumped into the bed, pulling the covers up to her shoulders, hiding her chemise.

"All right," she said. As Max turned back to her, she noticed her satchel on the floor, groaning when she realized it was beyond her reach.

"What's wrong?" asked Max.

"My hairbrush," she said. "It's in my satchel. Can you pass it to me, please?"

Max bent down and retrieved the bag from the floor, opening it on his lap and pulling out the hairbrush. He turned it over in his hand and then looked up to meet her gaze.

"Let me brush your hair," he said. As he rose and walked over to the bed, she stared at him. "Anna," he said, "I have already brushed your hair once. And I promise not to force myself on you," he added wryly.

Slowly, she turned around and presented her back to him, shuddering slightly when she felt his hands lift her hair. It was tangled after a day of riding in the wind, and he gently teased apart the knots before pulling the brush through her tresses. He worked slowly and rhythmically, and Anna could feel herself relax as he brushed. A few minutes passed before he spoke.

"Anna," he said, "I don't know what happened with Edmund, but you were no helpless damsel in distress this morning. I saw a young woman fighting to save herself, not a victim who could not fight back."

Anna was silent as she considered his words. At the first mention of Edmund's name she had felt the tension rise, but he continued brushing and she had slowly relaxed once more.

"Really?" she finally said.

"Yes. Don't allow the shadow of Edmund to defeat you. He is dead and gone, but even alive he was not worthy of your attention."

"Maybe not," she said, "but he still would have killed me."

"Perhaps," he replied, "but as it turned out, he was the one to lose his life, while you were given another chance. What are you going to do with it?" He paused for a moment. "You are no longer the girl that he kidnapped, but a young woman who has grown stronger because of it. But strength comes in many different forms. You can be a flame, destroying everything in your path, or water, which uses its strength gently, slowly shaping the rocks around it."

"Which one are you, Max? Are you not already fire?"

"I may be fire personified, Anna, but I can still be like a river, slowly carving out its path through the resisting rock, or a soft breeze, bending the trees to its purposes, rather than a fiery flame, which burns everything in its way."

He pulled the brush through her hair once more, his fingers following the strands, before placing it on the table next to the bed and moving away. Anna glanced over her shoulder, surprised to see him already seated in the chair across the room.

"Goodnight, Anna," he said.

"Goodnight." She lay down on the bed and pulled the quilt up to her chin, before rolling onto her side and peering at Max through lowered lashes. His eyes were closed, his head leaning against the back of the chair. His arms were folded across his chest, while his legs were stretched out before him. He had removed his boots, and Anna could see the muscles in his legs, taut against his breeches. She glanced away, embarrassed, and focused on his face. The light from the flames in the hearth danced over his skin, and for a moment she thought she could see flames responding from within, but it was just a trick of the light. She closed her eyes, capturing an image of him in her mind, and drifted off to sleep.

She slept restlessly, pursued by faceless men who would do her harm. She tossed and turned, until she felt in her dreams someone holding her tight, his soothing voice telling her that she was safe, and that everything would be all right. A warm hand rested against her forehead, and her heart slowed its racing as she settled back into a more restful sleep.

CHAPTER TWENTY-ONE

Keira saw little of Aaron over the next few days. It was often late when he came to bed, and he would leave early in the morning before the sun had fully risen. Dawn was the best time for hunting, and it also gave him time to catch up on dragon business with the dragon elder, but she was used to him being around and she missed his presence. She would watch through the window as two or sometimes three dragons flew through the open sky, their huge forms silhouetted against the rising sun. She could easily make out Aaron, shining gold between two red dragons, his wings stretching wider than either of theirs.

The days were spent in the company of the other two women in various pursuits. Keira had felt a kinship with Cathryn when they first met the previous summer, and as the days passed, she found that friendship growing. The mornings were usually spent with Margaret as Cathryn taught the children their letters and numbers, but the afternoons often found Keira and Cathryn together. When the weather was clear, Cathryn showed Keira the now dormant gardens, and led her into the forest, the trees bare of leaves, while the children trailed behind. A small river ran between the trees, and though the banks were covered in a thick layer of ice, a channel of water cut through the middle. One day Cathryn pointed to a large rock overhanging the water.

"That is where I was when I first learned that dragons were real," she told Keira.

"Oh? How? What did Favian do?"

"Not Favian. Aaron."

"Aaron?" Keira said in surprise. "What happened?"

"Favian and I were sitting on the rock when Aaron flew overhead."

Keira was silent for a moment. "Did Favian know Aaron was around?"

"No. He was furious."

"So why did Aaron do it?" Keira asked, as a yell cut through the air. Turning towards the sound, Keira saw Will hanging with his hands from a branch, his feet dangling over the narrow channel of water. Bronwyn stood on the ground below, her wide eyes watching her brother.

"Will," Cathryn said, her voice more exasperated than concerned, "what are you doing?"

"I slipped on the rock," he shouted. "Help me, I'm going to fall."

"Of course you slipped," Cathryn said. "It is winter, which means ice. Now hold on tight, let's get you down."

"I can't hold any more," he shouted.

Will's hands were slipping, and Keira could see that it was a matter of seconds before he tumbled into the frigid water. Cathryn was picking her way over the ice, trying to find a firm footing from which she could lift down her son, when a whoosh through the air had Keira looking up.

Two dragons, one gold, the other red, were speeding through the air toward them, their bodies scraping the tops of the trees. The red one reached Will first, and he wrapped his talons around the boy's wrists just as his hands slipped from the branch.

"Will-boy," said the dragon, lifting the boy into the air

116

and depositing him at his mother's feet. "What are you doing?"

"I just wanted to see from the top of the rock. Mama said she saw Uncle Aaron from the rock once, so I thought I would see him too. Besides," added the boy, "I was fine. I wouldn't have fallen."

"It would not have been anything to be ashamed about if you had," Cathryn said with a smile. She glanced up at the dragon. "I'm sure your father fell into the river many times."

"I would not recommend falling into the river in the middle of winter," said Favian dryly. He glanced around to look at Aaron, and the other dragon laughed out a stream of flame.

"At least we don't feel the cold," Aaron said. He looked at Keira before settling his gaze on Cathryn. "What exactly have you been telling my wife about me?"

Cathryn shrugged. "I haven't had a chance to tell her anything, yet." She gave Aaron a sly look. "Why, are there some things you don't want me to tell?"

"Yes, there are. But I suppose you still will." He sighed, sending sparks into the air, then turned his golden gaze on Keira. "Just remember, my sweet, that no matter what Cathryn tells you, I am not the beast I was before." Keira nodded, but before she could say anything, a little voice spoke up.

"Uncle Aaron, will you take me for a ride?" Aaron looked down at Bronwyn, who had crept up to stand beside her mother.

"Hey, that's not fair," shouted Will. "I want to go with Uncle Aaron. I asked first!"

"I'll tell you what, Will," Aaron said. "I will fly Bronwyn and your aunty back to the house, and then tomorrow I will take you for a ride all on your own. How does that sound?"

Will's scowl turned to a smile. "Good plan."

"All right." He turned back to the little girl. "Aunty Keira will pick you up, and then I will lift you both." The girl turned to Keira, her arms up as Keira hefted her onto her hip. In a moment Aaron swept his tail around them both and lifted them onto his back, while next to him, Favian lifted first Will then Cathryn onto his own back. Bronwyn leaned against Keira as Aaron rose into the air, Favian close on his tail. In a few short minutes they were back at the manor house, the passengers sliding off the backs of their massive mounts, and the dragons were off again.

The next afternoon, Cathryn asked Keira if she would like to accompany her while she attended to patients around the estate.

"It is usually a task that Margaret performs," Cathryn explained, "but she thought maybe you would enjoy getting out of the house. All we need to do is deliver the medicines with appropriate instructions on dosage."

"Let's go," said Keira, already on her feet.

"Right," said Cathryn. "We just need to get the supplies from Margaret. I believe she is in the parlor. Come along." Keira followed Cathryn out of the room, down the stairs, through the hall and into the corridor on the other side of the building. Cathryn pointed to the upper passage of the wing they had just been in.

"See that pillar," she said, indicating a carved wooden pillar that stood between the railings of the opposite passage, "that is where I saw Aaron for the very first time. He was in his human form, of course, and to tell the truth, he terrified me."

"Really?" said Keira. "Why?" Cathryn ducked into the parlor while Keira waited outside, staring at the pillar, and a moment later Cathryn reappeared, a basket over her arms.

"You know about Aaron's parents, don't you?" Cathryn said as they walked.

"You mean that they were killed by people in the village? Yes, I know that."

"And you know that Aaron would have nothing to do

with humans after that?"

"Yes."

"The first time I saw Aaron, he still despised humanity. Favian had convinced him to come to Drake Manor, but Aaron wanted nothing to do with people. And he had not been at the Manor for very long when Margaret invited me to come and stay. I was, at that time, betrothed to another man, but Favian had already made his feelings for me clear to his family, and Aaron was furious. I think Margaret thought he would stay away when he heard I was coming, but he didn't. The first time I saw Aaron, he glared at me across the courtyard, looking very much like someone I should be very afraid of."

"What did you do?"

"I mentioned it to Margaret and Owain, but I didn't know anything about dragons back then. Of course they assured me that Aaron wouldn't hurt me, but I'm not so sure. If he felt he was protecting Favian by doing so ..." Her voice trailed off as she stared unfocused into the distance.

"Did he hurt you?" Keira asked, bringing her back to the present.

"What? Oh no, he didn't even approach me, but he was very angry at Favian. Favian took me down to the river one afternoon, and it was then that Aaron decided to show himself, flying above us. Favian was livid, but I didn't know why. I still didn't understand that dragons could take on human form. And I certainly didn't know that the dragon was Aaron." Cathryn paused. "But later, when I thought I had lost Favian forever, it was Aaron who offered to help find him. So despite his anger, he still had a good heart. He loves Favian, and really wanted to see him happy." Cathryn stopped and turned to look at Keira. "Before you came along, I didn't think Aaron would ever find a mate. I thought he would never be able to love someone, especially not a human, in that way. But Favian always believed. He said he knew Aaron was capable of love, and just needed to find the right woman. And it is clear that Aaron loves you, more than even he ever thought was possible."

Keira smiled as a tightness she hadn't even been aware of eased slightly.

"You should ask Margaret to tell you some stories about Aaron," continued Cathryn. "He spent many of his childhood summers here, and from what I have heard, he and Favian were as thick as thieves."

The two women arrived back at the manor a few minutes before supper was about to be served, and they quickly hurried to the small dining room, arriving just minutes before Favian and Aaron walked into the room.

"Finally, the children have arrived home," Owain said, glancing up at the two men as though they were delinquents. Favian cast Aaron a look that spoke of mischief, and for a moment, Keira could only see two boys who had been up to no good.

Aaron laughed, then bent down to give Keira a quick kiss on the cheek before sitting down beside her.

"Where have you been?" Margaret asked.

"Fishing," Favian said with a grin. He caught Aaron's eye, and the two men started laughing.

"No!" Owain said. "Exactly how old are the two of you?" Keira glanced at Cathryn, who seemed as confused as she was, before turning to look at Aaron.

"I'll explain later," he said, leaning close to her ear.

The meal was brought in, and the conversation turned to other topics.

When the meal was done, Margaret led them into the parlor. The fire had died down in the grate, but there was no need for it with three dragons in the room. A flagon of spiced wine had been placed on a small table, and Keira helped herself to a cup before sitting down beside Aaron. Across from them she noticed Owain staring at Aaron intently. Aaron looked up, meeting his uncle's eye in bemusement.

"Owain? What is it?"

"You've changed, Aaron. Grown. I noticed it when you arrived."

"What are you saying, uncle?" Aaron said cautiously.

"You're stronger. Not in physical strength, but more powerful. I see you, Aaron, and all I see is pure, blazing white."

"White?" Aaron sat back in his seat, clearly startled.

"Wouldn't you agree, son?" Owain said, casting a glance at Favian.

"Yes. I also noticed it when you arrived," Favian said. "You have grown in power since I saw you at the binding."

"You weren't aware of this change?" Owain asked. He looked at Keira for a moment, before turning his gaze back to Aaron.

"No, I must confess I wasn't. How is it even possible?"

"I believe I know why," Favian started, but Owain held up his hand, stopping him short.

"No, Favian," he said. "A man must discover his source of power for himself." He glanced at Keira once more before turning to Margaret.

"What entertainments have you planned for us this evening, my dear?" Owain said.

"I thought perhaps you could read us a poem," Margaret replied. "He's got a splendid library," she said, turning to Keira as Owain rose with a nod and left the room. "Have you seen it?"

"I have," Keira said with a smile. She moved a little closer to Aaron, and he wrapped his arms around her. Owain returned a moment later, a large, hand-bound volume of *Beowulf* in his grasp. It was a story that Keira was unfamiliar with, and she listened with interest as Beowulf slew all manner of dreadful monsters. When he came to his final battle against a dragon, she smiled: always there was a dragon, and always, it needed defeating. She turned slightly, bringing herself even closer to her own dragon, and he glanced down at her with a smile.

"Feel sorry for the dragon, my sweet?" he whispered.

"I think I feel sorry for Beowulf, thinking he can fight a dragon and survive," she whispered back.

He laughed softly in her ear. "We all have to face our dragons, my sweet. It is just that some breathe more fire than others."

CHAPTER TWENTY-TWO

Keira woke the next morning with Aaron spooning behind her, his arms wrapped around her chest, his fingers trailing patterns over her skin. She smiled and turned around to face him.

"Good morning," she whispered.

"Good morning," he said, pulling himself forward on his elbow and leaning in to kiss her. She could feel the hard length of his body running down her side, and she wrapped her arms around him, pulling him closer. He lifted his head and she could see the flames swirling around in his eyes, and when he kissed her, his breath was hot. She ran her hands down his back, smiling when he released his wings. They stretched out around them, massive and gleaming, and when he wrapped his arms around her, pulling her close, she felt her body leave the bed as his wings held them aloft. Her head fell back as she lay helpless in his arms, while his mouth and fingers ravaged every part of her.

Later, as they lay tangled together, he stroked his fingers down her skin.

"I can't stop myself from loving you," he said, his voice low.

"Why do you want to?" she asked, but he silenced her with a kiss.

Still later, as the sun rose in the sky, beams of sunlight shone through the open window, landing on his skin, making it glow bright and golden.

"What did Owain mean when he said you had grown more powerful?" she asked.

"I told you before that dragons can see how powerful a dragon is by how hot he burns. Owain thinks I am burning with more power, but I don't know what it means."

"Does that happen often? Growing more powerful?"

"A young dragon grows more powerful as he matures, but most of our power is inherent, growing to a certain level, then no more. I reached my full level of power years ago, or at least I thought I did."

"Well," Keira said, wrapping her arms around him, "you are the most powerful creature I know."

Aaron laughed. "A resounding validation from the human who has met – how many creatures of power?" He caught Keira's hand as she raised it to smack him, then pulled her in for a kiss.

"Your love is all-powerful," she said a moment later, "and that is enough for me."

He stared at her, then pushed himself from the bed.

"It must be time for dinner, and I'm starving."

"Oh, good. You're having human food today." Keira rose from the bed and headed to the antechamber where she pulled out a dark red gown. She felt Aaron come up behind her, and shivered when he trailed his fingers over her skin.

"I've been neglecting you," he said. "I'm sorry."

Keira turned around, meeting his gaze. "Aaron, your family is important to you, and I don't begrudge you time spent with them," she said. She wagged her finger in his face. "Just as long as you don't forget about me."

"As if I could," he said with a laugh. "You are all I think about." He paused, then added, his voice low, "That's the problem."

His tone made her pause and she glanced up at him, but he stepped away and pulled on his tunic. "Take your time getting dressed. I will see you downstairs." Keira watched as he left, then turned to face the mirror with a sudden sense of unease. Tugging at the laces of her gown, she pulled them tight and tied a knot, before dragging a brush through her hair, but her mind was not on the tasks she was performing. Something was changing. She just didn't know what.

Keira headed out of the chamber and made her way towards the dining room, pausing at the entrance when she saw it was empty. Voices drifted down the dark passage from the parlor, and she turned towards them. She could hear Aaron and Favian talking, their voices low. She was about to push the door open when the sound of her name froze her in place. She stepped closer as Aaron's voice reached her through the door.

"It's not right, Favian. I shouldn't even love her." Keira held her breath and leaned forward as Aaron spoke again. "Just being with her is a torment."

She pulled back with a slight gasp, then spun around on her heel. As she ran back down the passage she heard the conversation stop.

"Keira?" Aaron's voice sounded through the parlor door. "Keira?" The door opened and then Aaron was behind her. "Keira. Stop." He grabbed her by the arm, forcing her to a halt.

"Let me go," she hissed, shaking her arm free.

"Keira, please, let me explain."

"What is there to explain?" She pulled in a deep breath. "Fine. Explain."

"Keira, don't you see? I love you too much, and it's consuming me. I cannot get you out of my mind when I'm away from you, and when I am with you, all I want to do is touch you. I never want to let you go, and it's wrong. No-one should love that much."

"How can you love too much, Aaron?" she said, her voice rising.

"I already do," he said. "I've already done things I shouldn't have because of my love for you."

"Like what? What have you done that you shouldn't have done?"

"I saved your father. I revealed myself to that man on the road."

"How was saving my father wrong?"

"I gave him my blood, Keira! A dragon should never share his blood with a human who is not his mate. And now he feels bound to me."

"You saved his life!"

"Yes. But only because of my love for you! I am the Master, responsible for my clan, and yet all I can think of is you! Don't you see how wrong this is?"

"It is wrong to love? No, Aaron, I don't see that. Love is a strength, not a weakness."

"Tell me, Keira, how did love make my father strong? He allowed himself to be killed. He could have saved himself, but he chose to die, leaving me to pick up the pieces. He abandoned me and abandoned the clan. I shouldn't even be Master, but I didn't have a choice!"

"You are not your father, Aaron."

"No? His blood runs in my veins. His love for my mother was a sickness, just like mine is for you!"

"A sickness, Aaron?" Keira shouted. "A sickness?"

"Yes," Aaron growled back. "I am Dragon Master, Keira, and you have crept into my veins like a poison. But what would you know? You are only human, after all, prone to the frailties of humanity." He glared at her, then turned around and stormed the opposite direction down the passage, brushing past Favian, who stood at the doorway to the parlor watching her with concern. Angry and humiliated, Keira turned in the opposite direction, passing through the hall and out the door.

She stood against the side of the house for a moment, before turning in the direction of the woods. The tears were stinging her eyes, but she brushed them away, stumbling through the scrubby grass. She headed towards the river, following the footprints left by someone after the dusting of snow they'd received the previous day.

She glanced up at the rocky outcrop, and carefully, mindful of the fact it was icy, pulled her way to the top of it. It was here that Cathryn had said she had first seen a dragon, and it was here that the dragon said he was no longer the same creature he had been twelve years previously. But as she gazed miserably over the trees, she wondered whether he had changed at all.

How long she had been sitting there, she didn't know, but she turned her head when she heard footsteps crunching through the snow. It was Owain, and in one quick leap, he was on the rock, his footing sure.

"It's a good place to think, isn't it?" he said, sitting down next to her. "I used to come here a lot when I was a lad, and Favian and Aaron used to get up to all kinds of mischief around here."

They sat in silence for a moment.

"You heard what he said, didn't you?" Keira finally said.

Owain nodded.

"Is it true? Does loving someone make you weaker?"

"No," Owain said. "If you allow it to, it makes you stronger. That stands true for dragons and humans."

"He said I am a sickness. A poison."

Owain looked at Keira for a long moment, his face sad. "Ever since his parents died, Aaron has been in control. Of the clan. Of himself. Of everything around him. Even in his anger, he was controlled. And now he finds himself unable to control his love for you, and he doesn't know what to do."

"He said he shouldn't even be Master."

"Aaron had Mastership thrust onto him before he was ready, but it was just a matter of time. The clan always knew that Aaron would be the next Master."

"Because his father was Master."

"No, because from the time Aaron was young, it was clear that he would be a dragon of power."

"So what am I to do?" she finally said.

Owain stared into the distance for a long moment. "Aaron's father was my brother," he finally said. "When we were children he was always the stronger of the two of us. He could run faster, fly faster, and hit harder. And it wasn't just me – Zachary could beat any dragon, even those more powerful than him, because what he lacked in inner strength, he had in brute force. So when the old Master died, Zachary was the logical choice to become the next Master. But as strong as Zachary was, he never seemed happy. Even as a child he seemed ... needy. Desperate for love; as though something was missing.

"And then he met Eleanor, and all that changed. He loved her with utter devotion, and she became his whole life. For a while everything was good. Aaron was born, and Zachary led the clan as a strong leader should. But then Eleanor lost the baby."

"Aaron had a sibling?"

"No. The baby died at birth, and Eleanor was devastated."

"How old was Aaron?"

"He must have been around fifteen. Zachary had sent him to stay with us long before the baby was due so he could devote his attention to Eleanor. I'm not sure Aaron even knew." Keira nodded as Owain continued. "After the baby died, everything changed. Eleanor was unhappy, which made Zachary unhappy. He started neglecting his duties as Master, and it fell on the elders to deal with issues. He withdrew to Storbrook, staying away for years at a time. Aaron remembers a strong leader and father who suddenly chose to die, but the truth was, Zachary had already given up as Master. Even if he had survived that day, it was just a matter of time before he was forced out and Aaron became leader in his place. Zachary didn't die because love made him weak. The weakness was already there, and he made a decision that day that he could not live without Eleanor.

"But Aaron is not his father. He is far stronger and far more resilient, but he needs to realize that for himself. He has the strength and power to love you and lead the clan, but he needs to see it within himself. In the meantime," Owain shrugged, "all you can do is love him and trust that he will figure it out."

"And if he doesn't?"

"He will. You have to believe that." He gave Keira a wry look. "You have dragon blood in your veins now, which means you have plenty of time."

"Wonderful," she muttered.

He smiled, then held out his hand. "Ready to head back indoors?"

"No," she said, "but I will come anyway." She placed her hand in his, gasping when he pulled her off the rock. He steadied her with a hand at her waist when she hit the ground, then stepped back and gestured for her to lead the way through the trees.

"Aaron said he should not have saved my father," she said as they walked.

"Perhaps not, but Aaron is making far more of the situation than necessary. It is better if we dragons don't draw attention to ourselves, but we have all done things we shouldn't have. And saving his father-in-law was probably the best decision at the time, even though it had some undesirable consequences."

They were close to the house when Will came running out, waving his arms in the air.

"Look, another dragon." Owain and Keira followed Will's pointed hand, and sure enough a dragon could be seen circling through the air.

"Max," Owain said.

"Anna," Keira said. She turned her gaze to the road, but did not see anything.

"Do you see them?" she asked Owain.

"Yes, I see them. Thomas, Anna, and two extra horses."

"Good," Keira said, lifting her skirts and hurrying down the road as the small party came into her view.

"Anna!" She waved her arms in the air as Max landed beside her. "You made it," she said, turning to him with a smile.

"Did you doubt it?" he asked.

"I did wonder whether you would make it one piece," she said.

"Quite intact, I assure you. I am a resourceful man."

"Should I be worried?" she asked, her eyebrows raised.

"No. Your sister's contempt remains as resolute as ever!"

Keira grinned, then turned her attention back to the approaching figure.

"Keira," Anna shouted, pulling the horse to a halt and sliding off her saddle. She ran up to her sister and gave her a quick squeeze. "I never want to see a horse again in my entire life. Nor," she said, turning a disdainful glare at Max, "that annoying, absolutely awful ... creature!"

"I see you've arrived safe and sound," Keira said as Max laughed.

"Yes," said Anna, looking at Max again before responding. "Quite safe and sound." She held his gaze for a moment before looking away.

"Anything untoward happen?" Aaron's voice behind her made Keira jump, and she dropped her eyes to the ground as she drew in a shuddering breath. Her gaze met Anna's as she looked up, and she gave a weak smile.

"One little incident, easily handled. Nothing to be concerned about," Max said.

"Good," Aaron said, before turning and walking away.

CHAPTER TWENTY-THREE

Anna looked at Keira curiously. Something was wrong, but she could not place her finger on it.

"Aaron seems in a hurry," she said, glancing at the retreating figure.

"Yes," Keira said, and the tone in her voice made Anna give her a second look. "He's been very busy with dragon matters lately." She took Anna by the hands. "Tell me everything about your trip. Was it long and tedious?"

"Very," Anna said, drawing out the word. "I think every item of clothing I brought is covered in mud, and" – she leaned closer to her sister, dropping her voice – "I'm not sure I will ever be able to sit comfortably again!"

Keira laughed, and linking her arm into Anna's, pulled her sister towards the house.

"Come and meet Margaret and Cathryn," she said. Max had already wandered over to the two women waiting at the front entrance, and Anna saw him give the older woman a quick kiss on the cheek. He laughed at something she said as Anna and Keira drew close.

"This is my most troublesome charge," he said, a grin tugging at his mouth when Anna scowled at him.

"Anna, welcome to Drake Manor," said the younger woman with a laugh. "And take no notice of Max. We certainly don't!"

"You know how to make a man feel right at home, Cathryn," Max said. Cathryn grinned, then turned to Keira.

"I'm sure you want some time alone with your sister, so would you mind showing Anna her chambers? It is the room two doors down from yours."

"Of course," Keira said, leading Anna into the building.

After a week of cramped rooms at inns of varying quality, Anna's chamber was wonderful. It was large and airy, with a huge fireplace where a fire crackled and blazed. A bed stood in the center of the room, while next to the fireplace was a wooden chair. Keira left her so she could freshen herself, and Anna stripped off her dirty clothes with relief. A basin of water stood on a washstand beside a ewer, a stack of linens piled next to it, and Anna scrubbed off the dust and dirt with a sigh of pleasure. A fresh chemise and gown made her feel transformed into a new, clean person, and she looked at herself in the mirror with satisfaction. Donning a fresh pair of slippers, Anna made her way down the hall in search of Keira. She found her in the courtyard, chatting to Cathryn while two children ran around their legs, playing a game of tag. Keira glanced up with a smile.

"Feeling refreshed?" she asked. "I thought we could go for a walk. Even though it is still winter, the gardens here are lovely."

It was wonderful to go by foot rather than horseback, and Anna spent the afternoon telling Keira about the journey. They walked to a small lake, their feet crunching through snow that had lost its fluffy softness, before turning back and walking through the woods that bordered the estate. There was little snow under the trees – instead the ground was covered in a thick layer of dried leaves. Anna could hear the sound of men laughing as they approached the house, and as they rounded the walls, she saw Max standing with another man in the courtyard. They both looked up at the sound of their approach, and Anna looked at the unknown man with interest. He was big, broader and taller than Max, with a shock of red hair.

"Anna, this is Favian," Keira said. "Favian, my sister, Anna." Favian turned to Anna with a smile. "Welcome to Drake Manor." He glanced back at Max. "And well done for putting up with this rogue on the road."

"Rogue?" Max's voice was indignant. "If you knew the cutting tongue that this woman possesses, you would know that it is I who deserves the congratulations!"

"Cutting tongue, eh? Well, Max, hopefully she cut you to size."

Anna smirked at Max's feigned look of dismay, but he soon started laughing.

"She put me thoroughly in my place," he said. He looked over at Anna, his gaze catching hers for a moment, and she looked away in confusion, unsure how to act towards him with all these people around.

"Come, Anna," Keira said, taking her by the hand and leading her to the house, "we should ready ourselves for supper."

Aaron was the last one to arrive at supper that evening, and he took a spot next to Thomas, who was seated at the opposite end of the table from Keira. Thomas looked at Aaron in surprise as Anna glanced at her sister, but her expression was unreadable.

"Anything happen on the trip I should be aware of?" Aaron asked his steward. Thomas shot Max a quick look, while Aaron turned to face Max with narrowed eyes.

"Max?"

"A small band of thieves tried to get the better of us, but they soon learnt the error of their ways." Max met Aaron's gaze steadily.

"Very   well.   Were   you   able   to   find   suitable accommodations?"

Max nodded, then launched into a brief description of some of the inns where they had stayed. After a few more questions, Aaron pushed himself away from the table.

"Very well. I'm going out. Alone," he added, waving his hand at Favian when he started to rise. The two men eyed each other before Favian dropped his gaze and slowly sat down again. Aaron glanced quickly at Keira, then strode out of the room.

Aaron's departure signaled the end of the meal, and the rest of the party soon retired to the parlor, but Anna did not linger. Her body ached and she was weary, ready for a night's rest in a comfortable bed. Smiling at the others, she excused herself from their company and made her way to her chambers. She sighed at the luxury of fresh, clean quilts and soft pillows, a mattress of wool instead of straw. Her hair had become tangled again, but she gave it a perfunctory brush before lying down on the bed. Her gaze fell on the empty chair as she pulled the quilts up to her chin. How wonderful to have the room to herself, she thought. She had suffered Max's presence in her chamber every night after the attack, but there was no need for him to protect her any longer, and she sighed at the thought of being in the room completely alone. It was so marvelously private. She closed her eyes, but opened them a moment later, peering into the shadows. The room was larger than she had at first realized. She rolled onto her side, and watched the embers glowing beneath the flames. Her eyes fell on the empty seat again, and the image of a man spread out in a wooden chair filled her thoughts, before she hurriedly pushed them away. She certainly did not want to think of *that* person.

She was still wide awake when she heard a tapping on the shutters outside her window. She froze, her heart suddenly racing, before a soft voice called her name. She jumped up from her bed and hurried to the window, pushing open the shutter.

"Max," she said, "what are you doing here?"

"Sshh," he said, "Aaron will skin me alive if he knows I'm here. Can I come in?" Anna stepped back as Max drew closer to the window, the light of the fire spilling from the room and across his frame. His torso was bare, and just before he passed through the window, Anna glimpsed wings spreading out wide from his back, shimmering in the dull light. She had seen him as a dragon before, and she had seen him as a man, but never before had she seen him as both, and she could not help staring. So beautiful, she thought to herself. He folded his wings against his back, where they disappeared beneath his skin, and hopped down onto the floor.

"I thought you might need help getting those tangles out of your hair," he said, stepping closer. She looked up into his face, then nodded silently. Without a word, she climbed back into the bed, handing Max the brush from the table. He sat down on the edge of the mattress as Anna turned her back to him, and lifting her hair, he gently began to tease out the knots. His touch was soothing, and she felt herself relaxing as he ran his fingers through her hair.

"Something is wrong between Aaron and Keira," Anna said as Max worked.

"I noticed," he said.

"What do you think it is?"

"I don't know, but I'm sure they will work it out."

"Keira looked so unhappy."

"So did Aaron. I saw him watching her when he thought no-one was looking. He looked so ... lost."

"Lost?" she said. "Aaron?"

Max was silent as he pulled the brush through Anna's hair.

"Max?"

"Hmm?"

"Do you think love can last forever?" There was a long silence.

"Yes," he said, his voice low.

"Have you ever been in love?"

"Just once."

"And do you still love her?"

"Forever, Anna. Forever."

Anna was silent as Max finished brushing her hair. He placed the brush on the table and went to the chair near the fire.

"I'll just sit here for a few moments."

Anna nodded and snuggled into the quilts, lying on her side facing him. He had stretched out his legs and crossed his arms, but she saw in the light of the flames that he was watching her. She met his gaze for a moment, then closed her eyes.

"Goodnight Max," she mumbled, but she was asleep before he replied.

CHAPTER TWENTY-FOUR

Keira sat at the edge of the bed, looking out the window. The moon was on the wane, little more than a sliver of light, but the stars shone brightly in the night sky. The fire had burned low in the grate, and she shivered slightly as she pulled the quilt tighter around her shoulders. It had been many hours since the household fell into silence, with only the occasional hoot of an owl outside the window to note the passing hours. Was Aaron going to stay away all night, she wondered? Phrases from their argument played through her mind, over and over again: *"I love you too much ... you are a sickness ... poison ..."* Tears were starting to flow down her cheeks again, and she scrubbed them away, pushing her fists into her eyes to stem her weeping. When Aaron returned – *if* he returned – she did not want to be a tangle of tearful emotion. She looked out the window again, focusing her mind on the long watch ahead.

A flash in the sky caught Keira's attention, and she looked up to see a golden light slowly dissipating in the dark sky. The source of the light was beyond her line of sight, but she knew it was Aaron, landing on the roof of the Manor. She smoothed down her gown, suddenly nervous. A long time passed before she heard footsteps in the passage outside their chambers, but when they did come, she turned to watch the door as it opened slowly.

At the sight of Keira sitting on the bed, Aaron paused.

"Keira," he said. Her name sounded stilted, unfamiliar on his tongue, and she looked down, twisting her hands in her lap. She felt the weight of his gaze as he took a step closer. "Keira, you were never meant to hear my conversation with Favian, and I should never have said what I did. Please accept my apologies."

"You said I was a sickness."

"I'm sorry. I should never have said that."

"You should never have said it," she said, "but you still believe it is true." Aaron looked away for a moment, then turned back to meet her gaze.

"Yes." He paused for a moment. "Maybe weakness would be a better word." Crossing to the bed, he sat down with a sigh, careful to maintain a few feet of distance. "Keira," he said, "I know you believe that love makes you stronger, and maybe in the human world it does, but I have seen firsthand what can happen when you love too much."

"You are not your father, Aaron."

"No? Perhaps not. But I am the Master of my clan, as he was before me. And you, well, you make me vulnerable. As much as I love you, you are also a liability."

"No," she whispered, "you are wrong."

"I have already made choices I shouldn't have, Keira."

"Like saving my father?"

"Yes."

"And tell me, Aaron, do you regret saving him?" Aaron turned away as he answered.

"No."

"So how is it wrong?"

"It's wrong because my first responsibility lies with the clan, with my own kind. This may seem like a simple thing to you, but if every dragon showed himself to humans, saved

138

their lives, it would be disastrous."

"And yet you only saved one human."

"One is too many for a Master."

"So now what? Are you going to go and kill my father?"

"No. I'm going to give up Mastership of the clan."

"What? No!" Leaping from the bed, Keira faced him, horror written across her face.

"Keira, it has to be one or the other. I cannot stop myself from loving you, although God knows I've tried. As soon as this problem has been sorted out with Jack, I will let the clan elders know my decision."

"Aaron, you are the Dragon Master! This is not something you choose to walk away from. Who else is as strong as you? Who else has the level of power that you have? Owain said he could see you are growing even more powerful – there must be a reason for that."

"What reason, Keira?" Aaron rose and clamping his fingers around her arm, bent his face down as he glared at her. "I don't have an answer. But I will not be like my father. I will step down before the clan is left leaderless."

"Aaron, no. This is wrong. Your father was weak, but you are not. This is not a choice you have to make." Releasing her arm, Aaron turned away, placing his back to her.

"The choice is already made, Keira. Unless you want to go and return to your family, I will follow through on this."

"Well, maybe I should, Aaron Drake," she shouted, stomping around the bed and climbing under the covers.

"Carry on like that, and perhaps I will send you myself," he said in a low voice. She pushed the covers back to glare at him. She was being immature, she knew, and this was not the time for childishness. But he was already gone, leaving nothing but a trail of light that disappeared out the window.

Aaron did not come back again that night, but he made an appearance when the morning meal was served. He took a seat beside her, and for a moment she thought he was going to kiss her, but then he looked the other way and said something to Favian. Keira longed to reach out and touch him, but a river of angry words lay between them, like a physical barrier that she couldn't cross. She picked at her food, aware of him sitting only a few inches away, but when the meal was done, he rose and left the table, and the opportunity was gone. Owain and Favian remained at the Manor all day, and it happened often that Keira looked up to see one or the other watching her. She was sitting in the library, a book in her lap, when the door opened to admit Favian.

"Ah, Keira. I didn't know you were here," he said.

"Liar," she mumbled under her breath, flushing when he laughed.

"Is it that obvious?" he asked.

"Yes. But don't concern yourself, I am quite fine."

"Good," he said, settling himself down on a chair opposite her. She looked at him pointedly, then set the book aside with a sigh.

"I know my father spoke to you," he said, "but I wanted to add my own weight to his words. You don't know how changed Aaron is because of you. There was little joy in his life before, but he is different now."

"He doesn't seem very happy with me in his life at the moment."

"Only because he fears being happy. Don't give up on him, Keira."

"Cathryn said the first dragon she saw in dragon form was Aaron," Keira said after a pause.

"Yes. I was very annoyed with Aaron."

"Why?"

"Because he was trying to force Cathryn away. He thought if she knew what I was, she would want nothing to do with me."

"But he was wrong."

"No, he was right, actually. At least at first."

"Well, she must have accepted you eventually."

"Eventually," he said with a laugh. "But when I thought our relationship was hopeless, it was Aaron who found me, lectured me and told me to go back to Cathryn. He knew, deep in his heart, that Cathryn and I were meant for each other, and that her love made me a better person." Keira looked down at the book on her lap, her fingers tracing the delicate patterns around the page.

"Thank you," she said. Favian nodded, and rising to his feet, left her alone with her thoughts.

Keira woke the next morning to the sound of Aaron moving around the room. She opened her eyes to see him pulling on a pair of trousers. Beside her the bed felt cold, a clear indication that he hadn't slept in it.

"Aaron?" she said.

"I'm going out," he said.

"Please, Aaron, talk to me," she whispered. He had been striding towards the door, but paused at the sound of her voice. He stood there for a moment, his back to her, as little wisps of flame curled around his body. Slowly he turned around and looked at her, his gaze capturing hers, and then he was by her side, kneeling next to the bed, his knuckles white as he clenched the wooden frame.

"Oh, Keira, I'm so sorry," he whispered. "I'm angry at myself, but I am just hurting you." He reached out a finger and trailed it down her cheek. His hand slipped around her neck and tangled in her hair, and then his mouth was on hers, hard and desperate. His other hand slipped down her back and he rolled over her, holding his weight on his elbows as he pulled her hard against his hot skin. His legs tangled with hers, and when he pushed up her chemise, his lips left hers and trailed a fiery path over her body. She moaned, lifting herself up to him, and he wrapped his arms around her, holding her weight. She felt a stirring in the air, and knew he had unfurled his wings. She opened her eyes and she saw them, huge and golden, hovering over them. She felt them brush against her hand, and she reached up to stroke them as he moaned her name. His eyes were bright white flames, and she could see the blaze just beneath his skin. "I love you," he growled, and then he took her, body and soul.

They lay in a tangled heap afterwards, his fingers hot against her skin. "I can't stay away from you," he said. "You are a drug running through my veins and I just want more." She rolled onto her stomach and looked down at him.

"Don't stay away," she said. "When we joined together we became one, and we are stronger together than apart." Aaron stared at her for a moment, before turning away and rising from the bed.

"I really do have to go. Owain is waiting for me – I think he wants to lecture his Master before we leave tomorrow."

"He just wants what's best for his nephew," she said.

Aaron gave her a bleak smile then turned towards the door.

"I'll see you later, my sweet."

Keira watched as the door closed behind Aaron, her eyes blurring with tears. What would it take for Aaron to love her freely, as he had done before? Was it only at Storbrook that he could be truly happy? Was this going to be the pattern of their lives? She could not allow Aaron to give up the clan, but she found she had no wisdom in how to negotiate the snares that seemed to be set around them. Rolling over onto the bed, she buried her face in the quilts and allowed the tears to flow.

CHAPTER TWENTY-FIVE

Anna couldn't wait to reach the city. She knew it was going to be the most wonderful place. So many people. So many buildings. And maybe Aaron would allow her to go to court! Max had told her that Aaron knew the prince. His Royal Highness Prince Alfred, first in line to the throne, to be exact. And it was because the prince had summoned Aaron that they were going to the city.

"Aaron will have to present himself at court," Max had explained one evening as he sat behind her on her bed, brushing her hair. "And if you behave," Max continued, "I'm sure he will take you, too."

"Have you been to court?" she asked.

"Once or twice," he answered. She was about to ask more when he pointed out a brightly shining star through the open window. "Look, the North Star," he said. "Do you know that the North Star guides mariners when they sail the oceans? A sailor told me once that without the North Star to guide them, mariners can become hopelessly lost when the sun is hidden behind cloud, sailing aimlessly towards the edge of the ocean. And that is not the only danger. Sailors can also fall victim to a siren's song."

"A siren?" Anna asked.

"Yes. A man cannot resist the call of a siren, and she will lead him to a watery grave."

"That's terrible. What do sailors do?"

"There is little they can do, because as soon as they hear the first note, all is lost."

"Did your friend ever hear the siren's call?"

"Anna," he laughed. "You aren't listening. If he had heard the call, he would not have lived to tell the tale." Anna blushed as Max continued.

"Should I tell you some other stories?"

Anna had nodded, smiling contentedly as Max spoke, all the while pulling the brush through her hair.

Every night since arriving at Drake Manor, Max had crept into her room through the open window. He would sit on the bed and brush her hair, then move to the chair while she fell asleep. He would be gone in the morning, the chair where he sat looking empty. She knew he was risking Aaron's wrath if he found out, but she could not bring herself to tell Max to stay away. Thinking about Max made Anna pause in the self-appointed task of repacking her trunk. Would she still see Max at night when they were in the city? The thought that she wouldn't made her feel a little sad, and she laughed at her silliness. Really, what did it matter if she never saw Max again? Sometimes she noticed him watching her – like this morning, before he and Favian went out together. She never spoke to him during the day except to pass insults, all of which, she thought, were quite true. He really was annoying, arrogant, and rude. Except at night, when he talked softly to her and answered her questions, his fingers in her hair. She sighed, pushing the thought from her mind. Max would have things to do once they reached the city, and she would be free of his annoying presence.

The small party that left Drake Manor the following morning consisted of Anna and Keira, Aaron, Max, and Thomas.

Anna and Keira rode on horseback with Thomas, while the two dragons flew overhead. It wasn't far to the city, Aaron assured them. They would be there in the early afternoon.

At the first sight of the city, Anna gasped. They had just reached the summit of a small hill, and the city lay in the valley below them, stretching into the distance on the other side of a wide river. A road led across a bridge to the heavy wooden gates of the city, which stood wide open. It was crowded with people, pushing and shoving as they made their way into the pulsing heart of the city, a tangled mass of alleys and lanes, twisting this way and that without any plan. Steeples rose above the low wooden dwellings that crowded the streets, while in the center of the city rose the cathedral, its spire reaching almost as high as the surrounding hills. It was built of golden stone, and it glittered in the pale winter sun. A low hum rose into the air, and despite the pall of smoke that hung over the buildings, it seemed to Anna that she had never seen anything so wondrous. The two dragons landed on the grass a little way behind the riders, their transformations flashing through the sky. Anna turned to Max as he joined them.

"Have you ever seen anything so amazing?" Max laughed.

"This is my home, Anna," he said, his eyes meeting hers. She blushed and looked away, turning back to look at the city again.

"It is incredible," Keira said beside her. "I didn't think it would be so big,"

"Come along," Aaron said. "If we stand here gaping, the gates will be closed before we get in." He turned to his steward. "Thomas, lead the way."

"Aye, Milord," Thomas said, urging his horse into motion.

They reached the entrance well before the heavy doors closed for the night, joining the throngs of people crossing the bridge, pushing and shoving as they tried to get ahead of others. All manner of people and beasts flowed through the gateway – peasant men and women on foot, lugging heavily laden baskets and huge bundles on their backs; farmers driving carts pulled by mules. Anna saw a knight, his chestplates of iron glittering in the sunlight, striding ahead on his steed while a page boy trailed behind leading a pack horse. A gentleman stepped lightly around piles of refuse that littered the road, handkerchief held delicately to his nostrils, while street urchins weaved between the crowds, bumping against unwary travelers before running away with their fists closed around the prize of a coin or some other valuable. Soldiers stood at the gates watching the people enter, and occasionally they made a grab at one of the young pickpockets, but all except the youngest were too slippery to be caught, and the soldiers would shrug their shoulders at the disappearing figures before stepping back to watch the seething mass once more.

The streets immediately beyond the gateway were dirt, tramped down to a surface as hard as rock by thousands of passing feet. Buildings blackened with soot crowded into every available spot, leaning against each other haphazardly. Anna ducked just in time when some foul-smelling liquid was thrown out the window of one of the houses, and Max threw a quick grin in her direction. Further down the road a main artery forked from the dirt road, leading into the center of the city, and it was onto this street that Thomas led them. It was paved with cobblestones, but Anna could see narrow dirt alleyways stretching out in every direction. Bells chimed every quarter hour, reaching Anna's ears from all sides, and each time the city dogs started barking in chorus. Every quarter of the city seemed packed with people as they passed: hawkers shouting out their wares, washerwomen stringing laundry between the buildings, and children darting around the ankles of passersby, causing them to trip and curse.

A woman approached Anna with a small posy in her fist, which she thrust into Anna's face. "Keeps you safe from the plague, my dear," she said, but Anna shook her head, and the woman passed by with a muttered curse. The mingled smells of smoke, sewage, and food prepared on the streets hung heavy in the air, while the odor of unwashed bodies added to the mélange.

After a while the buildings began to change, growing larger as they rose more evenly from the ground. Roads instead of alleys led from the main artery, wide and elegant. The clothes worn by the men changed, too. Practical tunics of browns and blues were less in evidence in this section of the city, replaced by two-toned hose, doublets that reached no further than the waist, and shoes with points that left Anna gaping. She glanced at Keira, smiling when she saw that her eyes seemed just as large as her own.

"How does it feel to be back, Aaron?" Max said, turning to look at his Master as they walked.

"I didn't think I would feel this way," Aaron replied, "but it actually feels good to be back. Like I'm returning home after a long trip away."

Max nodded. "I feel that way every time."

Anna felt a stab of envy. She wished that she too could call this huge, exciting city home. She glanced at Keira, wondering whether she felt the same, and was startled to see a strange, sad expression in her eyes. It was gone when Aaron turned to look at her, replaced with her usual, calm smile. Anna wondered what it meant, until she gave a mental shrug. Whatever it was, it was not her concern. As Max had said, Keira and Aaron would figure it out.

They walked along for a little further, until Thomas turned the party into one of the wide roads that led from the main artery, stopping outside a large house. The timber beams were black with age, while whitewashed walls glimmered in the sun. The second storey of the house overhung the street, creating a roof over the entrance. Thomas dismounted from his horse and rapped on the wooden door, as Anna slid down from her mount, ignoring Max's proffered hand. The door swung open and a woman in her thirties stood at the threshold.

"Thomas!" she said with a smile. "Milord Drake, Master Brant."

"Hannah," Thomas said. "Why are *you* opening the door? Where is Harry?"

"Heaven only knows," she said. She looked at the two women, and Thomas turned to introduce them.

"This is Milord's wife, Mistress Keira, and her sister, Mistress Anna."

Hannah dropped a quick curtsey, then stepped back, gesturing into the house. "Welcome to Drake House. Mistress Cathryn sent word to prepare for you."

"Hello, Hannah," Aaron said, stepping aside to allow Keira and Anna to walk ahead. The front door opened into a large hall, from which Anna could see various doorways along the one length.

"I'll just go call a boy to help with the horses, and will be back in a moment," Hannah said. As she disappeared through one of the exits, Max turned to Aaron.

"I'll take my leave now, Aaron. You know where to find me if you need me."

Aaron nodded. "I'll keep you apprised of any new developments," he said.

Anna looked away at Max's words. Of course he would not be staying with them at Drake House, since he had his own apartments in the city, but somehow this fact had escaped her till now. She was relieved, naturally. Max was far too annoying for comfort. She looked at him, meeting his gaze.

"At long last there will be peace and quiet," she said.

Max laughed, a humorless snort. "Oh, Anna, don't hold out too much hope. This city may seem very big to you, but it is not so big that you will avoid seeing me. And," he added with a glint, "I will be frequently at Drake House." He took her hand and brought it to his lips as Aaron and Keira looked on. She was embarrassed, but as his lips touched her skin, everyone but Max was forgotten. She stared into his eyes as his hands held hers. She felt like he was searing her, burning his touch into her skin.

At the sound of Aaron clearing his throat, she pulled her hand away as though she had touched a flame, and took a step back.

"Not too frequently, I hope," she said, but even she could hear that her voice lacked conviction.

Max grinned sardonically, turning once more to Aaron.

"Master," he said, raising his fist in a dragon salute of fealty, then nodding at Keira, turned and walked out the door.

CHAPTER TWENTY-SIX

Hannah led Keira and Aaron to a chamber that overlooked a small courtyard. There were stables at the far end, although the horses that had brought them into the city were being stabled down the road. Keira gazed out the window for a few minutes before turning to face Aaron.

"What is the plan, now that we are here?"

"I've asked Thomas to send a message to the prince, letting him know that we have arrived. In the meantime I need to find where Jack is hiding himself, and what he is up to."

"How do you plan to do that?"

"Favian and Owain have already told me what they know —"

"Which is what?"

"That Jack has been hunting within the city."

"He's been hunting?" Keira's faced reflected her horror. "Why?"

"To force my hand. Favian says that he's heard Jack plans to challenge me as Master."

"What are you going to do?"

"I cannot allow Jack to become Master of the clan. I will

find him and kill him." Aaron paused. "Word travels fast in the city. Max is not the only dragon that lives here. Jack will already know of my arrival."

"Are the other dragons in league with Jack?"

"I dare say some of them are. Favian cautioned me against a few."

"But they are all part of your clan?"

"Yes. But no clan is without its intrigues. Not all dragons like being restrained in their hunting. Jack may have promised them free rein in the city."

"But that's ... terrible!"

"Only for humans," he said wryly. He turned towards the door. "I'm going out for a while."

"Where are you going?"

"I thought I would take a walk. See what new information I can discover."

"Can I come with you?"

Aaron looked at her for a moment before answering. "Yes. Of course," he finally said. "Make sure you dress warmly."

Keira flung a cloak around her shoulders and followed him to the door.

"Where are we going?" she asked as they stepped onto the street.

"For now we will just take a walk. Show ourselves, just in case news hasn't spread to all corners of the city. Later tonight I will visit a few other places." He caught her expectant look. "Places too uncouth and uncivilized for a woman to be seen in," he added.

"Does Max live far from here?'

"About ten minutes away. Most dragons tend to live within this area." They walked down the road a short distance before Aaron led her into a much narrower street. It was late afternoon and the sun was already low in the sky, casting long shadows on the ground. The noises of the city seemed strangely distant on this street. Keira shivered and Aaron put his hand on her back, drawing her closer. There was only one other person on the empty road, walking towards them. He was shorter than Aaron, and his plain clothes were not enough to hide his well-built frame. For a moment he watched Aaron, then turned his gaze back to the road, looking straight ahead. It was only when he was a few feet away that his eyes flicked back to Aaron and he gave the tiniest of nods. His arms came up and crossed his chest, but as he drew parallel, Keira saw his right hand inch slightly higher while his fingers curled slightly. A salute to the Master. Keira looked up at Aaron, but before she should could say anything, he shook his head. Not now.

They reached the end of the road and turned the corner, and up ahead Keira could see the main road, filled with people as a city should be. They had just turned into the crowds when Keira heard a voice calling from behind.

"Aaron."

Another man approached them. At a glance, he looked to be in his forties, but Keira could see the glow that marked him as a dragon, which meant he was probably around two hundred years old, or even more. His dark brown eyes were creased with laugh lines, but his expression looked somber now.

"Oliver Calder," Aaron said. "What are you doing in the city?"

"I've heard rumors of a dragon disturbance. You will probably find many more clan members congregating within these city walls." He paused a moment, then placed his fist over his heart. "Master." Aaron nodded, and the man turned to look at Keira.

"Oliver, this is my wife, Keira."

"Mistress Keira." Oliver smiled. "I'm sorry I wasn't able to attend the binding ceremony. We had given up hope for Aaron, so it is with great pleasure that I welcome you to the clan."

"Thank you, Master Calder."

Oliver looked back at Aaron, his expression growing serious again.

"I heard what happened at the binding, Aaron." He flicked a glance at Keira. "Not that I can blame Jack," he said, a slight grin tugging at his mouth. It was gone a moment later when he caught Aaron's look. "Er, well, it seems Jack is eager to see you gone. And although most of us see the folly of his cause, there are some who have been enticed to his side by promises of freedom in their hunting both within the city and beyond once you are dead."

Aaron nodded. "I thought as much."

"He has also killed two dragons who would not take up his cause." Aaron's eyebrows shot up at this piece of news.

"He's grown in strength, then. Who were they?"

"His cousins Hillary and Benjamin." Aaron turned and gazed into the distance, his face troubled. Oliver watched him for a moment. "Aaron," he said finally, "you need to know that rumors have been spreading about you."

"What kind of rumors?"

Oliver shifted uncomfortably. "Some dragons are saying that you have given your blood to humans, binding them to you." Aaron shot a glance at Keira before replying.

"Just one. Keira's father was mortally wounded when trying to reason with his neighbors about their plan to kill me. I gave him my blood to save his life." Aaron ran his hand through his hair. "I cannot regret it, and despite his desire to serve me, I have made no demands of him."

"And he was the only one?"

"Yes."

Oliver nodded. "Given that it was your father-in-law, I can understand your actions. But there is more. A tale has been spreading amongst humans about a golden dragon that not only talks intelligently, but has a human wife."

Aaron ran a hand over his eyes with a groan. "That was a mistake." He dropped his hand and met Oliver's gaze. "After we left Storbrook we ran into a young man determined to save Keira from the beast that held her captive. He was very determined, and I'm afraid I lost patience."

"Ah! Well, it is not my place to judge your actions, Aaron, but if I have heard of this, chances are Jack has too. He is probably using this information to make clan members question your leadership."

Aaron nodded. "Of course he is. Do you have any idea where Jack has made his lair?"

"No. But I don't think it is within the city."

"Where can I find you?"

"I'm staying on River Row," he replied. "Number ten."

"Very well. I will be in touch. And if you discover anything more, let me know. You can find us at Drake House."

"Yes, Master," he said. He briefly touched a fist to his chest once more, then turned away, walking briskly in the opposite direction.

"A member of the clan?" Keira said as she watched the retreating figure.

"Hmm? Yes. A clan member."

"And the other person?"

"Also a clan member. We were being followed, and he didn't want our interaction observed. If Jack is hunting dragons who have turned against him, then I cannot blame his desire for secrecy." Aaron led Keira to the other side of the street. "We're still being watched, so let's keep going."

The rest of the walk passed without incident, and soon Aaron was opening the door to Drake House. They had just entered the hall when Thomas came in from another doorway.

"Milord," he said, walking towards them.

"Thomas. Did you deliver my message?"

"I did, Milord. The prince has asked that you be in attendance at court tomorrow morning. With Mistress Keira." Aaron looked at Thomas in surprise.

"With Mistress Keira?"

"Yes." Aaron cast her a speculative look, then nodded his head.

"Very well. And did you discover anything else?"

"People are saying that a large black dragon has been killing and eating people on the street."

"How many?"

"Over a dozen. Men. Women. He even killed a man while his son looked on. The boy had been injured, but for some reason, the dragon let him go free."

Aaron raised his eyebrows in surprise. "He allowed a child to go free?"

"Yes. But not before he, uh, disposed of the father's body."

Aaron turned and slammed his hand against the wall with a growl, sending shards of whitewashed stone tumbling to the floor. "He wants to instill as much fear as possible. He's provoking me into an attack, rather than attacking me first."

"What are you going to do?" Keira asked.

"First I need to find him. But I will fight him on my terms, not his."

"Didn't you say his father died because he refused to eat human flesh?"

Aaron turned to look at her. "Yes. You are right. This is just as much about his father as it is about me. And he's not going to stop until I stop him."

CHAPTER TWENTY-SEVEN

Keira tied the laces of her chemise as Hannah waited behind her with hairbrush in hand. Hannah had been Cathryn's lady's maid for many years, she explained, since before Favian.

"Usually I return with her to Drake Manor," Hannah said, "but Mistress Cathryn knows I've met someone here in the city."

"So she lets you remain at Drake House so you can be with your beau?"

Hannah blushed, but return Keira's gaze steadily. "That's right."

"Well, I'm glad you are here, Hannah, as I have no idea what to wear before a prince."

"A prince isn't that different from any other man," Hannah said. "He just thinks he is. Now let's see. This one, I think." She pulled out a gown of dark crimson velvet, trimmed in gold. She slipped it over Keira's outstretched arms. "Perfect. Now sit down while I do your hair."

Half an hour later Keira left the room and went in search of Aaron, finding him pacing the hall.

"Come," he said. "Let's get this over with." They stepped

out onto the road, turning in the direction opposite to the one taken the previous day. As they walked, Aaron instructed Keira on how to greet the prince.

"He has no inkling of who, or what, I am," Aaron explained. "If he did, then he would be showing me fealty, rather than the other way around. But we enter his court as subjects, and as such we will give him the respect required of his subjects. However, since he calls me friend, and you are my wife, one shallow curtsey will do."

Aaron led Keira to the river, where he tossed a ferryman a coin. "To the palace," he said. The ferry was a long, flat-bottomed boat with planks that spanned the width of the craft, serving as seats. Thin cushions lay on the planks, offering a small comfort to the traveler. Aaron held Keira's hand as she stepped into the rocking boat, while the ferryman jumped with ease into the back, his nimble feet barely rocking the craft. Aaron settled next to Keira as the ferryman thrust his long pole into the water, pushing them away from the bank. The noise of the city disappeared as the boat slipped down the river, carried along by the current, and as they glided around a bend the palace suddenly came into view. A wide swath of lawn stretched from the edge of the water to the red-brick palace that rose from the countryside. Chimneys and spires competed with each other as they reached into the sky, while huge windows filled with leaded glass made the building glitter in the sunlight. Open fields stretched in all directions beyond the palace, dotted with grazing sheep, huddled together for warmth. Their noisy bleats, which drowned out all other sounds, spoke of their displeasure at being left in the cold. An area of wilderness had been carefully cultivated beyond the formal gardens that lay on the other side of the palace, while in the distance Keira could see a dark stretch of forest with hills rising behind it. The ferryman deftly maneuvered the boat to a wooden platform where Aaron jumped out, reaching back to steady Keira. She turned to look at the enormous building towering above her. Directly ahead of them was a huge archway, through which Keira could see the courtyard bustling with activity.

"Come along, my sweet," Aaron said. "A human prince is not nearly as terrifying as a dragon master."

"Spoken like a true dragon," Keira said. She turned to look at Aaron. "I feel like such a country maid," she said. "I don't want to shame you."

"You could never do that," Aaron replied. He took her hand into his and gave it a gentle squeeze, before pulling it through his arm and starting down the path that led through the arched entryway. The palace surrounded the courtyard on all four sides, with numerous doorways leading into the building. Another archway was built on the side across from where they entered, flanked by elaborate doorways. Aaron led Keira without hesitation to one of these, and a liveried footman silently opened the door for them to enter. Once inside, they found themselves in a long passage that stretched the length of the building, while to their left was a large staircase to which Aaron headed. They had just climbed the first stair when a voice trilled behind them.

"Aaron Drake, is that you?"

Keira felt the muscles in Aaron's arm tense, but he turned to the voice with a smile. "Madame Pritchard. Delighted, I'm sure. Now if you will excuse us –"

"Why, Milord Drake, surely you can spare a few minutes? Elise will be delighted –"

"Yes, I'm afraid we are in a hurry. We have an audience with His Royal Highness." With a quick nod in the woman's direction, Aaron spun around and took Keira's arm, dragging her up the stairs.

"Who was that?" Keira asked as she stumbled onto the grand landing. Aaron caught her before she fell and pulled her arm into the crook of his own, leading her at a more sedate pace up the next flight.

"That was Madame Pritchard."

"Ah, yes. So I gathered."

Aaron looked down and gave her a reluctant smile. "Let's just say this place is a piece of my past best left forgotten."

"Aaron –"

"Forgotten."

Keira looked at the set of his face and nodded. "Very well," she said.

At the top of the stairs was another passage, and once more Aaron led her without hesitation through a doorway into a small, square, windowless room. A closed doorway was on the opposite end, while benches lined the wall on one side, and cushioned chairs lined the other. Aaron led Keira over to a chair where they sat down. There was only one other person seated on the chair side, and he glanced up at Aaron before returning to his reflections. The benches, however, were filled with people sitting silently. They were a ragtag mix of individuals, young and old, men and women, well dressed or shabby. Most of them ignored Keira and Aaron, but a few of them looked up, their gazes ranging from wary to hostile. There was a young woman directly opposite Keira, and Keira smiled, but the woman just stared at her vacantly before looking away. The door opposite the one they had entered opened, and a man stepped into the room. His expression was dispassionate as his gaze ranged over the people on the benches, but when he turned towards their side, his eyes stopped at Aaron.

"Aaron Drake."

Aaron rose to his feet and bowed his head slightly. "My Lord Chamberlain. Allow me to introduce my wife, the Lady Keira." Aaron's hand was on her shoulder, pressing her down when she would have stood. She nodded as the other man turned to her with a bow.

"Madame." He looked back to Aaron.

"I will advise the prince of your presence."

He disappeared through the door once more, but was back a moment later. "Come," he said.

Aaron rose and held out his hand for Keira. She took it, walking beside him as they followed the chamberlain into the next room. It was large and rectangular, with soaring, arched ceilings. The badge of each noble knight was carved into the beams, painted with bright hues, while the rest of the surface was covered in gold. Long narrow windows, made up of hundreds of small, square panes of glass, ran down the length of one wall, and in the corner stood a massive gold clock, with a long pendulum that swayed hypnotically. Paintings taller than Keira were mounted on the walls, depicting pastoral and spiritual scenes, while at the far end were portraits of monarchs who had reigned before. In the middle of the room was a raised dais, covered with a purple canopy, while heavily embroidered drapes hung down the sides and back. Two chairs, elaborately carved and gilded with gold, stood on the platform. At least a dozen men stood about the room, huddled in pairs or small groups, whispering between themselves while on the dais, upon one of the chairs, sat another man with a heavy ermine fur draped over his shoulders, secured with a heavy chain from which hung a huge, glittering ruby. On his head he wore a thin circlet of gold. He was whispering behind his hand to a man at his side, and together they looked up as the chamberlain entered the room, Aaron and Keira on his heels.

"Master and Lady Drake," the chamberlain said in a loud voice.

The prince nodded, then rose to his feet as Aaron bowed. At his side, Keira dropped a shallow curtsey.

"Your Highness," Aaron said. He watched as the prince made his way across the floor.

"Aaron!" The prince was a young man in his mid-twenties, with muddy brown hair that hung in curls to his shoulders. He was at least six inches shorter than Aaron, with a thin, lean face and a narrow frame. He clasped Aaron's shoulders, and looked up into his face. "You look quite unchanged." He glanced at Keira. "It must be this lovely wife of yours. Although I fear news of your arrival with a wife in tow has cast quite a pall over the women at court." The prince turned and walked back to the dais, sitting himself down on his ornate throne, and with a glance at Keira, Aaron followed. Keira stood unsure for a moment, but when Aaron made a motion with his hand, she quickly followed.

It did not take the prince long to apprise Aaron of the situation with the black dragon.

"It is terrorizing my people and causing great distress in my city," he said. "When the royal archers were unable to subdue the creature, I offered all knights of the realm a reward if they could kill it. But ten have already lost their lives, and the zeal and bravery of my remaining knights has fled. What am I to do, Aaron? Is there any way to subdue this monster?"

"There is always a way," Aaron replied, "but more lives may be forfeited before this beast is defeated."

"And how will you defeat it? Surely you do not mean to engage this beast."

"We will fight fire with fire. A dragon with a dragon."

"Is that possible? Without bringing further devastation to my people. And where will you find such a dragon?"

"It is possible. And rest assured, Your Highness, that I can find a dragon willing and able to defeat this black beast." He paused as the prince slowly nodded. "Do you know where the dragon has made its lair?"

"No. Somewhere beyond the city."

"Very well. I will find and kill this dragon."

"I know you will, Aaron. I know you would give your life for the love of your prince." Keira glanced at Aaron, but he nodded solemnly, and she returned her eyes to the man on the throne. He had leaned back in his seat and was looking at Aaron affectionately. "I am hosting a small soiree this evening, Aaron. Why don't you and your lovely wife," he flicked a finger in Keira's direction, "join me."

"Thank you, Your Highness," said Aaron. "We would be

honored." He bowed his head, then with a quick glance at Keira, stepped back a pace before turning around and grabbing her hand, and heading towards the door. Keira heard a sudden burst of laughter from one of the huddles of men as Aaron's grip on her hand tightened, and then they were out of the room. Keira could feel the tension in Aaron as he marched her along the long passage.

"I should never have allowed you to come here," he said. "I had forgotten what it is like."

"What are you talking about, Aaron? It seems fine to me." But shaking his head, Aaron led her towards the stairs.

"Let's go home," he said.

CHAPTER TWENTY-EIGHT

Anna was frustrated. Being in the city was not nearly as much fun as she had thought it would be. Before Aaron and Keira had gone to court, leaving her behind, Aaron had strictly forbidden her from leaving the house unattended. At least at Storbrook she had the freedom of the estate, but a house in the city meant there wasn't even a garden to walk in.

She fell onto her bed in a huff. It had been difficult to sleep last night as well. She had been in a strange bed, and things just didn't seem the same. The memory of Max brushing her hair crept into her thoughts, but she pushed it away.

A soft knock sounded on her door, and Anna looked up to see Hannah enter the room. "There's a gentleman downstairs waiting on you," she said.

"A gentleman?" Anna said in confusion.

"Master Max," Hannah clarified.

"Master Max?" Anna jumped off the bed and smoothed down her hair, hurrying out of the room. She paused at the top of the stairs, then slowly descended the narrow staircase that led to the ground floor. Max turned to look at her as she entered the hall, his face breaking into a smile.

"Max," she said, "what are you doing here? Aaron is out."

"It isn't Aaron I came to see," he said.

"It isn't?"

"No, I came to see you."

"Oh. Why? Perhaps I don't want to see you."

"Well, in that case, I'll just take my leave." Max swept her a low bow, and turned towards the door. Anna watched as he strode away, her lower lip caught between her teeth, then called out.

"Wait. Why did you come to see me?"

Max paused and turned to face her again. "There's a jousting tournament later today, and I wondered if you would like to go watch, but since you seem to have an aversion to my company –"

"I didn't say that!"

"You didn't? I thought that's what you meant, but I must have misunderstood." He walked back towards her. "Mistress Anna, would you give me the pleasure of accompanying me to a joust this afternoon?"

Anna glanced down, debating the alternatives. Going out with Max, who, she reminded herself, was arrogant and rude, or staying at Drake House alone.

"I'll come with you," she said. "Just wait while I get my cloak."

Anna stepped onto the street a few minutes later with Max one step behind, and ignored the proffered arm.

"Which way?" she asked. Max gestured down the street.

"Since the joust doesn't start for another few hours, I thought we could go via the marketplace." Anna nodded and set off in the direction he indicated. As they walked, she could hear the sounds of the market growing closer, and soon she could see the slanted slate roof of the tall stone market cross rising from the center of a large square. At least, Anna guessed it must be a large square, but it was so packed with merchants and hawkers selling their wares that it was difficult to tell. In every direction, stalls and tables were vying for space, even disappearing into the alleys that fanned out from the central square. Wheels of cheese and aromatic spices, nuts, herbs, and pickled vegetables all added color and aroma to an otherwise gray day. And it seemed as though the entire population of the city had congregated in this one square, because as far as Anna could see, crowds of people were pushing and shoving each other.

"Stay close to me, and watch your purse," Max whispered in her ear, and when he pulled her hand through his arm, she didn't protest. Pushing his way into the crowd, Max led her through the throng, leading her past the different stalls. He bought some roasted nuts from a hawker, holding the hot treats in his hand without a wince, and waited patiently when she stopped at a table spread with fox and rabbit pelts. The textures were soft and inviting, and she ran her hand through them with pleasure. By the time they had reached the other side of the market, Anna felt like everything that could possibly be sold in the world was collected within the square mile of the market.

The opposite side of the market square bordered the church yard where wide stairs led up to enormous, arched wooden doors. The doors were closed, but the stairs before the church were a hive of activity as a troupe of mummers re-enacted the martyrdom of an archbishop, murdered within his own cathedral, to a delighted crowd. Max and Anna stood and watched for a few minutes, but another form of entertainment caught Anna's eye, and she turned to see a man standing on his hands, balanced on a pair of swords. She gasped when it seemed that he would lose his balance, then breathed a sigh of relief when he nimbly somersaulted onto his feet, the swords still in his hands.

"Come along," said Max. "We have some time before the joust, so let's get something to eat." He pointed to a tavern which could be seen near the church, and led her away from the noise and crowds. The door to the tavern was low, with stairs leading down as soon as the threshold was crossed.

Max had to duck his head to avoid the low ceiling beams, blackened with age and smoke, as he led her to a table beside a leaded window. A long bar ran the length of the tavern, and Max waved his hand, gaining the attention of a short, balding man wearing a leather apron.

"Wine, my good friend, and a plate of your best venison for the lady and myself." He turned back to Anna. "This establishment is renowned for its roast venison, and John does not water down the drinks."

The tavern buzzed softly with the sounds of people conversing, tankards hitting the table and logs falling in the fireplace, but after the cacophony of the market place, it was a haven of tranquility. Anna tugged at the ties at her throat and shrugged her cloak onto the bench behind her with a sigh.

"There are so many people," she said to Max. "And is there anything you cannot buy in the city?"

Max shrugged. "Probably not. Did you enjoy the play?"

"It was wonderful! The city must attract a lot of troupes."

"Troupes like that don't leave the city. They perform every day wherever they can find an audience. In fact, you could probably find a dozen such plays on any one day."

"It is so wonderful here," Anna said, her eyes shining. "How can you ever bear to leave?"

"I didn't have much choice when it came to spending Christmastide at Storbrook. When Aaron summons you, you go. But as it turned out, I'm glad I went."

"You are? But why? If the city is so wonderful in the middle of winter, it surely must be even more wonderful on feast days." Max leaned forward, his gaze capturing hers as he answered slowly.

"That is true. But you weren't in the city, Anna. You were at Storbrook." Anna's forehead creased in confusion.

"Me?" The confusion cleared and she pulled back in a huff. "Can you not be serious for once?" She glanced out the window, then back at Max, startled to see him watching her

166

intently.

"I am being serious," he said softly. Anna stared at him for a moment as a flush crept into her cheeks. For a fleeting moment she was tempted to believe him, but it passed as soon as a buxom serving maid slammed their plates and cups down on the table, sloshing wine onto the waxed surface and glaring in Max's direction. Max held Anna's gaze for a moment longer before turning to the woman with a wry grin.

"Molly. Your service is impeccable, as usual." Molly leaned forward, resting her elbows on the table as she drew closer to Max. Her breasts strained against the dull blue fabric of her gown, threatening to overflow it as she slowly ran her hand down the side of her neck, curling a brown strand of hair around her finger.

"Why, Master Max, you know I'm 'appy to provide whatever service you require." Anna turned to look out the window as the color flared in her cheeks.

"Thank you Molly," she heard Max say, "As I have told you before, I require no other services from you." Out the corner of her eye, Anna saw Molly pull herself up with a huff before turning on her heel and marching away.

"I'm sorry, Anna," Max said.

"Really, Max," said Anna as she turned to look at him, "It's no concern of mine if you choose to associate with every wench in every tavern or bawdy house across the city."

"Oh?" he said. "Then you wouldn't want to know that I have never associated with any wench from any bawdy house?"

"No," she said, with an airy wave of her hand, "no concern of mine." But when she turned away, she smiled to herself, glad of his words.

The venison turned out to be as good as Max had promised. Served with parsnips and bread, it was covered in a rich gravy that was as good as the meat itself. Washed down with a glass of wine, it was a most appetizing meal.

It was not far from the tavern to the jousting arena, and

as they left the establishment and started walking, the brightly colored tents where the jousters prepared themselves for the competition ahead soon came into view. Raised platforms ran along the length of the arena on either side, but while one side had open benches, the other had cushioned chairs beneath a covered canopy. In the center stood a platform raised above the rest, where the guests of honor would sit. It was to the covered side that Max led Anna, squeezing past the people already in their seats.

"Have you ever seen a joust?" Max asked as they sat down. Anna shook her head. "The aim is to unseat your opponent," he explained. He pointed to a rope that ran the length of the field. "The knights will face each other across the rope, each holding a lance. The victor proceeds to the next round."

"But they don't kill each other, do they?"

"No, the tips are capped. But a man could still die falling off his horse." Anna shuddered.

A movement on the raised platform caught Anna's eye, and she turned to see a middle-aged man mount the stairs with a young woman trailing behind him.

"Who's that?" she asked Max. Max turned to look at the newcomers.

"Duke Farrand and his daughter, the Lady Isobel. The duke is the tournament sponsor."

Anna nodded, taking in the young woman. Lady Isobel, who looked similar in age to Anna, was beautifully dressed in a gown studded with jewels. Her long, yellow hair was flowing loosely down her back, but was pulled away from her face with a hair net that covered the crown of her head. In her hand she held a white handkerchief trimmed in lace, initials embroidered in the corner. Anna was still looking at the woman when a trumpet sounded the start of the tournament.

"These are unknown knights," Max whispered as the first two jousters entered the arena. "The knights who have earned honors and awards will come out later." Each man was dressed in armor that covered his chest, arms, and legs, and carried a helmet under his arm. Neither man looked above the age of twenty.

"Why would they enter a joust?" Anna whispered to Max.

"Fame, glory, and prize money," he replied.

The two men clanked over to the raised platform and gave a stiff bow to the duke and his daughter. Lady Isobel smiled at each of them, then leaned back in her seat as they moved away to opposite ends of the field. They mounted their horses, which were draped in brightly colored cloth. Anna watched as the knights pulled their lances close to their bodies.

A flag was dropped and the men charged down the field, their weapons lowered and turned toward their charging opponent in the other lane. It was over in a few seconds when the man closest to Anna and Max hit his opponent squarely on the chest with his blunted lance, the tip ringing loudly against the heavy metal armor. The blow knocked the man off balance, and despite his attempts to keep his seat, the charging pace of his mount rendered his efforts useless and he fell to the ground with a clang. His foot remained caught in the stirrup, and he was dragged across the ground, his armor bouncing and scraping over the hardened dirt, until someone finally caught the bridle and brought the horse to a halt. Two pages ran onto the field, and lifting the fallen man onto their shoulders, carried him from the arena into a tent beyond. The victor marched over to the platform again, and received the congratulations of the duke while Lady Isobel once more bestowed a smile.

The next pair of knights entered the field and mounted their chargers, and once more one emerged victorious. Over and over again knights charged down the field, and over and over one was knocked from the tournament while one progressed.

"How many knights are there?" Anna asked.

"It depends on the size of the prize. The big tournaments are usually held in summer, but this is a smaller tournament, so the first round should be almost done."

As he was speaking a loud cry went up from the crowd, and Anna turned to see the next two knights enter the field. One of the knights, like those who had gone before, entered with his helmet off, his dented and scratched armor glowing dully in the winter sun, but the head of the second knight was covered with his helmet, the visor pulled down. As strange as that was, it was his armor that immediately drew attention, however, as it was as black as night from head to toe.

"Who's that?" asked Anna.

"I have no idea," Max replied. "I have never seen him before." He turned and whispered to his neighbor, then turned back to Anna.

"No-one has been able to learn his identity. It seems he entered the Christmastide tournament, which he won, and has won every tournament since. People are calling him the Black Knight."

"No-one has seen his face?"

"Apparently not."

Anna watched as the two knights faced each other. The flag was lowered and the knights charged. As unfamiliar as Anna was with jousting, it seemed clear from the start that the Black Knight was going to win the round. Despite the heaviness of the armor, he moved effortlessly, and with a speed that defied belief. His back remained straight and tall, and in his posture there was no hint of tension. His lance hit the other knight square in the chest, knocking him from his horse, and he then leapt from his own mount with an ease that seemed impossible given the armor he wore. He gave a low bow to the duke and his daughter, then turned and exited the field as a cheer went up from the crowd.

The Black Knight won each of his rounds with the same graceful ease as the first. Each time he came onto the field, Anna held her breath, releasing it when he unseated yet another opponent. She joined in the cries of the crowd, ignoring the looks of amusement Max cast her way.

"Enjoying your first taste of blood sport, are you?" he said with a grin.

"Max! It's not a blood sport! No-one has died!"

"Not yet," he said.

The light was beginning to fade when the final two knights still remaining entered the field, one at a time. The first knight was an experienced soldier, who had fought many infidels in the Holy Lands, earning glory and honor for himself and his family. A shout went up from the crowd as he moved to the platform, bowing low to the duke and his daughter. The duke rose, moving to the railing to speak to the knight. He nodded and stepped back as Lady Isobel waved and blew him a kiss.

"What did the duke say?" Anna asked Max.

"The gist of it was that if he didn't unseat the Black Knight, he would need to find another patron."

Anna was shocked. "That's dreadful."

Max shrugged. "That's the nature of the game, Anna." Another shout arose from the crowd, and the Black Knight entered the field. Like the other knight, he strode over to the platform, but it seemed to Anna that his bow was shallow, lacking proper respect for the duke. This time the duke remained seated, but Lady Isobel rose to her feet and moved over to the railing. She waved her handkerchief above her head; then crumpling it in her hand, she threw it at the Black Knight. Behind her, the duke glared at her back.

Max leaned towards Anna, his lips close to her ear.

"What are the chances Lady Isobel will be sent to an invalid relative in the country tonight?" he said.

Anna turned and smiled at him, her eyes sparkling. "I think she should pack her chest as soon as she gets home."

The charge was over almost as soon as it started, the Black Knight flowing down the course as though riding the wind rather than a horse. He unseated his opponent in one quick move, so fast Anna did not even see the lance move forward, and then it was over. The Black Knight once more walked over to the platform as Lady Isobel rose to her feet and blew the champion kisses. The duke stared at the knight for a long moment before also rising to his feet and coming to stand next to his daughter.

"Well done, Sir Knight," he said. "You have bested my champion and earned another prize. But before I hand over the purse, you need to reveal your identity."

"No."

The crowd gasped at the single word.

"I insist," said the duke.

"No."

"Then you will forfeit the prize."

"Very well. But be very sure you are willing to accept the consequences of that choice."

"What consequences?" Anna whispered to Max. Max turned to his neighbor, then a moment later he whispered in her ear.

"The last sponsor was killed two days after denying the Black Knight his prize."

"Killed?" Anna turned to meet Max's gaze. "How?"

"By a dragon." Max's voice was grim as he returned his gaze to the knight. The Black Knight was still before the platform, but his gaze, hidden by the visor, was roving over the crowds. It stopped when it reached Max, then moved slowly to rest on Anna. Even though she could not see the knight's eyes, she knew with complete certainty that the knight was looking at her. She felt Max glance down at her, then back at the knight, and sensed him stiffen beside her. The knight faced the platform once more, but in the instant before he turned, Anna saw a glint of light behind the visor.

"I refuse to be cowed by the likes of you," said the duke. "And let all here know that if I die before the week is out, by whatever means, it will have been at the hands of this so-called Black Knight who is too cowardly to show his face."

The Black Knight stared at the duke, then nodded.

"Very well." He turned and walked down the field, the crowd suddenly silent as it watched. He was a few feet away from the competitors' tent when the duke signaled with his hand, and within moments the knight was surrounded by a dozen guards. Anna heard Max groan.

"What is it?"

"This will not turn out well." He pulled her to her feet. "Come, we need to find Aaron."

"Aaron? Why?"

"Because," Max said, holding her hand as he moved between the seats, "that is no human knight."

"No human knight? You mean he's a dragon?"

"Yes."

"But those guards —"

"Are as good as dead."

CHAPTER TWENTY-NINE

"It must be Jack," Aaron said, pacing the hall floor as Keira watched. Max had arrived just a few moments before, pulling along a breathless Anna.

"I agree," Max replied. "But why is he doing this?"

"I don't know." Aaron sounded frustrated. "It is one thing to challenge me for Mastership, but another to target the city."

"Maybe he's just doing it for amusement," Anna said. "Something to pass the time until you arrive." Three sets of eyes turned to stare at her.

"It's possible, I suppose," Aaron said slowly. He looked at Max. "Our hands are tied until we can discover where Jack is hiding. Contact everyone and let them know I will be waiting for them at Drake Manor at midnight."

"Yes, Master."

"When you're done, I need you to return here, Max," Aaron continued. Max opened his mouth, then closed it as his gaze dropped to the ground. He remained silent for a long moment, then slowly lifted his eyes to Aaron's once more.

"Yes, Master."

"I cannot leave Keira and Anna unprotected, Max. Apart

174

from Favian and Owain, there is no-one I trust more with this task. I need you here, but I will not leave you uninformed."

Max nodded. "I will obey you in whatever task you give me, Aaron. You can trust me, and I will not fail you."

Aaron nodded and clamped his hand on Max's shoulder. "Thank you, Max." He turned to Keira. "Come along, my sweet. We need to get ready for an evening with the prince."

The palace in the evening looked completely different from the daytime. The walk from the river to the courtyard was lined with long rush torches, staked into the ground and gleaming against the stone walls of the palace. Keira couldn't help stopping to stare as she climbed out of the ferry.

"It looks so magical," she said, looking at the wavering lights.

"Nothing magical about being at court," Aaron retorted dryly. He turned to face Keira. "Those women in there, they are nothing like you. Don't allow them to intimidate you."

Once inside the courtyard, Aaron led Keira towards a different entrance from the one he had taken that morning.

"We are going to the prince's private apartments," he said in response to her look of enquiry. The doorway led into a narrow passage with a carved stone staircase spiraling upward at the end. There was no light in the passage, but Aaron led her unerringly up the stairs.

"How do you know the back corridors so well?" she asked. He glanced down at her, before pulling her hand through his arm and heading down the next passage.

"I spent a lot of time at the palace once," he said. Keira was about to enquire further when Aaron stopped outside a set of closed double doors where liveried guardsmen stood on either side. At their approach, they stepped forward and held out their lances, crossing the doors with an X.

"Sorry, Sire, you cannot enter."

"We are here at the invitation of the prince," Aaron said.

The guards looked at each other, then pulled their lances back to their sides.

"Your name?"

"Aaron Drake."

"Wait here, Sire," one of the men said, before slipping through the doors. He returned a few moments later and nodded to the other guard, pulling open the door and gesturing for Aaron and Keira to enter.

They passed through into a narrow anteroom. Two footmen stepped out from their places next to the door.

"Your cloak, My Lady," said one, holding out his hand. Keira handed him her cloak, then nervously smoothed down her gown. Made of dark blue silk, it was cut close to her figure, while a white linen chemise, lined with lace, peeked out from beneath the neckline. At her hips she wore a jewel-studded belt, and her hair had been braided on either side of her head and pinned in the latest fashion.

"You look beautiful," Aaron assured her. His eyes held hers for a moment, then he turned toward the door being opened by the footmen. He extended his hand, and she lightly laid her own upon it, turning towards the entrance as their names were announced.

"Master Drake and Lady Drake."

The room they stepped into was large and ornately furnished. Tapestries in bright hues covered every wall and thick rugs covered the stone floor. Candles lit every corner, while a huge chandelier hung from the ceiling blazed with dozens more. Benches and stools with richly embroidered cushions were neatly placed along the walls, and crowded throughout the room people were chattering and laughing.

"Aaron!" The prince's voice rang out over the crowd. "And my Lady Drake. Welcome. Welcome."

Keira turned to see the prince making his way towards them. He wore a courtepy, or short doublet, of dark green that was so short it hung only a few inches below his waist, while his breeches of bright crimson were so tight, Keira felt herself blushing. On his feet he wore shoes of the latest fashion, with points so long they were tied back in a circle. As he drew close, he was joined by a young woman who looked Aaron up and down in frank admiration.

"Aaron Drake," said the woman. "Well, well. Back in town I see. Does Elise know?" At the mention of the name, Keira glanced at Aaron. His mouth had tightened slightly, but he returned the woman's look steadily.

"Your Highness," Aaron said with a shallow bow, "allow me to introduce my wife, Lady Keira." The woman turned an appraising look on Keira as she dropped into a curtsey.

"Your Highness," Keira murmured. Aaron had told her that Princess Matilda would be in attendance, but she still felt a little intimidated by such an important personage.

"Pretty young thing, Aaron," the princess said. She looked to be about the same age as Keira, or maybe a year or two older. She wore a long gown of crimson, the same color as the prince's breeches, while over it she wore, like the prince, a hip-length courtepy of dark green, trimmed in white fur. Her braided hair was pinned over her head and covered in gold gauze, studded with jewels. Keira glanced down at her own gown, suddenly feeling very plain, but she lifted her chin and looked at the princess as Aaron's hand rested lightly on her back.

"She is indeed very beautiful, my lady," Aaron said. "I must be the happiest man in the kingdom." Keira could feel the heat from his hand spreading through her back as Aaron held the gaze of the woman before him. She glanced at Keira, then nodded slowly as the prince clasped Aaron by the arm.

"Come, Aaron, everyone is abuzz with the tournament. You heard what happened, did you not?"

"I heard that the duke refused to pay the Black Knight when he refused to reveal his identity."

"Farrand tried to arrest him but was unsuccessful. The Black Knight got away, but not before killing three of his men."

"How did a single man overcome three trained guards?"

"That is a mystery to which we don't have an answer. The men who survived said that when they tried to grab the knight, they were burned by his armor, but that of course is quite impossible. The man himself could not have survived within armor that hot."

As the prince led Aaron away, he shot a glance at Keira, his eyes meeting hers. There was no doubting *what* the man was, even if they couldn't say for certain that it was Jack wearing that armor. Keira was still looking at Aaron when she felt a hand on her arm.

"Come Keira," said the princess, "let's join the other ladies and leave the gentlemen to their tales of jousting and Black Knights." She led Keira over to a group of women who were standing near the fire watching her curiously.

"Ladies," Princess Matilda said, "allow me to introduce Keira Drake." She gestured towards each woman. "Lady Elizabeth, Lady Joan, and Lady Blanche." Keira resisted the urge to look down as the women continued to stare at her.

"Keira Drake," Joan finally said. "We heard that Aaron had finally got himself attached, but I must admit, you are nothing like I expected."

"Yes," Blanche added. "So different from Elise. I wonder what he sees in her." Keira recognized the immediate antipathy in the woman's gaze.

"Don't concern yourself with Blanche, my dear," Elizabeth said. "I'm certain Aaron Drake saw something that made him desirous of marrying you. Now sit down with us, and tell us all about it." She pulled Keira over to a chair and pressed her down onto the seat. "Where are you from, my dear?"

"A little village near the mountains," Keira said. "You wouldn't have heard of it." She looked down when she saw the women glance at one another.

"A girl from the country," Joan said as Blanche tittered.

"Now, now," Elizabeth said, "she can't help where she

comes from." She turned to Keira. "How did you meet Aaron?"

"I ... uh ... I met him in the market."

"In the village market?"

"Yes."

"Ah! You were out shopping?"

"Something like that," Keira said. She glanced over to where Aaron was standing with a group of men. He had his back to her, but as she looked at him, he turned and met her gaze, holding it with his own. From the corner of her eye she saw Blanche follow the direction of her gaze, then turn away with a soft snort.

"Did you hear what happened at the joust today?" Blanche turned back to the other ladies. "Isobel threw her handkerchief at the Black Knight, in defiance of the duke's wishes!"

"I heard he's sending her out of the city for a while."

"But who do you suppose the Black Knight could be?"

"Mary Pritchard says" – Joan leaned forward and lowered her voice – "that he is not a knight at all. She says she knows who he is, but promised to keep his identity secret."

"How would she know?"

"Because," Joan whispered, "she's sleeping with him."

"No! What if Wesley finds out?"

"Wesley is in the country." Joan leaned back with a satisfied grin. "And even if he did find out, he is too well satisfied with Agnes to care."

"Agnes?"

"The daughter's governess."

As the ladies digested this new piece of gossip, a tinkling bell sounded from the doorway.

"Ladies and gentlemen," a footman intoned loudly, "supper is served."

Keira glanced around the room to see Aaron coming towards her. She took his arm gratefully, smiling at him when he squeezed her hand. A long table was laid with silverware that glittered in the light of a multitude of candles, standing in gold candelabra, and at each setting were elegantly-written name cards. Aaron had been placed near the head of the table, close to the prince, while Keira was seated at the opposite end, with men she didn't know on either side of her. She drew in a fortifying breath and took her seat with the other guests.

The meal was a sumptuous affair, with each course quickly following the previous one. Keira soon gave up any efforts to make small talk with the men on either side of her, and instead listened to the conversation flowing around the table. Speculation was rife about the identity of the Black Knight, but the main topic of conversation was the dragon. It did not take long before the prince was plying Aaron with questions on how he would deal with the threat, but when Aaron gave no further indication of his intentions than he had that morning, the prince launched into his own narrative about Aaron's skill with dragons.

"The first time I met Aaron Drake," he said, "was when my royal person was threatened by a dragon. When Aaron appeared before me, insisting he could chase the dragon away, I must admit I was disinclined to believe him. But he walked right up to that monster, said something to the beast, and it left." He turned to face Aaron.

"Tell me, Aaron, what did you say to the creature?"

"I can no longer recollect the words, Your Highness," Aaron said.

Prince Alfred turned back to the other guests. "That is what he has been saying since the day I met him. Very well, Aaron, keep your secrets. Just don't fail me now when I need you the most."

"I won't, Your Highness," Aaron replied.

Keira knew it was customary in large households for the women to leave the table first, allowing the men to their conversations, and it was with relief that Keira finally rose and followed the women from the dining room. Being at the far end of the table, she was the last to leave, and the other women were already seated when Keira entered the parlor. Elizabeth beckoned to her and patted the empty seat at her side.

"Don't be shy, my dear." Keira took the seat, listening in silence to conversations that meant nothing to her. Who the father of Katherine's child could be, how Lord Harris had beaten his wife for talking to Lord Snow, the terrible shade of purple Martha had been wearing at the last ball. How long, she wondered, had Aaron been part of this world? Eventually the conversation turned to her.

"How long does Aaron plan to remain in the city?" Elizabeth asked her.

"Just until he has dealt with the dragon," she replied.

"What a shame," Joan said. "We will all be distraught when he abandons us again."

"Why?" Keira asked. Her question was met with blank stares for a moment.

"Aaron was always a favorite at court," the princess finally said. "Especially," she added with a significant look at Joan, "amongst the women. But of course he is married now, so I suppose we should expect things to be different." There was an awkward silence as Keira examined her hands.

"Did I hear Max traveled with you?" Elizabeth said.

"You know Max?" Keira asked in surprise.

"Yes, indeed, we all know Max," Elizabeth replied as the women laughed. "I understand he spent Christmastide with you."

"That's right. He and Aaron are distantly related."

"Of course they are," Blanche said. "And I'm sure they had plenty of shared experiences to reminisce over." Again, the women laughed, glancing at each other in amusement. Keira returned her attention to her hands.

"Do you have any family?" Princess Matilda asked.

"Yes. My parents are still in the village, but my sister traveled to the city with us."

"Your sister? And how old is she?" Elizabeth asked.

"Seventeen."

"Seventeen? A bit young, then," Blanche said with a snigger.

"That will do, Blanche," Elizabeth said, patting Keira's hand soothingly. She looked up at the sound of the door being opened. "How marvelous. Here are the men," she said.

Keira looked up to seeing Aaron walking towards her, a slight frown marring his forehead.

"I'm afraid we need to leave this pleasant gathering," he said as he drew near. He turned with a bow towards the princess. "I'm afraid other business calls me away."

"There's no need for Keira to leave," she said. "We can send someone to escort her home, or order chambers prepared and she can stay the night."

"Yes," added Blanche, "I'm sure there is plenty for us to discuss."

But Keira had already risen to her feet. "Thank you so much for your kind offer, Your Highness, but I must return with Aaron. My sister will be wondering where I am."

"Yes, of course. Your sister. Perhaps I will have the pleasure of making her acquaintance sometime."

"Thank you, Your Highness," she said, dropping a low curtsey. She nodded to the other ladies as Aaron made his own bows, and a moment later they were out the door.

"That," she said as they walked towards the ferry, "was the most awful evening I have ever endured."

"As bad as that?" Aaron said with a slight smile, but it quickly disappeared. "I'm sorry. I heard some of their insinuations, and took my leave as soon as I could." Keira looked at him curiously.

"How many years did you remain at court?" she asked.

"Three," he said.

"Three years? Really? I wouldn't have thought you could endure it for more than a few weeks."

"I was a different man, then, and there were

complications."

"Did that complication involve a woman named Elise?"

There was a moment of silence. "Keira," he finally said, "what happened before is of no concern. All that matters to me now is you. And you know I love you."

Keira stopped, turning on the path to face him. "Yes, I know you love me. But I also know that you are distancing yourself from me. And the women I met this evening know more about you than I do. I may be a simple country girl, but I am not so naïve as to think that nothing happened in the hundred or so years before you met me. For all I know, the things those women were referring to happened before I was even born. But the thing is, I don't know!"

"That's because they are of no importance."

"If they are of no importance, why are you hiding them from me? Do you think I will run away screaming when I hear what you did? I can handle the fact that you are a man-eating, fire-breathing dragon, but you think you need to protect me from your life as a man. I would rather hear about these things from you, than learn about them from a group of mean and malicious women who use the knowledge to taunt me."

"I had a few affairs, Keira, but as I said, they meant nothing. They are all in the past. You are the only one I care about."

"Who is Elise?"

Aaron glanced away, looking out over the river. "She's just one of many women I slept with," he said.

Keira stared at him. "You know," she finally said, "I think it is easier for you to be with women like that." Aaron turned a startled glance on her.

"How can you say that?"

"They make no demands of you beyond physical pleasure, and you remain in control of your feelings, because you feel nothing for them. But Aaron, you chose to marry me. You say you love me, and I believe you, but love also means being open and vulnerable. It means trusting the other person enough to share your deepest secrets. It means letting go. I have trusted you in everything, Aaron. Don't turn away from me now."

"I'm not turning away from you. I love you. I choose you. I am giving up Mastership for you."

"Aaron, that is not a choice! You are giving up Mastership because you feel compelled to. And you will hate me every day because of it. Because you know you are the Master. You, and no-one else."

Aaron turned away as she spoke, his jaw set as he looked over the river. A soft splash sounded behind them, and Keira turned to see a light bobbing in the water, growing closer as the ferry pulled up beside the dock. She stepped into the craft without another word, and sat down. She felt Aaron settle next to her; but wrapping her arms around herself, she turned to look at the dark water lapping gently against the long boat.

CHAPTER THIRTY

Anna watched Max as he reclined on the parlor floor next to the fire, while she sat on some cushions across from him. The stone floor was warm, but whether it was from the fire or the dragon, Anna wasn't sure. Max was staring into the flames, his expression distant as the light of the fire flickered against his skin. He had barely said a word to Anna all evening. He's probably frustrated at being left to babysit, Anna thought.

"You're being terribly rude," she finally said. Max looked up with a faint smile.

"My apologies, Anna. I was thinking about Jack."

"Oh." She watched as he turned back towards the fire, flipping a log with his bare hand. "Max," she said, "why do you live in the city?"

"This is my home," he said, looking at her in surprise.

"How long have you lived here?" He shrugged.

"Oh, I don't know. About twenty years."

"Twenty years? How old are you?"

"Thirty-five," he replied in amusement. "I'm a lot younger than Aaron," he added when she stared at him in shock. Anna slowly closed her mouth.

"You must have been very young when you moved here. Did you come with your parents?"

"No. My mother lives in a small town on the moors, while my father lives" – he waved his hand vaguely – "somewhere else."

"They aren't married?"

"No. My father had a brief affair with my mother, then left her with a child to raise on her own. A child whose true nature she knew nothing about."

"That's … terrible."

"It wasn't so bad when I was small. He left her with enough money to buy a house and support herself and a child. It only became difficult when I turned twelve."

"Twelve? Why then?"

"Because that was when I realized I was a monster." Anna stared at him in horror, and he gave her a wry smile. "At least, that was how it felt to me."

"You didn't know what you were?"

"No. My father omitted that small detail about himself when he seduced my mother. She had no idea what manner of creature she had slept with, and I certainly had no idea what I was."

"So what happened?"

Max sighed. "A dragon child only starts changing at the onset of puberty. I knew something was happening to me, but had no idea what it was."

"What was happening?"

"My entire body was changing from flesh and bone to flame. I felt like a fire was raging through me, which of course it was. My skin itched from the scales forming beneath the surface. And then, instead of the fire being inside me, it was all around me. I started fires just by breathing, but the flames didn't burn me. Fire would burst from my hands, but my skin was unsinged." He opened his hand, and Anna's eyes widened when she saw flames burning in the palm of his hand. "Other things were happening, too. I noticed ridges forming on my back. I could suddenly see better, could smell better. I could even smell people's emotions. And then, one day ..." His voice trailed off.

"One day?" Anna prompted gently. He looked up and met her gaze.

"Then one day I turned into a monster. I was with a girl. There was no warning. One moment I was myself, and then I was a beast, standing ten feet tall. All I was aware of was a ravenous hunger. And that there was something on the ground before me that could satisfy my appetite. I could hear her screaming, could smell her fear, and that just sharpened the hunger."

"No," Anna whispered.

"Now you know," Max said softly. "A monster." Anna could feel her heart pounding as she looked away. He was right; a monster. She glanced back at him. He had turned away and was looking into the flames, his expression sad. And for a moment she saw someone as adrift as herself. She reached out and placed her hand over his.

"Not a monster," she said. Max swung a startled gaze around to look at her, then dropped it down to where her hand covered his. Slowly, he turned his hand over and he twisted his fingers around hers.

"What happened next?" she said softly.

"When I realized what I had done, I fled. Or rather, I flew. I found a cave deep in the mountains and hid myself away. The following morning I was back in my human form. My first thought was that it had been a terrible dream, but I just had to look around the cave to know it was real. And I felt different. Powerful. Invincible. And monstrous." Max frowned. "The smell of blood excited me. Taking to the air thrilled me. I was a predator. The most dangerous hunter in the world. Just the thought of killing my prey, their hot blood spilling into my mouth, made me eager to do it. But my human emotions were horrified at what I had become." He looked at Anna askance with a wry smile. "I think you are horrified, too."

"No," she said. "Not horrified." She paused. "What did you do?"

"I stayed in the cave and learned to control my hunger. The blood lust lessened as time went on. And I discovered I could control my transformations. I fed on wild animals in the woods, and found that they satisfied my appetite. And after about three weeks, I went home."

"You went home? Why?"

"I had never met my father, but I was sure that he had the answers to what was happening to me. I found out all I could about him from my mother, then set off to find him."

"And did you find him?"

"Eventually."

"And did he tell you what you wanted to know?"

"He told me that I was a dragon, not a monster. But it was Beatrix who helped me the most. She's my step-mother, and Aaron's aunt. She's also a dragon. James was married to her by then, and she was horrified to learn that he had left me without any way of discovering what was happening to me. She was even more dismayed when she learned there was a younger daughter as well. She made James find her, and she also came to live with us. But I couldn't bear to be near James, so I moved to the city as soon as I could. James tried to stop me, but he hadn't been a father before, and I wasn't about to let him start then."

"And you've lived in the city ever since?"

"I have."

"You must enjoy it here to have stayed so long."

"I suppose I enjoy it well enough. But that isn't what keeps me here."

"Then what?"

Max looked down at their entwined hands. "A lack of purpose, I suppose. Nothing better to do."

"Everyone has a purpose. You just have to find yours."

"Really?" Max looked up at her with a grin. "And tell me,

oh wise one, what is your purpose in life?"

"I'm still trying to figure it out. Maybe I will take holy orders."

Max grimaced. "Definitely not."

"No? Then perhaps I am meant to stay with Keira. Help her when the children come."

"A kind, sweet, docile aunt? I don't think so."

"Why not?" Anna asked, a little piqued.

"You, darling Anna, were made to love. Passionately. Wildly. Completely." Anna stared at him, trying to decide if she felt offended, or something else, but before she could say anything, a sound at the front of the house had her pulling her hand away from Max.

"Aaron and Keira must be back," she said. Max just grinned, his eyes on her, as Keira walked into the room ahead of Aaron. She stopped at the sight of Anna and Max on the floor, her face registering her surprise.

"How was your evening?" Max asked, finally dragging his gaze away from Anna.

"Fine," Keira said. "Dreadful. What awful people." Max laughed, then turned to Aaron.

"Did you learn anything of interest?"

"No. It seems like our mystery dragon killed three of the duke's guards. The duke's fortunate that they weren't all killed." He looked at Keira as he spoke, but she was examining a rip in her gown.

"Look at this, Anna," she said, showing her the tear. "I wonder how I got that."

"Probably a nail," Max said. "Happens all the time." Keira nodded, her attention still on the rip.

"I will be on my way, then," Aaron said. He was still watching Keira, but she was preoccupied with the tear in her gown. He waited a moment, then with a nod in Max's direction, left the house. At the sound of the door closing, Keira looked up.

"I am exhausted," she said. "I think I will retire. Come

with me, Anna," she said, "and I will tell you about the dreadful women I met this evening."

"All right," said Anna. She rose to her feet, and linked her arm into her sister's. "Good night, Max," she said as they exited the room.

CHAPTER THIRTY-ONE

The room was cold when Keira woke the next morning. She rolled over in the bed, seeking out Aaron's warmth, before remembering the events of the previous night. Aaron had called a meeting of dragons at Drake Manor. And before that ... Keira shivered, remembering the evening spent at court.

The fire had burned low in the grate during the night, and Keira stared at it for a moment, willing it to burn higher, before pushing back the quilts with a sigh and padding over to the hearth. Kneeling down on the stone floor, warmed by the glowing coals, she stoked the embers and added another log, watching as the flames slowly licked around the dry surface, lighting bits of loose bark, before finally spreading to the rest of the log. She pulled a cloak around her shoulders, shivering as the cold fabric touched her bare arms. Placing her feet into a pair of slippers, she slowly opened the door to the chamber. The passage outside was quiet, but Keira could hear the household sounds drifting up the stairs. She left the room and made her way down the staircase, pausing to look into the hall. Hannah was sitting on one of the benches, Keira's torn gown on her lap, plying a needle and thread. She looked up, catching sight of Keira, and quickly stood.

"Mistress, you should be in your chambers, not wandering around the hall in your chemise and cloak. Let me help you back upstairs and see you dressed."

"No." Keira waved her hand in dismissal. "I was just looking for Master Drake. Has he returned?"

"Well then, he's in the parlor," said Hannah, sitting down again and picking up the gown. Keira nodded her thanks and headed towards the parlor, pausing at the open door. Aaron was sitting on a chair, his face lined with thought as he absentmindedly tossed a ball of flame from one hand to another. Keira watched from the doorway for a moment and Aaron looked up to meet her gaze. He stared at her, his eyes flaring into flames as his gaze held hers. Keira nodded at the flames in his hands.

"What are you doing?"

He looked down at the fiery ball and shrugged. "A parlor trick," he said, lobbing it into the fire.

"When did you return?" Keira asked.

"Shortly before dawn."

"You didn't come to bed."

"I wasn't sure you wanted me to." He glanced at her again, then looked away. She stared at him, unsure what to say. She loved him, and every fiber of her being yearned for him, for his touch, for his love, given freely and openly. She walked over to the chair, knelt down on the ground and rested her head in his lap.

"I love you," she said. A shudder passed through him, almost a sob, and his hand brushed her neck, twisting into her hair, before falling back to his knee. She pulled away to look into his face. He was staring into the flame once again. "What happened last night?"

He took a deep breath and rose to his feet. "Our first priority is to find Jack. It seems that he has been moving from place to place, but I intend to spend the day tracking him. He cannot hide forever." He opened his palm, throwing a flame from hand to hand as Keira watched. A light tap sounded on the parlor door, and Aaron closed his hand over the flame as Thomas entered the room.

"Milord," he said, nodding at Aaron. "Milady."

"Thomas. You have news for me?"

"I do, Milord." He paused and looked uncomfortably at Keira as he cleared his throat. "The, uh, black dragon was in the city again last night. There were some" – he glanced at Keira once more – "casualties."

"The duke," Aaron said in resignation.

"No," Thomas replied. "The duke's daughter, Lady Isobel." Keira gasped as Aaron looked up sharply.

"Lady Isobel? Wasn't she the one who gave the Black Knight her token?"

"Yes. But she wasn't the only one to lose her life. Another five people were killed, but she was the only one who ... whose body was touched."

Aaron turned away with a growl as flames escaped from his mouth, the air shimmering around his body. His fingers stretched into talons as he curled them into fists, the muscles straining against his skin. A falling log pulled Keira's attention to the fire, and she drew in a breath when she saw the flames in the grate rising higher, spreading beyond the confines of the fireplace and up the length of the wall, leaving a black scar on the whitewashed surface. Aaron was pacing the small room, his face a mask of anger. His face was changing as he paced, half dragon and half human, and Keira could see his teeth, sharp and pointed between wisps of flame.

"Jack has gone too far," he snarled. "He will be begging for mercy by the time I have finished with him." He turned to Thomas. "Go find Max and tell him his presence is required." Thomas nodded, but made no move to leave the room. "Is there something else?" Aaron said.

"A messenger from the palace delivered this first thing this morning." Thomas held out a small scroll of paper, tied with a leather thong. Aaron stared at it for a moment, then took it between his claws.

"Go find Max."

"Yes, Milord." As Thomas left the room, Aaron slid the cord off the scroll and unrolled the heavy sheet. He stared at it for a long moment, then handed it to Keira. Written in elegant script and embellished with purple and gold was an invitation to the annual winter ball at the palace. Keira studied it for a moment before looking at Aaron.

"It includes Anna," she said.

"So it would seem," Aaron said. "We won't be going, of course."

"Why not?"

Aaron turned to her with eyebrows raised. "Because I have no desire to return to the palace, and even less to take you there. Besides, why would you even want to go?"

"Because I have never been to a ball." She took a step towards him and laid her hand on her arm. "Please?"

"No." He glared down at her. "I have no time for a ball."

She dropped her hand. "Very well. There is no need for you to go. Max can escort us."

"He will do no such thing," he said. His eyes blazed, matching the flames that suddenly flared once again in the grate. Keira darted a look at the fire, but Aaron did not seem to notice as he clenched his hand around her arm, his talons scraping her skin. His skin was hot, hotter than she had ever felt, and his palm seared into her skin through the fabric of her cloak. "Are you going to burn me where I stand?" she said, lifting her chin to look at him.

He glanced down at where his hand was clamped around her arm. Releasing it, he stepped away from her at the same instant, a look of horror crossing his face. The fabric where his hand had been was scorched, and beneath it Keira could feel the pain of burnt flesh. She pushed the cloak aside and watched as the blistered skin slowly smoothed over, turning from red to pink as the dragon blood in her veins healed the wound. She looked up to meet Aaron's appalled gaze.

"You burnt me."

"I'm so sorry." His voice shook slightly. "I had no idea. I don't know what's happened." He opened his hands and stared down at them as his talons receded. "Something is changing within me. As though I am becoming one with the flame."

"Like you were in the cave?" Keira whispered.

"Yes." His voice was low. Keira stepped closer.

"Do you know you did something to the fire in the grate?"

He had been examining his hands, but he lifted his gaze to hers. "What do you mean?"

"You were angry, and the flames suddenly flared up." She pointed at the black streak on the wall. "That wasn't there before. You made that happen."

"That's impossible," he said. He turned back to the fire, his eyes narrowing as he stared intently into the blaze. The flames suddenly grew, reaching higher than they had before. As Aaron fell back in shock, the flames dropped down again. He glanced back at Keira, his eyes wide, then looked back at the flames once more. As Keira watched, a small ball of fire left the grate, drifting higher into the air, and then as Aaron stepped back, it followed him into the room. He held out his hand and the flame landed on his palm, vanishing when he closed his fingers over it. For a long moment Aaron stared down at his hand, then turned towards Keira as she stared at him in shock.

"How ...?" she said.

"I'm not sure. I used my mind to imagine what I wanted to happen, and then ..." He shrugged. Keira took a step back as a wave of uncertainty rushed over her, but in two long strides Aaron was before her, and grabbing her by the shoulders, dropped a quick, hard kiss onto her lips. He stepped back as the door opened and Max stepped into the room. He paused, looking between them, before closing the door.

"You wanted me, Aaron?" he said. Aaron stared at Keira for another long moment, his eyes holding hers as she gazed at him wide eyed, before finally turning to Max. He drew in a deep breath before responding.

"Yes. I need you to go to Drake Manor. Owain needs to know what Jack is doing. Tell Favian I'm going to spend the day tracking Jack, starting at Potters Field, if he wants to join me. Come back here as soon as you're done – I don't want Drake House left without security."

"Very well," Max said with a nod. Aaron turned back to Keira, tapping his finger on the scroll still in her hand.

"I believe we are done discussing this," he said as he followed Max out the room. Keira watched as the door closed behind them.

"For someone who has lived over a century," she said under her breath, "you don't know very much, Aaron Drake."

CHAPTER THIRTY-TWO

Anna could not believe she had been invited to a ball at the palace.

"How does the palace even know about me?" she asked Keira. Her sister laughed.

"I already told you, Anna. Princess Matilda asked about my family and I said you were in the city with us."

"But what am I going to wear?" she said.

"We will ask Hannah to help us," Keira replied, smiling at Anna's excitement.

"Is Max going?" Anna asked.

"I believe so. Why, do you want him to?" Keira asked. The color rose in Anna's cheeks, but she waved off the question.

"It doesn't matter to me whether he goes or not," she said. "I was just curious." She pulled a gown out of her chest and held it up against her shoulders. "What about this one?" she asked.

"Maybe." Keira tilted her head as she examined the gown.

"What did Aaron say when he read the invitation?" Anna asked as she twirled around the floor.

"He was ... less than enthusiastic. But he finally agreed

to escort us when he realized it would offer him an opportunity to check in with other dragons who had been invited."

Not only had Aaron agreed, but he decided that Keira and Anna needed to be suitably attired for a royal ball. The following morning, Anna's chamber was filled with different fabrics while Hannah directed a small army of seamstresses as they cut, fitted and sewed. It was only three days until the ball, but somehow they accomplished the impossible. Of Aaron, Anna saw very little, and even Max seemed preoccupied. She overheard him talking to Keira one afternoon as she was fitted for her gown yet again.

"Has Aaron managed to track Jack at all?" she heard Keira asking.

"He's tracked down his lair in the mountains, but Jack has been keeping to the city since Aaron arrived." Max sounded frustrated. "He keeps himself surrounded by humans, making it almost impossible for Aaron to do anything without revealing himself and other dragons. But Aaron has dragons watching him continually, so Jack has been keeping to his human form."

"But he's no longer killing?"

"He's not killing."

"So what is he doing?"

"That's what Aaron is trying to figure out. He thinks Jack is just biding his time, but he doesn't know why."

The river was a sea of bobbing lights on the evening of the ball as boats plied the waters, ferrying the royal guests to the palace. Anna could not help staring at the people stepping gingerly into the floating vessels, their jewels and finery sparkling in the light of the swaying lamps at the end of each boat, but when the palace came into view, she gasped. Thousands of lamps lined the path that led to the palace courtyard, making the night seem as bright as day, while hundreds of footmen stood on guard. There were people everywhere, streaming from the river towards the palace, or appearing through the trees that surrounded the walls.

Anna felt as though they were being swept along in a tide, unable to change course, even if they wanted to. She glanced at Keira, who looked back with eyes shining, her face reflecting her own excitement as their gazes met for a moment.

They followed the crowd through a door where still more footmen were waiting to greet the guests. One of them stepped up to the small party, and Aaron held out their invitation. Max had his own, and these were both duly inspected. Satisfied with their authenticity, the footman bowed low, as another liveried servant stepped forward to lead them up the huge staircase and through the doors of the hall.

"Master and Lady Drake, Anna Carver, and Max Brant," he shouted out before stepping back and gesturing for the group to enter. For a moment, Anna could only stare as she looked around the enormous hall. Intricately carved wooden beams curved over the room, while along the top half of the whitewashed walls were huge arched windows, the leaded panes filled with colored glass. The lower half of the walls were covered in wood paneling, carved with scenes of hunting, romance, and nature. The walls were lined with torches, while above them were silver chandeliers filled with brightly burning candles. At one end of the hall was a raised dais with a long table covered in a white linen cloth, in front of which were two ornately gilded chairs, carved with a pair of lions. Behind the dais stood an embroidered screen, and strains of music could be heard coming from behind it, almost drowned by the general hubbub. Further down the hall were trestle tables, each lit with dozens of candles, while at the other end of the hall was another elaborately decorated screen. In the center of one wall stood a huge stone fireplace, so big a person could stand upright within it, while flames blazed and flickered behind an iron screen.

Aaron and Keira were moving into the room, and Anna followed at Max's side, her eyes darting to take everything in. People crowded into every corner, chatting and laughing. Someone was calling Max's name, and Anna turned around to see a woman pushing her way through the crowd.

"Max, darling, you're back! We have been so forlorn without you." At the sound of the voice, Max paused, but when Anna glanced up at him, she was startled to see he was looking not at the woman but at her. His eyes met hers for a moment, his gaze unfathomable, and then he was turning to the woman with a smile.

"Jane. As you can see, I am back for now."

"For now? Oh Max, you cannot leave us again. We are lost without you." She was right upon him now, her hand stretching out to take his arm. He took a small step back as she touched him, creating a space between them. The woman's eyebrows went up, and her gaze shot over to Anna, whom she looked at thoughtfully. Stepping back, she dropped her hand.

"Ah. I see," she said. Max inclined his head slightly, meeting her gaze.

"It is lovely to see you again, Jane," he said. Anna looked at him in confusion. She felt like a child watching through a window, seeing something just beyond her ken, but when Max pulled her hand through his arm and turned to follow Aaron, she allowed herself to be led away. A footman walked past with a wooden tray in his hands, and Max passed her a silver goblet of wine. More and more people were joining the crowd, spilling from the hall into the passages beyond. Anna was sure that no more people could squeeze in when a clarion sounded and a hush fell over the company. A man stepped onto the raised dais, his voice ringing over the crowd.

"Their Royal Highnesses, Prince Alfred and Princess Matilda."

The clarion sounded again as the eyes of everyone in the room turned to follow the pointed hand. There was a wide doorway through which a man walked into the hall, a crimson robe falling from his shoulders and a chain of office around his neck. Following behind were the royal couple, the prince beaming at his loyal subjects as he led his wife to the raised dais and sat down on the larger of the gilded chairs, while the princess sat down next to him.

The entrance of the royal couple marked the official start of the evening, and it was not long before people were instructed to take their seats while food was served. Anna could not believe the variety of dishes offered – fish, peacock, woodcocks and swan, venison, lamb and suckling pig. Fruit, nuts and cheeses, baked quince, fruit compotes and spiced baked apples. It seemed like the fare was endless as each course was removed and another brought forth. Ale and wine flowed from the jugs held by servants as they hovered around the tables, and when the spiced wine was served at the end, Anna felt like she would not be able to eat again for a week.

The meal done, servants entered the room and removed the trestle tables, clearing the room for dancing.

Max was already at her side when the music started, and grabbing her hand in his, he pulled her into the line of dancers who were forming a large circle that wound its way around the room. Her feet flew as they executed the simple steps, moving first one way and then another. She laughed when her other neighbor tripped over his own feet, knocking her off balance, but in a moment Max's hands were at her waist, keeping her steady. She felt a flash of heat where his hands touched her, and she pulled away in momentary confusion before returning her attention to the steps of the dance. The musicians were skilled and it was difficult to tell when one piece of music ended and the next began as they flowed from one tune to another. By the time they finally stopped, Anna was panting from the exertion.

"Wait here," Max said. "I will return with some refreshment." Anna watched as he weaved his way through the throngs of people, pausing to speak with Aaron who was on the other side of the hall. Anna had seen him and Keira dance for a while, before Aaron left to speak to some men who had arrived later. Anna wondered if they were dragons, but couldn't be sure. The music struck up again as the royal couple made their way onto the dance floor.

"We have a new dance to teach all our friends," Princess Matilda said with a smile at her guests. "It is already being danced in all the royal courts across the continent." She looked at the prince, holding out her hand to him; he took her hand in his and held it at shoulder level. Facing each other, she made a slight curtsey while he made a bow, and then they repeated the movement facing outwards. Taking a few steps forward, they repeated the action once again, then released hands and circled around to meet up once more further down the hall.

"The Basse Danse," a voice said close to her ear. "They probably learnt the steps from their lovers." Anna turned around to look at the man standing near her shoulder, her eyes widening as she took in his visage. He was dressed in black from head to foot, the only relief to the dark color being a silver ribbon that held his black hair at the nape of his neck. His lip curled as he looked down at her, and Anna felt a thrill of fear run the length of her spine.

"Are you enjoying yourself, Mistress?" he asked, bending closer to her ear.

"I am," she said, pulling back to look into his face. The man was darkly handsome, and looked infinitely dangerous, but when he smiled at her it softened his whole face, and she smiled back.

"Good," he said. "A girl should always enjoy her first ball." He held out his hand. "Will you join me in a dance?"

Anna glanced around, uncertain, but the man seemed to understand her hesitation. "You are Aaron's new sister-in-law. Anna, is it?" She looked back at him in surprise. "I know Aaron well," he said.

He placed his hand at the small of her back, and brought his head close to hers again. "Please don't refuse me," he coaxed. "I promise to be on my best behavior." He smiled at her again. "And we should not go against the wishes of the princess. She wants her guests to dance with her, so let us dance."

Anna felt her resistance fading, but she still glanced in the direction where she had last seen Max. He was making his way towards her with an angry scowl, and his expression made up her mind. She turned to the dark stranger with a smile and held up her hand for him to take in his. He smiled back and led her into the line of dancers that was forming on the floor. The music struck up, and she was moving, following the simple steps demonstrated by the royal couple.

"I think Max is in trouble," the man said, and Anna looked across to see Aaron bearing down on Max, his brows drawn together in anger.

"Why?" Anna asked, turning back to her dance partner.

"Oh, I don't know. Perhaps Aaron would prefer not to see us together." He glanced down at her, and Anna felt a sudden shiver of trepidation.

"Why?" she whispered. The man smiled sardonically, his gaze holding hers.

"I'm sorry, I forgot to introduce myself. My name is Jack Drake." His hand tightened around Anna's as she tried to pull away from his grasp. "Now, now, my dear, no need to make a scene." Anna looked back at Max, her eyes meeting his as he stared at her. His glance flicked over to Jack, before landing on her once more. Aaron was standing next to him, his hand heavy on Max's shoulder. Neither man spoke as they watched the pair dancing.

As soon as the music was over, Anna jerked her hand away as though she had been stung, and turning on her heel, walked away from Jack without another word. Max was by her side in a moment, his voice low and angry.

"How could you, Anna?"

"I didn't know," she said, swinging an angry glare at him.

"Surely it's obvious," he said, glancing back at the man swathed in black. Anna stared at Max in silence before turning her back to him and marching across the room. She listened for the sound of his pursuit, but heard only the mingling throng.

CHAPTER THIRTY-THREE

Keira stood in a corner of the hall, watching Anna as she danced with Jack. She could see Aaron and Max watching them, too, their expressions furious. Jack would be enjoying this moment, she thought, knowing Aaron would not retaliate with so many people present. She wondered how Jack had managed to gain entry into the ball, before remembering Blanche telling the ladies a few nights before that Mary Pritchard was sleeping with the Black Knight. Mary probably thought she knew the secret Jack, not realizing that Jack's secrets were multi-layered.

Keira returned her attention to Anna and Jack. From the way Anna was woodenly moving through the steps of the dance, it was clear she had discovered the identity of her dance partner.

It was soon over, and Anna fled the floor. Keira watched as she exchanged a few words with Max before heading towards a table with a jug of wine.

Pushing her way through the crowds, Keira headed to her sister. Anna was trembling as she turned to Keira.

"I didn't know," she said, her voice pleading for understanding.

"I know," Keira said. "It's all right. Aaron and Max are angry with Jack, not you."

"It wasn't just *him* Max was angry with," Anna said bitterly.

"He was concerned about you."

"Why would he be concerned about me? He doesn't even like me."

"You know that's not true." Anna glared at Keira for a moment, her gaze challenging, but a moment later her shoulders slumped, the fight suddenly gone.

"I know," she said.

Keira and Anna both looked back at Max, who was once again standing with Aaron. Aaron was stiff with tension, his hand on Max's shoulder. Another man joined them, and they talked together in earnest for a few moments, until the other man nodded and turned away. Aaron was still talking to Max when a woman approached, and Keira watched with interest as she stopped before the two men. Her figure was presented in profile, and Keira could see the woman was a beauty, despite the fact that she was not in the first bloom of youth. The long, dark hair that framed her face had been braided and wound into a coil at the top of her head, then covered with a net that sparkled with jewels, while the rest of her hair hung loose down her back, twined with dark green ribbons that matched her gown. Long eyelashes fluttered over her cheeks, her nose was small and straight, and her neck was long and graceful. She placed a hand on Aaron's arm and when she smiled up at him, Keira could see a row of straight, white teeth between full, rosy lips. The tension melted from Aaron's shoulders as he looked down at the woman with a warm smile, and Keira felt the breath catch in her throat.

"Who's that with Aaron?" Anna asked.

"I don't know."

"It seems he knows her."

"Hmm, so it would appear," Keira said. The woman's hand was still on Aaron's arm, and Keira watched as he covered it with his own, holding her close. He bent down and said something in the woman's ear, and she pulled back with a smile, glancing around the room. Keira turned away and stepped around Anna, hiding herself from Aaron and the woman as her heart pounded furiously. She could only guess the identity of the woman, but none of the possibilities pleased her.

"I need some fresh air," she said over her shoulder, heading towards an open door that led to a balcony overlooking the gardens, not waiting to see if Anna followed. She glanced back once as she reached the door, and caught Aaron laughing at something the woman said, his face lit with genuine pleasure. She bit her lip as she turned away and stepped out into the cool night air. The gardens below were laid out in a symmetrical pattern, lit with hundreds of glowing lanterns. There were stairs leading down, and she headed over to these.

"Where are you going?" Anna asked, following close behind.

"Let's take a walk through the gardens," Keira said. "They look so beautiful."

"Is this about that woman?" Anna asked. "Because you know Aaron loves you." Keira was silent as she descended the stairs. "Just ask him who it was," Anna said as she stepped onto the grass. Keira turned to look at her sister.

"Please, Anna, I really don't wish to discuss this with you." In the faint light she saw Anna flush slightly.

"Of course," Anna said.

It was quiet in the gardens, the sounds from the hall becoming a distant murmur as they walked. There was no-one else around, and Anna glanced around nervously.

"Shouldn't we be getting back? Aaron and Max may be wondering where we are."

"Aaron and Max know exactly where to find us if they choose," Keira retorted. She looked at Anna, noting her confusion with a sigh.

"They can track us by our scent as easily as I can see you," she explained.

"Oh. Of course."

They walked a little further, meandering along paths that wound through the gardens, until Keira came to a stop. She turned around to face the palace. They had walked further than she realized, and suddenly the building seemed a long way off.

"Let's go back," she said. They had just taken a few steps when two men, their chests bare, stepped out in front of them, blocking their path. Keira knew at once that they were dragons, and a sliver of fear wound through her.

"Let us pass," she said, but the two men just stared at her in silence, their arms crossed against their chests, their feet firmly planted. She glanced around, wondering how they could make their escape, when she heard a laugh.

"Aren't you happy to see me, cousin?" Jack said, stepping in front of the two men. "I must admit I have been eagerly anticipating this reunion. You and me, all alone." He glanced at Anna. "Well, not quite alone, I suppose."

"Jack," Keira said angrily. "What is the meaning of this?"

Jack looked at her with a smile that was both charming and sinister.

"You and I have unfinished business," he said. He took a step towards her, then laughed when she stepped back, dragging Anna with her.

"There is no escape, Keira," he said. Keira drew in a deep breath and opened her mouth to scream, but before she could make a sound, Jack was behind her, his hand covering her open mouth.

"I look forward to meeting Aaron in a fight," he whispered in her ear, "but it will be at the time of my choosing." With a snap Keira closed her mouth behind his hand, clamping her teeth against his skin. He snatched his hand away, and Keira drew in a breath to make another attempt at screaming, but before she could make a sound he slammed his hand against her mouth again. His fingers wrapped around her cheeks, holding tight as he brought his mouth to her ear. "I can be pleasant or unpleasant," he growled. "Do something like that again and I will be very unpleasant."

He glanced again at Anna, trembling beside her sister. "I've already had the pleasure of meeting your sister," he said to Keira, "and I'm sure I will find her willing to give me a few moments' pleasure, with just the slightest persuasion." Keira darted a quick glance around the gardens, but apart from Jack's two henchmen, there was no-one else to be seen.

"It seems that Aaron is too caught up with his mistress to notice your absence," Jack said. He watched as Keira's eyes widened. "Ah, you don't know, do you? That woman he was with is Elise, the Duchess of Southbury. His affair with her lasted close to three years, until she finally broke it off. I heard he was devastated." Keira closed her eyes as the image of the woman standing next to Aaron rose in her mind.

"I don't believe it," Anna said. Keira glanced at Anna in surprise as she continued. "Anyone can see that Aaron loves Keira. I don't know why he isn't coming, but it is not because he has a mistress."

"Brave words," Jack said. "Time will reveal the truth." He turned to the two men. "Take them," he said.

In a flash of light the two men transformed into their dragon forms – one dark brown, the other tan. A slight shimmer in the air was Keira's only warning of their change, and she cried out to Anna to cover her eyes, breathing a sigh of relief when Anna dropped her face into her hands. Relief was short-lived, however, as the dragons caught the two women in their talons and swung them into the air. Keira thought about trying to shout for Aaron again, but the veiled threat against Anna had her holding her tongue. The glittering lights of the palace quickly faded into darkness as the dragons rose higher and higher, the whoosh of their wings sweeping through the air the only sound.

The darkness pushed in on all sides as the dragon holding Keira flew through the silent night. She peered into the inky blackness, trying to spot Anna and the other dragon, but could see nothing beyond a few feet. She had struggled at first, trying to break free of the dragon's grip, but even as she made the attempt, she knew her efforts were in vain. All she had accomplished was a tighter grip that chafed against her skin. The dragon was gripping her around the waist, her legs and arms dangling free, their weight dragging against her stomach. Her back ached from being bent over, her eyes stung from the wind around her face, and nausea made her stomach heave. Her head felt detached from her body but still managed to pound relentlessly. She had thought, at first, that Aaron would be close on their tail, but as the hours dragged by, she felt that hope fading. For all she knew, Jack was right and he hadn't even noticed her disappearance. The bitter thought rose unbidden and she pushed it away.

A few hours into the flight the air changed, becoming colder, damper and salty. And still the dragon flew on and on. Keira felt the darkness overtaking her, and for a while she lost consciousness, but when she awoke, she could see the light of dawn pushing away the darkness. The dragon was starting to lose altitude, and through the gray light she could see a pile of rock protruding from the ocean's surface. Waves pounded against the high cliffs that presented an obstacle to the current of the water, while birds flew around the shore, screaming at one another as they dove between the cliffs. A building rose from the rock, austere and formidable, and Keira realized that this was to be her prison.

CHAPTER THIRTY-FOUR

Keira was thrown into a small stone cell beneath the fortress. It lacked all manner of furnishings, but she was beyond noticing as she lay on the cold floor, vomiting over and over, the effect of being carried around by her stomach for hours on end. She passed out after that, waking to the feel of coarse hands pulling her roughly into a corner, while a bucket of water was sloshed over the floor. The water was a poor substitute for a scrubbing brush and soap, but it cleared away some of the muck, washing it into the drain that ran along the outside wall. The heavy wooden door banged shut, and Keira passed out again, only rousing to consciousness when a bowl was pushed through a slot in the door.

The days passed slowly. Twice a day someone pushed a bowl of gruel through the door, sometimes retrieving the bowl later on, sometimes not. Once Keira called after her jailor, asking for news of Anna, but she was ignored.

Staring up at the ceiling, Keira counted the cracks yet again. She knew that there were eighty-three, just as she knew that one hundred and fifty-seven stones had been used to construct her cell, and that nine bars covered the open window and forty-three flagstones were in the floor. She counted them continually, only stopping to pull herself up to the window, set just above the ground outside, and hanging onto the bars, peer through at the never-ending ocean, until she dropped back to the floor, her energy spent.

A blast of wind blew through the uncovered window, and she shivered. She had no clothes apart from the gown she had worn to the ball, and she was given no other covering. The gown was stained and ripped, and she knew she probably stank of dirt and vomit. Her hair lay in a tangled mess on her shoulders, and she pushed it away with a shaking hand. She sat in the corner below the window, hoping to find a little warmth between the walls, but the effort was futile. She wasn't sure what Jack intended to do with her, but at this rate she would either freeze to death or go insane.

On the first day of her incarceration, Keira had been determined to find a way from her cell. She had examined every stone, traced every crack and shaken every bar, but despite increasingly desperate searches, it had soon become clear that without the power and strength of a dragon she was securely imprisoned. Her only hope lay in Aaron coming to rescue her in some spectacular fashion. But thinking about Aaron brought with it other, unwanted thoughts. The memory of him with that other woman just kept creeping into her mind. Jack had called her Elise, the woman Aaron had not wanted to talk about. And the longer Keira lay in her cold, empty cell, the more insidious her thoughts became. For she could not forget the shared smiles, the easy touch and the laughter between them. Jealousy snaked through her, that green-eyed monster, and she shoved it away with determination. Whatever Aaron had shared with Elise was over, of that she was sure.

But at night, as she lay shivering in the cold, unwanted memories lodged in her mind. He had called his love for her a poison. A weakness. Would he deny her now? The days dragged by, hour after endless hour, and the chill of the stone room seemed to seep into her bones and into her heart. Why had Aaron not come? And as her mind wandered through a landscape that wavered between reality and fantasy, part of her wondered if what she had shared with Aaron had just been an illusion.

The sound of boots scraping against the stone floor of the passage had Keira lifting her head. Supper had been pushed through her door a few hours before, and usually the only time anyone ventured into these passages was when someone was bringing her food. The footsteps stopped outside her cell, and she heard the jangling of keys before one was pushed into the lock from the other side. A moment later the door swung open, and Keira blinked as the light of a torch met her eyes. The man holding the torch was unfamiliar to her, but he motioned with his head.

"Come," he said, his voice rough.

Keira slowly pushed herself to her feet, her cold, aching limbs protesting at the effort. She stumbled slightly as she stepped from the wall, and it took a moment to regain her equilibrium. The man was watching her, not unkindly, but made no move to help her. Slowly she made her way to the door, following him when he turned and marched down the passage. She could not keep up, but he waited for her at the end before turning the corner and leading her up a long flight of stairs.

He led her down another passage, the light from his torch wavering against the dark stone walls, before pushing open a door and gesturing for her to enter. Keira walked through the door and paused at the threshold, taking in the scene before her.

The room was large, with windows that overlooked the ocean crashing hundreds of feet below. A stone fireplace was set between the two windows, a huge fire blazing in the grate, drawing Keira's eyes as she looked at it longingly. A round table was in the center of the room, high-backed chairs pulled around it. Jack was sitting in one of the chairs, while in another sat Max, his long legs stretched out before him and a glass of wine in his hand. He met her startled gaze steadily, but with a frown between his brows. Her gaze moved over to Jack, who was watching her intently.

"Ah," Jack said. "Keira dear, how lovely to see you again." He smiled as Keira returned his gaze through narrowed eyes. "You are probably wondering why you are here. And Max, too, of course. Well, I'm delighted to inform you that Max has seen the benefits of following my claim of Mastership." Keira's eyes widened in shock as she glanced back at Max. He was still watching her steadily, his eyes holding hers.

"With conditions," Max said, finally turning to look at Jack.

"Ah yes, those conditions," he said. "They concern the girl, don't they?"

"That's correct." Max nodded. "Anna."

"Hmm. Then let's get her to join our little party as well," Jack said. He turned to a man standing against the wall whom Keira had not noticed before, and gestured him towards the door. Keira watched him leave the room, bemused. She was sure he was human, but why would Jack use humans, and why would they help Jack? He had not been the only human in the room, either: another half dozen stood silently against the wall.

Keira turned back towards the two dragons as Max waved his hand in her direction.

"What have you been doing with her? She looks a little the worse for wear."

"Does she?" Jack said. "Yes, I suppose you are right. She's been locked in the dungeons."

"Ah." Max paused. "You may want to keep her in good health if you wish to use her to force Aaron's hand."

"She's alive, isn't she?"

"Yes, but for how long?" Max pushed himself from the chair and walked over to her, pacing around her in a circle. "I could feel the blast of cold air as soon as she entered the room." He stopped in front of Keira and placed a hand on her arm. His eyes flared for a moment, and Keira could feel the warmth suddenly spread through her. Jack rose to his feet, and Max dropped his hand, his eyes turning back to their regular shade of gray.

"What are you doing?" Jack said. "I thought you were here to offer your allegiance."

"I am," Max said. "But my argument is with Aaron, not his wife."

"Hmph," Jack said, returning to his seat. The door opened and Anna was pushed into the room.

"Keira," she gasped. Anna took a step towards her sister then stopped as she caught sight of the two dragons. "Max. What are you doing here?"

Out of the corner of her eye, Keira saw Jack smile. "Isn't this a lovely reunion," he said. He turned to face Anna. "Max is joining me, my dear."

"No!"

Max was staring at Anna, but he dropped his eyes at her exclamation of horror.

"Oh yes. Tell her, Max."

Max glanced at Keira, his eyes meeting hers for an instant, before turning his gaze back to Anna. "It's true," he said. "I refuse to support Aaron any longer."

"But why?" Anna said.

"Because I am tired of Aaron telling me what I can and cannot do." He turned towards Jack. "He humiliated me in front of humans. He would have me babysit the women, and he blamed me when you danced with Anna. I cannot take it any longer."

"I quite understand," Jack said with a tone of sympathy. He turned to Anna once more. "You see, my dear, it is quite true. What I cannot understand, however, is Max's obsession over you." Anna glanced at Max, startled.

"Obsession?"

"Jack, you misunderstand," Max said. "This chit needs to

learn a lesson, and I intend to teach it to her. She has been a thorn in my side since Aaron ordered me to Storbrook." Anna glared at him, her fury evident.

"And how do you intend to do that?" Jack asked.

"I plan to teach her that I am her master, and that she needs to serve me."

"Ah," Jack said. "And when she has learnt this lesson?"

"Then I don't care what happens to her," Max said. "Give her to one of your human minions, if you choose."

Keira heard Anna's sharp intake of breath, and felt her own catch in her throat.

"You wouldn't," Anna whispered.

"Quiet," Jack said with a glare in her direction. He turned back to Max. "And this is your condition?"

"It is."

"Very well," Jack said slowly. "You can have her until her usefulness runs out, but she is not to leave this island. And I will be watching you, too."

Max nodded.

"Of course."

CHAPTER THIRTY-FIVE

Anna stared at Max in horror. She could not believe the words she was hearing. Surely there must be some mistake! But when Max glanced at her, his eyes hard and cold, she knew there was no mistake – Max meant every word he said. He turned back to Jack, who was pulling a knife from his pocket. He held it against his wrist and looked at Max, who nodded.

With a quick motion, he pulled the blade over his skin, then extended his wrist to Max. Lifting the wrist to his mouth, Max clamped his lips over the bleeding wound, his eyes not leaving Jack's as he swallowed, over and over. Anna watched for a moment in disgust, before glancing at Keira. She was watching the scene wide-eyed, a look of dread written across her face. Anna turned back to Max. He was pulling away from Jack, his eyes burning as he wiped the back of his hand across his mouth, the blood staining his skin red.

Jack turned to face Keira with a look of triumph.

"It won't be long before you're wearing a widow's weeds," he said with a grin, "but I am happy to take Aaron's place when he's gone." A shudder passed through Keira.

"Never," she hissed. Jack shrugged.

"Oh well." He motioned a man forward, and nodded in Keira's direction. "Take her back to her cell."

"Wait!"

Jack turned to Max in surprise. He compressed his lips as Max walked towards Keira, but did nothing to stop him. Max picked up a cup of wine, and stopping just a few inches away, he pressed it into her hand. "Drink," he said. Keira took the cup, her gaze flying up in surprise to meet his before she tipped back her head and drained the contents. She held the cup out to Max, but instead of taking it, he placed his hands behind his neck and pulled off his tunic in a quick motion.

"What are you doing?" Jack demanded.

"As I said before, my argument is not with Keira," Max replied. He pressed the tunic into her hands, and then she was being led away, prodded by the man Jack had motioned forward. Keira turned and looked at Anna, their eyes meeting for an instant before Keira was pushed from the room.

Anna felt tears welling up as her sister disappeared from view. When would this nightmare ever end? Jack turned to one of the people standing at the wall.

"Francis. Give him your tunic," he said, nodding at Max. "I really have no desire to see your bare chest, Max," he said. The man, Francis, was shorter and skinnier than Max, but his tunic hung loose around his waist and reached to his knees. He stepped forward and quickly pulled the garment over his head, handing it to Max without meeting his gaze. Max stared at the man for a moment, before pulling the garment over his head.

"So what can you tell me about Aaron's plans?" Jack asked once Max was suitably attired.

"I'm happy to tell you," Max said, "but first, send the girl to my chambers." Jack snapped his fingers and once more Francis stepped forward.

"Take her to the chambers on the second floor," he said. "And make sure the door is properly secured when you leave." Francis took Anna by the arm and pulled her from the room, dropping his hand when they were out the door. His touch was cold, and Anna stared at him as he walked ahead of her.

"You're human," she said. "Why are you doing this?"

"Jack is my master," Francis replied. "I would do anything to serve him."

"Such as hold a woman against her will," Anna said dryly.

He shrugged. "If that is what he asks me to do."

"And would you kill someone if he asked you to?"

"Yes." Francis gestured with his hand. "This way," he said.

Anna followed him up the stairs and through the door into the chamber. A huge bed took up most of the space, but Anna noted a chair and a long table with a ewer and basin. There was a grate in the wall, stacked with wood, but no fire burned. She stepped into the room, turning when the door closed behind her. Francis had gone, and she could hear him dropping a plank over the door. She was trapped, but at least the room was more comfortable than what she'd had before – that room had only had a narrow bed with a dirty straw mattress, a thin rag for a quilt, and a rickety chair in the corner. She rubbed her eyes as she sank down onto the chair, waiting for the inevitable to arrive.

A few hours had dragged by before Anna finally heard the sound of Max's footsteps outside the door. She rose and went to stand against the wall opposite the entrance. The bar against the door lifted, and the door swung open with a creak as Max stepped into the room. He stopped at the threshold, pushing the door closed behind him, before turning to meet her gaze.

"Anna," he said, taking a step towards her, but she held up a hand to stop him.

"Don't come near me," she said, her voice low. "Don't even talk to me."

"Anna, please."

"Please, what? Please understand that you're a traitor? Please understand that you are going to use me then discard me? Please understand that you have no human feelings? That you really are a monster?" She turned her back to him and looked out the window, unwilling for him to see the tears shining in her eyes, but she turned back in fury when she heard him drawing closer.

"Don't come near me," she shouted. Max stopped, then spinning around, strode over to the fire grate. A blaze of flame shot from his hand, igniting the twigs and kindling.

"Anna, I'm not going to hurt you," he said, turning from the fire and pacing the room.

"Of course not," she said in a withering tone. "You're just going to use me."

"I'm not going to touch you," he said.

"That will be interesting," she sneered. "How are you going to make me serve you without touching me?"

"I'm not," he said with a sigh. He stopped pacing and sat down in the chair, dropping his head into his hands. "I am not going to force you. I'm not going to touch you. I'm not going to come anywhere near you. I'm going to stay right here, while you stay" – he waved a weary hand around the room – "wherever you want." Anna stared at him in confusion.

"What do you mean?" she said slowly.

"I mean just what I say. I wanted to keep you safe from Jack, and this was the only way I knew how."

"Safe from Jack? You betrayed Aaron, choosing to serve Jack instead, and now you want to keep me safe from him?" Something flashed in Max's face, but it was gone in an instant.

"What happens between me and Jack, or me and Aaron, has no bearing about how I feel about you."

"Do you really think I could feel anything but revulsion for the person who betrayed my sister's husband?" she demanded. "The man who welcomed you into his home?"

Max glanced up at her, then dropped his head back into his hands.

"I suppose not," he said.

Anna nodded, but the fight had suddenly gone from her. Walking over to the bed, she lay down, dragging the quilt over her body.

"Goodnight," she heard Max say, but she did not respond. She did not want to respond to Max ever again.

He was still in the chair the following morning, his legs stretched out in front of him, his arms crossed over his chest. She opened her eyes to see him watching her, and she turned her head away. His betrayal had come rushing back to her as soon as she'd opened her eyes and seen him sitting there. She pulled the quilt over her head as the questions pounded through her mind. How could he have done that? Aaron had trusted him. Tears sprang into her eyes, and she blinked them away, furious at herself. Hearing Max rise from the chair, she pushed the quilt down to see him approaching the bed.

"Go away," she said. "You're a traitor. I hate you." Max stopped, his eyes narrowing.

"No, you don't," he said. "Don't say that."

"I do," she said. "Just leave me alone." She turned her head and buried it in the pillows, and after a moment she heard Max move away. There was a splash of water, and a short while after, the sound of the door being opened.

"I'll see you later," he said, and then the door was closing, leaving her alone with her thoughts. She lay in the bed, weeping silently into the pillows for a long time; and when the tears finally stopped flowing, she stared at the ceiling, counting the cracks.

A long time had passed before she sat up in the bed, her face turned towards the window, and looked down at her gown. It was the one she had worn to the ball, although it was now grubby and torn. Her hair fell tangled around her face, and she pushed her fingers through it, trying to tease out the knots. It seemed she could not pull her fingers through even the smallest hank of hair without meeting with a tangle, and she longed for a comb to aid her in her efforts. A slight rustling sound made her jump, and she turned to see Max standing at the door, bare-chested, watching her futile efforts.

"How long have you been standing there?" she demanded. "And where is your tunic."

Max shrugged. "I went for a short flight, and lost my tunic along the way." He walked over to the jug of water and dipped a linen cloth into it. He wrung out the excess water and moving towards the bed, held the cloth out to Anna.

"Clean yourself up," he said. "Jack has requested your presence at dinner."

She eyed the cloth suspiciously for a moment, then took it from him gingerly, careful not to touch his fingers.

"Why?"

"He wants to see if you are suitably chastened."

Anna laughed sardonically. "Then he is in for a surprise."

Max looked at her carefully. "Anna, I cannot tell you how to behave or what to say, but if Jack knows that I have not carried out my threats, he may decide it would be more entertaining to pass you along to someone else."

"But you made an agreement with him."

"When you make an agreement with the devil, it is foolish to think he will uphold his end of the bargain. Right here, in his lair, he is king, and he can and will do whatever he chooses." Anna looked down, her mind racing as she wiped the cloth over her face and down her neck. She could do nothing about the state of her gown, but she smoothed it down with her hands regardless.

Standing, she nodded to Max, indicating that she was ready to go, then followed him as he led her out the door. As they walked along the passage, they were passed by one of Jack's humans. Stopping him, Max pointed to his tunic.

"Your master will not wish to see me only half dressed," he said, as the lackey quickly handed over his garment.

"Thank you," Max said with a grin. It vanished a moment later as he strode ahead of Anna, heading down the stairs to the same room they had been in before. Jack was seated in the same spot as the previous day, his eyes watching her closely as she entered the room. As she passed the threshold, Max pushed a hand against her back, causing her to stumble. She reached out to catch Max's arm, but he stepped away, allowing her to fall to the floor. Anna bit her lip in anger at the humiliating display, but kept her eyes down as she slowly pushed herself onto her knees.

"It looks like you have begun your lessons well," Jack said. Max didn't reply, and Anna glanced up to see him nod grimly. His eye caught Anna's for a moment, and she hurriedly returned her gaze to the floor.

"You've seen her, now," Max said. "We don't need her presence here to spoil our meal. Let me send her back to my chambers."

"No," Jack said. "It will be entertaining having her here. Perhaps she can amuse us while we eat."

"Amuse us, how?"

"Hmm, let's think. She can serve us our food … after she's removed those rags she's wearing."

"No!" Max took a step towards Jack as the other man turned to him with raised eyebrows.

"No?"

Max stopped, his eyes meeting Jack's as Anna glanced up in dismay. "I cannot, of course, tell you what to do, but I for one will not enjoy the display. Just look at her – she is dirty and unkempt, her hair is tangled, and she does nothing but scowl. I find I enjoy her best when it is dark." Max walked to where Anna knelt on the floor, and wrapping his hand in her hair, pulled up her head. Anna kept her gaze on the ground but could feel Jack's eyes on her, and when Max released her hair a moment later, she allowed her head to fall to her chest. "Furthermore," Max continued, "I had to use some rather, er, extreme methods of persuasion, and her body may be a little marked."

Jack laughed. "Well, I can see your point. She does look too scared and unkempt to be much entertainment anyway."

Anna felt a wave of relief wash over her, but she kept her eyes cast downward as Jack waved someone over. "Take her back to his chambers," he said. Someone tugged her arm and she rose from the ground, keeping her gaze carefully on the floor as she was led from the room.

CHAPTER THIRTY-SIX

Keira sat on the cold stone floor, holding Max's tunic over her chest and across her shoulders. Beyond the confines of the castle, the wind howled, whipping around the scrubby bushes that clung tenaciously to the sandy soil. There had been a violent storm the previous night that drove the rain through the bars of her cell, soaking her meagre coverings and leaving a puddle of water in the corner of the room. The tempest had lashed the waves into a frenzy, and the roaring of the ocean had been incessant until it finally died down shortly before dawn. The gray bank of cloud remained, however, preventing even a single ray of sun from breaking through.

The tunic did not offer much warmth, but every added piece of protection against the cold helped. She was grateful for the little bit of aid that Max had rendered her, though she was still in shock at his desertion from Aaron's side. She could not believe that he had chosen to align himself with Jack, knowing the terrible things he had done. When he had spoken in anger about Aaron's treatment, she had thought he might be bluffing and that his promise of loyalty was a ruse.

But she knew the significance of the blood bond. Max had willingly drunk Jack's blood, binding himself to the other dragon and throwing off Aaron's claim over him. He had broken his vow of fealty and proven himself a traitor. She pulled her knees up to her chest, fighting the wave of nausea that had suddenly welled in her stomach.

"Keira? Keira? Are you there?" A soft voice broke through the silence and Keira rose to her feet, wrapping her hands around the bars in the window to hold herself up as she looked for the person behind the voice. As he dropped into a crouch, Max's face appeared at the bars. She pulled away, but not before Max's hands clamped down on hers.

"Keira. Listen to me." He glanced down at her hands, then back to her face. "You're freezing. Is there nothing in that cell of yours to keep you warm?" He peered through the bars, then pulled back in shock.

"I cannot believe Jack would be this cruel. Crouch down low and I'll heat the room for you." Keira glared at him for a moment, then did as he instructed, watching as flames swirled through the air above her then dissipated. Her clothes were steaming slightly, and the room felt a little warmer, but she knew it would not last. She rose and looked at Max, still crouching outside the window.

"How could you, Max? How could you betray Aaron like that? He loves you!"

"Keira, I —" Max glanced around. "Someone's coming," he hissed. "Here, take this." In a quick movement he yanked his tunic over his head and thrust it through the bars. Before she could say another word, he launched himself into the air, his bronze wings opening wide and carrying him away from her and over the ocean. Keira pulled herself away from the window as two pairs of feet walked past.

"Look at that," said one of the men. "Wish I had wings."

"Wonder what he was doing here," the other said.

"Don't know. Think we should tell Jack?"

There was a moment of silence, and Keira peeked her

head around the wall to see the men walking away.

"No, I'm sure it's fine," the man finally replied.

Keira slipped down onto the floor and pulled the tunic over her head. It still held Max's body heat, and she wrapped her arms around her chest, eager to keep the warmth. The other tunic had slid to the floor, and she placed it over her legs, feeling warmer than she had in days. Max's blast of heat had dried off some of the dampness and left the stones warm to touch. She leaned her head against the hard wall and closed her eyes, allowing her thoughts to drift.

The sound of a voice outside her prison door startled Keira, and it took her a moment to recognize Jack's voice.

"Open the door," he commanded, as someone scrambled to carry out his order. The door swung open and Jack stepped in with an expression of distaste. "This place is ghastly," he said. He glanced at Keira huddled against the wall. "How do you stand it?" he asked. He turned back to the man who had opened the door. "Why is there no furniture in this room?"

"You told us to put her in an empty cell," he mumbled.

Jack rolled his eyes. "Go find a mattress and a blanket. And a stool too," he added as the man turned away. "I refuse to sit on the floor." Keira heard the sound of footsteps fading down the passage as Jack turned to face her.

"Why are you doing this, Jack?" Keira asked wearily.

"Getting you a mattress? If you don't want it –"

"You know what I mean."

"Ah. You are wondering why I have you imprisoned on this pile of rock." The sound of returning footsteps had him turning away. A man Keira recognized as Francis entered the room with a rolled mattress and blanket in one hand, and a stool in the other. He threw the mattress and blanket to the ground, then placed the stool next to Jack.

"Roll out the mattress for the lady," Jack said. The man paused, his eyes downcast, then picking up the mattress, laid it carefully against the wall with the blanket on top. He glanced up at Jack, who nodded, and left the room. Hitching a foot around the stool, Jack pulled it towards him and sat down. He stared at Keira for a long moment, then turned towards the window.

"I was married once. Did you know that?" He glanced back at Keira as she pulled in a sharp breath. "Of course you didn't. Aaron barely spared a thought for my wife before, so why would he think to tell you about her now?" Jack cocked his head, his eyes narrowing slightly as he looked at her. "You have her eyes, you know. Not the color – hers were blue – but the same look. Frank and honest."

"Is that why you kissed me?" Keira asked dryly, instantly regretting the words as she waited for an angry response. Instead, Jack just laughed.

"Perhaps that was a small part of the reason, but it was mainly to annoy Aaron. I knew he would banish me when he heard what I had done. I wasn't prepared for your response, however. Quite a little tiger, aren't you." He lifted his hand to his cheek and ran his fingers along the spot where she had scored him with her nails.

"Back a cat into a corner," Keira said with a shrug.

Jack laughed. "Quite."

"What happened to your wife?" Keira asked. Jack stared at her for a long moment.

"My father killed her," he finally said.

"Your father? But ... why?"

"Perhaps Aaron told you about my father. That he refused to eat human flesh?" Keira nodded. "Of course he would have," Jack said dryly. "It drove my father crazy, denying himself, but I didn't know that when Aaron called me away."

"Aaron ... called you away? Why?"

Jack rose and went over to the window, gripping the bars as he stared across the ocean.

"Aaron and I used to be friends, once. Not as close as he and Favian, but close enough. He had just become Master, and there were troubles at some of our borders." He turned to face Keira, leaning against the wall. "You must know that dragon territory extends far beyond human territory, and our lands cross over many human kingdoms. There were skirmishes between our clan and the clan whose territory bordered ours, and Aaron went to deal with it. He called me and a few others to join him, but instructed us to leave all humans behind." He walked back to the stool and sat down once more. "I wasn't the only one with a human wife, but I had only been married for a few years. I loved her, and leaving her behind was the hardest thing I had ever done. But I knew Aaron was concerned about the safety of the humans if they came with us, so I left May with my father."

"May?"

"Yes. That was her name." Keira nodded. "Aaron should have known that it wasn't safe to leave her with him, but he gave no word of warning, so I went away, thinking she was safe. But she was in more danger there, from my father, than if I had taken her with me." He looked down at the floor, his voice softer as he continued. "My father loved May, but he was losing his mind. He hadn't eaten human flesh in over two years, and it was driving him crazy." Jack looked up at Keira with a wry expression. "Dragon lore says that there will be one who will break the dragon curse, but it didn't come soon enough for my father. He was consumed with hunger, and he killed her. The funny thing is, he realized straight away what he had done, and refused to eat her remains. She died in vain. He threw her body down the well, covered it with a rock, and locked himself into a cell, throwing the key out the window. By the time I returned, he was already halfway dead, but he still kept calling her name."

"What did you do?"

"What did I do? May's remains had been preserved in the cold water of the well, so I retrieved them and ate them." Jack looked at Keira in amusement as the color drained from her face. "That disgusts you, doesn't it? But it was the only way I could keep her with me. She's a part of me now, forever. Wouldn't you want Aaron to do the same if something happened to you?"

Keira closed her eyes. "No," she whispered. She opened them again, and stared at Jack, her voice loud and firm. "No, I would not."

"Ah, well. I wouldn't expect you to understand. I'm just a monster, after all." Keira turned to look at the wall, swallowing the nausea that rose to her throat.

"I still don't understand why you are going after Aaron."

"May would be alive today if it wasn't for Aaron."

Keira narrowed her eyes in confusion. "How?"

"If Aaron had not called me away, had not made me leave her behind, my father would not have killed her."

"But … you cannot blame Aaron for your father's actions."

"It was Aaron's father, Zachary, who first insisted that humans were worth saving. That we should only eat when absolutely necessary. And Aaron did nothing to change that."

"But he didn't stop your father from, uh, eating when he needed to."

"Until Zachary came along with his absurd directive, my father had never even given humans the slightest consideration. He coupled with my mother, and after I was born, killed her and ate her. It was Zachary who made him think humans were more than just a meal."

"Or maybe it was May?"

Jack rose to his feet in anger, his eyes narrowing as he glared at Keira. "May was not like other humans. She was different; special. And my father knew that. He never even considered her as human. But Zachary and Aaron whispered words that reached into his mind, making him crazy. And then he killed the one person he loved like a daughter – the woman I loved more than life. Aaron is going to know what it feels like to lose someone he loves. Not even death can break the bond a dragon makes with his mate, and when I kill you," Jack's lips curled into a cruel smile, "he will know the same anguish I felt when I found out May was dead. He will suffer, and then I will kill him."

Keira stared at him in horror, fear making her press her back against the wall. Jack laughed.

"You have a few days yet to live. I will kill you while Aaron is forced to watch, and will feast on you before his eyes." He smiled, then turned and left the room.

CHAPTER THIRTY-SEVEN

Anna paced up and down the room, unable to keep still. A fire burned in the grate, courtesy of Max, and she scowled at it. As much as she enjoyed the warmth, she did not want to feel even the slightest sense of gratitude towards him. She wondered for the hundredth time where Keira was being held, and hoped she had a fire to keep her warm. She longed to ask Max for news of her sister, but that would mean speaking to him, something else she did not want to do. A cold blast of air blew through the open window, bringing with it the smell of the ocean, which crashed relentlessly against the rocks far below.

Anna walked over and stared out the window, watching the birds that screeched as they flew between the cliffs. She wished she could fly as they did – then she could fly away from this prison. Being a dragon would be even better – then she would be able to kill Jack as well. But of course, she was neither a bird nor a dragon. She sighed loudly, cursing both Jack and Max for keeping her here. Far below she could see a small white strip of beach, with a boat pulled up onto the shore. Lying partly in the water, the boat rocked as the waves knocked against the stern. If she could only get to the boat, she would be able to row away. She turned and walked over to the bed, falling backwards onto the mattress. She had never tried to row a boat before, but how difficult could it be? Surely she would reach land somewhere. She had no idea how large the ocean was, but men traveled by ocean all the time, and always arrived *some*where. She lay on the bed for a while, pleasantly imagining herself rowing across the ocean into the arms of safety, before finally rising to her feet again. She paced around the room, then crossed over to the window once more, staring at the small craft placed so tantalizingly close, and yet so far.

If only there was a way to escape the room, but such thoughts were pointless. Unless ... she had heard a story once about a princess who escaped a castle by tying together the quilts from the bed. But just one glance out the window had her shaking her head ruefully. She would need a mountain of quilts to make a rope long enough to scale these walls. If only Max didn't keep the door barred, she would have a chance. She turned to look at the door, wondering if there was a way to shake the bar loose, when her eyes slowly widened. Max had left the room hurriedly that morning, called by one of Jack's minions to attend him in the hall. She could not remember the sound of the bar dropping against the door when he left, but surely he would not have left it open.

She quickly walked across the room, stopping in front of the door with a raised hand. She placed it against the solid surface and gave a slight push. The door held, and she breathed out a sigh of disappointment. Of course Max would not have been that careless. Turning around, she leaned her back against the door – gasping when it suddenly gave way, then grabbing at the frame to stop her fall. Pushing herself back to her feet, she stared at the door in disbelief, then shook her head as she started to smile. A quick glance down the passage assured her that no one had been roused by the noise, and she pulled herself back into the room and took a deep breath.

It could be a trap, and as soon as she left the room, Max – or even worse, Jack – would come and hunt her down. But just as quickly the thought crossed her mind that it was a chance, an opportunity to escape, that she could not afford to pass up. She glanced down the passage once more, and the silence that greeted her made up her mind. Running over to the bed, she dragged the quilt off the mattress and wrapped it around her shoulders. It would be cold on the open water, and she did not want to die of exposure.

She was back in the passage in a flash, and she glanced up and down, wondering which way to go. The passage was brighter to the right, so she chose that direction, walking as quietly as she could while still moving with some speed. She reached a spiral staircase cut into the stone, and steadying herself with her hand, cautiously made her way down the dark, narrow stairs. She was about halfway down when she heard voices, and she paused, pressing herself against the stone wall, but they passed and grew fainter. Leaning forward, she glanced down, and seeing no-one else, continued her descent. She had to pass a landing, but that too was empty, and she made it down to the bottom floor without being seen.

The staircase spilled into a dark passage, and Anna paused once more. In the one direction she could hear the banging of pots and pans, so she turned the other way, hopeful of finding a door that led outside. There were no candles in the passage, so she walked cautiously, running her fingers along the walls as she moved forward. Her head knocked against an unlit lamp that protruded from the wall, and she froze, groaning silently as she waited for footsteps to come chasing after her – but all was quiet. She moved forward again. There was a door ahead, and she fumbled with the latch, wincing when it squeaked. The door swung open, and she stepped outside, her heart pounding.

She glanced around, trying to get her bearings. The

ground was bare and rocky, with a few scrubby plants that lay close to the ground. About twenty feet in front of where she stood the ground suddenly dropped away, and beyond she could see the ocean. To the side, close to the castle wall, was a clump of large bushes. There was no cover where she stood, and after a moment's hesitation, she headed towards the bushes, sidling her way along the wall. She needed to figure out where the beach with the boat was, but knew that she was far too exposed where she stood.

She made the bushes just in time and huddled under the prickly branches, the cold of the ground seeping through her thin slippers, as the sound of voices headed in her direction. Two men passed by and after a few moments she risked a quick look around to make sure they had gone, breathing a sigh of relief when she saw they had. She waited a moment before crawling out of her hiding space, then holding the quilt around her shoulders, quickly dashed to the edge of the cliff and looked down. She could see the beach, but it was not right below her. It would take a scramble over some rocks to reach the path that led to it. She dropped her foot over the edge, wincing when she heard her gown rip up the side, but did not pause. She was at her most vulnerable now, and there was not a moment to lose. Scrambling over some rocks, she ducked down low as she made her way in the direction of the path she had seen from the top. She was about halfway down, when the thought of Keira made her stop.

How could she escape this place and leave Keira behind? But if she could just reach Aaron and tell him where she was … Anna quickly continued moving forward. She had reached the path, and the going was easier now. If she could just make it to the beach, she would be free.

The tide was coming in when Anna made it to the boat, and it bobbed and swayed in the water. The rope was wrapped around a rock, but Anna freed it easily. She threw the quilt into the boat and climbed in after it, turning around to face the rocky cliff. Her heart sank when she saw Max standing on a rock where the beach met the cliff, his arms crossed over his bare chest in amusement.

"I'm quite impressed, Anna," he said with a grin. "I wasn't sure you would make it all the way down."

"You were watching me?" She bit down on her lip to stop the tears of anger and frustration that threatened.

"I returned to the room moments after you left," he explained. "You've forgotten that dragons can track someone by their scent, but I already had an idea of where you were heading. I gave you a few minutes' head start and then followed you. I wanted to see how far you would get."

"Argh!" Anna stamped her foot in frustration, making the boat rock beneath her. She turned to look out at the water, drawing in a deep breath.

"Please, Max," she said, "let me go. You have no use for me here." Max's expression turned serious.

"I'm sorry, Anna, I cannot do that. Do you think Jack will just let you go? As soon as he knows you are gone, he will send his henchmen after you. No, you are much safer here with me."

"But ..." Anna's words trailed off as she realized the futility of her argument.

"You were hoping to reach Aaron?" She nodded, refusing to meet his gaze. Max turned and looked out over the water for a long moment.

"Aaron already knows where we are," he said softly. Anna looked at him in surprise.

"How do you know?"

"You will just have to trust me."

"Trust you?" she said bitterly. "How can I possibly trust a traitor?"

Max's gaze bore down on her, and she looked away.

"Come," he said, "grab the quilt and I will take you back to the room." He held out his hand to help her from the boat, but she ignored it and jumped unsteadily to the ground. Max stepped closer and wrapped his arms around her stiff, unyielding body as his wings stretched out from his back. His chest was firm and warm, and despite her best intentions, Anna relaxed against him ever so slightly. She felt his hand on her back as their feet left the ground, and he pulled her closer, his lips in her hair. She heard him breathe in deeply, and drew back slightly to see his face, drawing in a sharp breath when she saw his eyes blazing as he looked down at her. He was flying up the side of the building towards the window of their chamber, and as she glanced away, her eyes fell on the gray stone-face of the wall; she stiffened, her anger returning. She was locked in a prison, and it was Max who was keeping her from escaping. Max sighed, and then he was lifting her through the window that opened to their chamber. He set her on her feet, and she walked away, holding herself erect. He said her name, but she refused to turn and look at him.

The door opened and he left the room, dropping the bar against the door behind him.

CHAPTER THIRTY-EIGHT

The hours dragged by as yet another day passed. Keira wondered what Aaron was doing, then pushed the thought away. It was painful to think of him while she lay in her cold prison. As much as she longed to just feel him near, such thoughts were useless. Instead, she turned her attention back to Max and his betrayal. He seemed genuinely concerned about her, but if he hated what Jack was doing why had he aligned himself with the man? She still could not believe he felt the depth of animosity towards Aaron that he described. But no matter how much she thought about it, she could not come up with an answer that made sense. If only he hadn't drunk Jack's blood, she could believe it was just an act. But he had. Still, he had done what he could to help her, and for that she was grateful.

A scratching noise had Keira glancing around, and she jumped to her feet when she saw a rat scurrying along the gutter that ran the length of her cell. The creature turned and stared at her, raising itself on its back paws as it watched her impassively with its beady eyes. She breathed a sigh of relief when it dropped down once more and ran through the small gap that led to the next cell. She slid down onto the cold floor against the opposite wall, unwilling, for the moment, to risk another encounter with the rodent. Her eyes closed briefly, but flew open as a bird screeched outside her window. Along with the ocean, the birds provided a continual backdrop of noise, but they usually stayed on the cliffs, not venturing so close to the building. Keira pulled the blanket closer around her shoulders as the cold wind gusted though the open window. The blanket was damp, as was her gown, from the moisture-laden air, and caked in a fine layer of salt. The salt covered her, too, making her itch, and when she licked her lips, she could taste it on her skin.

Keira dozed a little more before a sound at her door had her turning to watch the gruel being pushed through the slot in the door. She had given up trying to communicate with her jailors, knowing she would get only silence for her efforts. The tepid gruel was thin and watery, pale brown in color. A single slice of limp carrot and a few pieces of cabbage lay at the bottom of the bowl, while a few globules of half-congealed fat floated on top. She wrinkled her nose in distaste, but forced herself to eat, knowing it was the only nutrition she was going to get. She finished the meal and pushed the bowl away with relief, glad to be done with the torment of eating, before curling herself into a ball on the mattress.

Her thoughts wandered to her sister, and she wondered how she was faring. At least she was in Max's care. Despite Max's words to Jack, she was confident he would do nothing to harm Anna. And at least she was in more comfortable quarters.

She closed her eyes and imagined that she was in more comfortable quarters, too – that the mattress she was lying on was really made with feathers instead of dirty straw, and that Aaron lay beside her, holding her tight. All she had left was her belief in him and their love. After the first few terrible days, when her mind had betrayed her and her body seemed incapable of the slightest exertion, she had slowly regained her sense of reality. Perhaps it was seeing Max that had wrought the change. Or perhaps it was just that his presence brought Aaron closer. But whatever it was, she had absolutely no doubts about Aaron's love for her. He might call his love a weakness, but he would never abandon her. However much he might deny it, they shared a bond so deep it could never be severed.

It took a while for Keira to fall asleep. Despite Max's tunics and the thin blanket Jack had provided her with, she was still cold. She shivered on the thin mattress, until she finally fell into a restless sleep. Just before dawn she began to dream that she was in a warm bed, with a fire blazing in the grate and warm quilts wrapped around her. She woke slowly, when the cold light of day filtered through the window, and it was only when she was fully awake that she realized she was still cocooned in a blanket of warmth. She opened her eyes a fraction, and then wider when she saw the light that surrounded her. Her name weaved through her mind, and the light around her caressed her, stroking her with warm fingers. She turned to see a pair of brightly flaming eyes of white staring at her.

"Aaron?" she said. She stared into his burning gaze, as warm tendrils brushed over her cheeks. She smiled, and some of the tension that lay coiled in her stomach eased slightly. "You're here," she whispered.

"*I'm here,*" he said. She gazed at him, still not quite believing, as tears started spilling down her cheeks. Blazing hands dried them as soon as they fell, while lips of flame brushed against hers. She lay wrapped in his warmth as Aaron slowly took on his human form, his arms steady bands around her as he held her close. His hands stroked her hair, brushing strands from her face.

"I love you," he whispered. She smiled.

"I love you too."

It wasn't until footsteps sounded in the passage outside that they pulled away from each other, and Aaron lifted an enquiring eyebrow.

"They must be bringing dinner," she whispered. "Stand behind the door." He moved to where she indicated, his face wrinkling in distaste when he saw the bowl of gruel that was pushed through the slot.

"What is this?" he said as the footsteps faded away.

"Dinner," Keira replied.

"That is dinner? Oh, Keira, I'm so sorry." His serious tone made Keira laugh, and he looked at her in surprise. "What's so funny?" His question made her laugh even more, and his expression grew even more perplexed when the tears started streaming down her face, the stress of the last few days finding a means of release.

"Oh, Aaron," she gasped, "I'm imprisoned in a stone cell in a dungeon, and you're worried about the food?" He grinned, unable to resist her laughter, then a moment later was laughing too. Keira sank down to the floor, her back against the wall, holding her sides as the giggles refused to stop, until eventually she was panting for breath. Aaron sat down next to her, watching her as she hiccupped. When she had finally regained some measure of self-control, he pulled the watery gruel towards her.

"Eat," he ordered. "You need every bit of nourishment you can get." He placed his hands around the bowl, then with a slight expression of distaste, blew onto it, making it steam. She sighed when the warm liquid hit her stomach. The gruel had never been more than lukewarm.

"Why are you wearing Max's tunic?" Aaron asked as she ate.

"He gave it to me to keep me warm." She dropped the spoon in the bowl and turned to him, her expression distressed.

"Oh, Aaron, I'm so sorry. Max is here," she said.

"I know."

"He gave his allegiance to Jack."

"Oh, I know that." His tone was relaxed, and Keira

frowned.

"You know he's –"

"He hasn't betrayed me, Keira. I knew he was coming here. It's a ruse."

"But he drank Jack's blood."

"Yes. But Max had been drinking mine every day since our arrival in the city. There is so much of my blood running through his veins, if he drinks any more he stands in danger of becoming me!" Aaron smiled and ran his fingers over her hand. "It is virtually impossible for him to bond to another dragon."

"Oh." She paused to consider this. "But why was he drinking your blood?"

"It was his idea, actually. We anticipated that the time might come when he would be more useful on Jack's side than on mine, but we knew that Jack would demand a blood bond. Drinking my blood was to ensure that his tie with me could not be broken."

"So he's been working for you all along?"

"Yes. Although I think Anna was also a strong motivation."

"So he hasn't been abusing her as he threatened to?"

Aaron laughed. "Is that what he said? No, I don't think he would lay a finger on her."

Keira smiled. "I didn't think he would, either. So how did you find me?"

"I tracked Max. He had already been spreading the word that he might switch his allegiance. Two days after your disappearance, someone contacted him with a message from Jack to meet him in one of the city taverns, and when he offered to support Jack against me, Jack brought him here."

Keira pulled away with a look of surprise. "So you've known for a few days I was here?"

"Yes." He took her hands in his. "I'm sorry. I wanted to give Max time to discover the full extent of Jack's plans. I couldn't come any earlier in case I was discovered, which would, of course, give up the game. I knew Jack wouldn't hurt you, although," he glanced around the stone cell, "I didn't think he would throw you in a cold, stone dungeon. There was nothing I wanted more than to storm in here, rescue you, and leave the other dragons to sort things out themselves. When I realized that Jack had taken you and Anna, I was more enraged than I have ever been. Max and I tracked your scent in the gardens, but scent disperses faster in the air, and the trail had already grown cold. When I realized there was nothing I could do, Max and a few other dragons had to force me away from the palace before I hurt someone. They dragged me away from the city." Aaron smiled wryly. "Even then, I managed to burn down a forest and cause an avalanche. After that I hunted, desperate to release my anger on something. On anything that moved. And it wasn't just Jack I was angry with. I was furious at myself. I had failed to protect you again —"

"No —"

"Yes." Aaron leaned closer, forcing her to look him in the eye. "Keira, you always try and relieve me of blame, but the truth is I failed to protect you and your sister. Jack should never have been able to get anywhere near you." He placed a finger on her lips when she would have said more. "But I didn't just fail to protect your physical person. I had also failed you by pulling away from you, trying to deny how much I love you. When Jack took you, all I could think was that you might die not knowing I finally understood that it is our love that completes me." He smiled. "I knew I would be lost without you. But I also knew something else: Jack needed to pay for what he had done. Now, more than ever, I had to lead the dragons and ensure that Jack never has a chance to become Master. And I realized that Owain was right. I am stronger than my father. I could not walk away from my responsibilities to the clan. So I went back to Drake House and began to lay my plans."

"So what are your plans?"

"I can finalize them once I've had a chance to see Max."

"So you are here to rendezvous with Max?"

"Yes. But more importantly I needed to see you."

"So how will you manage to see Max?"

"Like this," Aaron said, opening his hand. Keira watched as it turned to fiery tendrils that disappeared into his wrist, before becoming solid once more. Her eyes flew up to his.

"How did you do that?"

Aaron leaned his head against the wall and closed his eyes. "Owain thought I should work on harnessing my growing power, but when I tried, it seemed that I could do nothing differently." He looked at Keira. "You remember how I controlled the flames?"

Keira nodded.

"Try as I might, I could not do it again. No matter how long I stared at the fire, willing it to bend to my control, I could not do it. I tried using my mind, I tried using my voice, to the point where I was yelling and screaming like a frustrated child, but all to no avail. It was Owain who suggested what I was doing wrong." Aaron lifted his hand and trailed his fingers over Keira's cheek, the light from the blaze within him glowing on Keira's skin. "Owain said my strength came from you, and instead of focusing on the flames, I should try focusing on you, on our love. I must confess it took a while to work through all the anger and frustration. I locked myself away in our room and breathed in your scent. I imagined your body lying next to me, and the soft look in your eye when you are satisfied." Aaron smiled when Keira blushed. "I remembered that night in the caves," he said softly. "I thought about how I had touched you and caressed you. And then ..." He paused.

"Yes?"

"The flames in the grate came alive. I looked at them, and with a flick of my finger, they responded to me. I moved them around the room and made them return to the grate. And I became one with the flame."

"Like in the cave?"

"Yes, but even more. I didn't just take on a fiery form for a few minutes. I *became* the flame. I could remain in that state, and even though I could not communicate with others the way I can with you, I could move around undetected by both sight and smell."

"So Max won't be able to hear you?"

"No, although he is more attuned to me than anyone else, since he has had so much of my blood. But the connection I have with you is shared with no-one else." Keira smiled.

"So that is how you are going to see Max?"

"Yes. He already knows I'm here because of his bond with me, and will find a way to let me know what is happening. But before I go in search of Max, I want to hold you in my arms a little longer." He wrapped his arm around her and pulled her onto his lap, pretending to shiver when her cold legs met with his warmth. "Brrr, you really are in need of warming," he said, pulling her closer.

Keira smiled and leaned her head against his chest. "Jack's crazy, you know. He blames you for the death of his wife."

Aaron pulled back in surprise. "He told you that?"

"Yes. He also blames you and your father for what happened to his father."

"Yes, I know that."

Keira paused for a moment. "He said you used to be close."

"We were good friends, once. He never had much respect for humans, but we got on well enough. But when May died, and then his father ... well, he changed."

"He went a little crazy, like his father."

"I suppose so. And a crazy dragon is the worst kind to fight against."

"He said he was going to kill me. He wants you to feel the pain of losing someone you love."

Aaron's eyes flared in anger as he turned away. "Jack will die because of this."

"How?" she said. "How are you going to kill him?"

"When I know what his plans are, I can finish my own. And when I see him again, I will rip him apart limb by limb."

CHAPTER THIRTY-NINE

Keira watched as flames spread over the floor, heating the stones in every corner except the one where she stood.

"I saw you with Elise," she said. "At the ball. She had her hand on your arm." The flames stopped moving and Keira felt Aaron's attention turn to her. "You were smiling and laughing." She paused for a moment. "Jack said she was your mistress."

The flames pulled together, and Aaron's fiery form rose before her. "*Keira.*" The single word that wound through her mind was tinged with sadness, regret, and admonishment. "*Is that the reason you left the hall? Because you saw me with Elise?*"

"I was jealous," she whispered. "You looked so happy to see her. So familiar with her."

"*Oh, Keira.*" Fiery arms reached out on either side of her, trapping her against the wall as blazing eyes stared down at her. "*There is no one but you, my sweet,*" he said.

"But you cannot deny she means something to you."

Skin and muscle formed around the flame as Aaron gained more form. "She was my lover," he said, "but it was many years ago. She was widowed, and we were both lonely. She gave me friendship when I needed it, but although we took comfort from each other, she was never more than a friend. She was the one who brought it to an end. She had met someone, and was going to marry him."

"Jack said you were devastated when she left," Keira whispered.

"She had become a part of my life, and I suppose I felt a sense of loss, but I always knew she and I were never meant to be."

"But you still care for her."

"I do. As I care for all my friends." He stared down at her. "In fact, I was telling her about you." Keira's eyebrows rose, but she remained silent as he continued. "I was telling her how much I love you. How you have changed my life. She was happy for me."

"Does she know what you are?"

"No. I told you before, that is a secret I never shared with any other woman." He shrugged. "She probably suspected I was different from other men, but never questioned why, and I never said anything. You are the only one I have shared that with. And you are the only one I want to share my life with. I have never loved anyone the way I love you."

He wrapped his arms around her, and bringing his lips down to hers, kissed her. Keira could feel the warmth spread through her limbs. He was dissolving once more, but she could still feel his lips on hers. Breaking the kiss she pulled back to look in his eyes. They were burning white, reflecting brightly against her skin. He placed a glowing hand on either side of her face, then pushed his fingers into her hair as she stared at him. His arms were bands of flame, but she could still feel the weight of them around her.

"How can you do that?" she whispered. She moved her hand over his belly, watching as the flames rolled away, insubstantial once again. She saw him smile before his face dissolved into burning flames that swirled around her.

"*I've been learning greater control over my powers,*" he whispered into her mind.

"I could feel you holding me – not as flames but as though you are flesh and blood."

"I've learnt to use my mind to control my actions. I can be like a breeze, blowing any which way, or like a rock, a barrier that none can pass."

"This is …"

"A lot to take in?"

"Yes."

"I'm still me. That hasn't changed." He wrapped his arms around her and pulled her close. *"I love you, Keira. That is all that matters. I promise I will never try and deny that love again."*

"I love you, too," she whispered.

He held her for a long time before pulling away reluctantly. *"I need to go find Max."*

"Of course," she said. Another thought occurred to her. "How can you manage to keep changing without hunting? Is it because you have grown so much more powerful?"

"Yes, I think so. I'll still need to hunt again soon, but I'm finding that my strength remains longer each time."

She gazed at him. "You are truly amazing. Now go."

He smiled, then dissolved in a blaze of flame. *"I'll be back,"* he said, before swirling into a fiery mist and disappearing through the crack under the door.

It was already dark by the time Aaron returned, a spreading blaze that swept under the door and wrapped around her like a quilt.

"I'm afraid you will have to endure this hellhole for a few more days, my sweet," Aaron said as he blazed before her.

"You saw Max?"

"I did. And Jack too. He's planning to use you to lure me to a place of his choosing." Aaron ran his hand over her cheek. *"I wish there was another way, but I have to leave you here. But what Jack doesn't know is he will be walking into a trap of our own."*

"Do you know where he plans to lure you to?"

"Not only where, but when as well." Aaron smiled grimly. *"And I will be ready and waiting."*

Keira nodded. "Of course you will, and Jack will learn that he should never have challenged such a powerful dragon!" Aaron smiled. "Did you see Anna?" she asked.

"I did. She is in far more comfortable quarters than you." Aaron glanced around the bare cell with a frown. *"But she is furious with Max. I expect she is making his life quite unpleasant."*

"He hasn't told her the truth?" Keira asked in surprise.

"No. She still thinks he's a traitor."

"But why?"

Aaron shrugged. *"Perhaps he doesn't know if he can trust her."*

Keira opened her mouth to protest, and then closed it again. She didn't think Anna would betray Max, but Anna had given Max little reason to think well of her.

"I need to go, my sweet," Aaron said. *"But before I do, I want you to drink my blood. You need to be as strong as possible for whatever lies ahead."* He became more substantial as he spoke. He stretched his hand into a talon and scored the palm of his hand, holding it up to her mouth. She placed her lips over the wound and allowed the blood to flow into her mouth, warm and sweet. As before, she could feel it spreading through her, reaching into every part of her body and warming her from within. Stepping closer, Aaron wrapped his free hand into her hair, pulling her closer when she lifted her head from his hand.

"I don't want to leave you," he whispered.

"Go," she said. "I will be fine."

He nodded, then brought his lips to hers for a kiss before taking a step back, dropping his hands slowly from her body. He turned towards the window and then, as she watched, he dissolved into flames, disappearing between the bars into the night.

CHAPTER FORTY

Anna could not understand Max. He had betrayed Aaron, yet he wanted to keep her safe. She didn't completely understand everything about dragons, but she knew Aaron was important in the dragon hierarchy. And by turning against Aaron, Max was doing more than just betraying a friend. And what did he think would happen to Keira if Jack killed Aaron? The questions swirled around as she sat alone in the room. She wished she could put him from her mind, but it was impossible. If only he hadn't betrayed Aaron – but what was the point of 'if only'?

He had come and gone just shortly before, but had been acting rather strangely, grinning and whispering to himself. She could not make out the words, but the way he spoke made her look around to see if there was someone else in the room. They were alone, of course, but it had been most peculiar.

Stretching out her arms, she climbed off the bed and walked over to the window. It had grown dark outside, but the light of the moon reflected against the water. She could see the beach where Max had interrupted her escape attempt, and she shivered when she recalled his strong arms carrying her back. It was a rough night out at sea, and the waves crashed loudly against the boulders far below. As she watched, a faint glow of light caught her eye. It was spilling out a window near the base of the building, casting dancing shadows against the castle walls. She had not seen Keira since the day Max arrived, and she wondered if this was where Keira was being held. Anna knew there were cells in the dungeon – she had stayed in one for the first few days of her incarceration until Max's arrival. She shuddered to think that Keira could still be locked up in something so squalid. She looked back at the light, pulling back with a start. It was no longer a faint glow, but was growing in intensity. Was there a fire down there? Did she need to call for someone? The door to the chamber opened, and Anna turned to see Max enter the room.

"Max," she called, turning back to the window and leaning out again. Max was at her side in an instant, his hands at her waist as he held her steady, but Anna barely noticed. "Look down there," she said, pointing to the growing light. "I think it's a fire!" Max watched in silence for a moment.

"It's not a fire," he finally said.

"It is! We need to sound an alarm!" Anna leaned even further forward as Max tightened his grip, but then gasped in surprise when the light suddenly shot out from the window, spreading out in a blaze as it sped over the ocean.

"What was that?" she gasped. She pulled back into the room as the light disappeared in the distance. Max's hands were still on her waist as she turned to him, his face just a few inches from hers. She took a hurried step back, freeing herself from his grasp, and turning around, walked over to the bed. She sat down and looked at him.

"What was that?" she asked again.

"A signal," Max said with a grin.

"A signal? A signal for what?"

"A signal that events are moving forward."

"What are you talking about?"

"This issue between Aaron and Jack will soon come to a head. Jack plans to lure Aaron into a trap."

"But then we must warn …." Anna looked away. "Never mind."

"Anna." Max took a step towards her, but Anna held up her hand. She had forgotten for a moment what Max had done, but she would not make that mistake again.

"Stop, Max. You have nothing to say that I want to hear. You are a traitor, which is worse than the most despicable monster. When this is over, I never want to see you again."

"Anna, please listen —"

"Stop," Anna shouted. "I don't want to hear it. Just go away. I hate you." She turned around on the bed and placed her hands over her ears. She heard the door open a moment later, and then softly close, and she collapsed onto the bed in a flood of tears.

Sleep eluded her as she lay tossing and turning, but when she heard the sound of the bar being lifted, she closed her eyes, curled onto her side and pretended to be asleep. She listened as Max came into the room, pausing to pull off his boots. She sneaked a quick peek at him, pulling in a breath when she saw the light of the fire dancing over his golden skin. She quickly closed her eyes again when he rose to his feet once more. He walked over, and she could feel his gaze resting on her as he stood at the end of the bed. It was a long time before she heard him move again, but when he did, it was to throw a log onto the fire. As it crackled and hissed, he walked over to the wooden chair and sat down, and Anna risked another peek. He stretched his legs out before turning and looking at her, catching her by surprise when his gaze caught hers. He stared at her in silence for a moment, then leaned his head back and closed his eyes. She could feel her pulse racing as she closed her own, and it was a long time before she finally fell into a troubled sleep.

CHAPTER FORTY-ONE

Another two days had dragged by since Keira had seen Aaron. Max had been by again and given her yet another tunic, which she had pulled gratefully over the others. All the warmth that Aaron had left behind was gone, but Max had told her, in a whispered conversation through the bars, that today was the day. Jack had already sent out a pair of dragons to deliver a message to Aaron: Come with us now or Keira will be killed.

A rattle in the passage outside her door brought her to her feet. Aaron's blood had restored a lot of her strength, although it hadn't helped with the occasional bouts of nausea that assailed her. The door swung open and a human guard stepped into the room.

"Come, Jack wants to see you."

Keira followed him in silence as he led the way along the passage and up the stairs, retracing the steps she had traveled before. They reached the room, and as she entered, Keira saw there were a number of other dragons in the room apart from Jack and Max. Jack was standing behind a chair at the table, while Max stood at the window, his back to the door. He had found another tunic somewhere, Keira noticed. He glanced over his shoulder, meeting her eye for a moment before turning away again. The two dragons that had brought her and Anna to this fortress stood near Jack, while three more she did not recognize sat in seats around the table. As she entered the room, all eyes except Max's turned to stare at her.

"She lives," Jack said, raising a cup of wine and saluting her before tipping back the contents. The other dragons laughed as they watched her. Returning his cup to the table, Jack stalked up to Keira, lifting her chin with his finger.

"I'm not sure what Aaron sees in you," he said. "I thought I saw a spark of something before, but I was wrong. There is nothing of interest in there." He dropped his finger and stepped away as Keira kept her eyes on him.

"Max," Jack said, turning to where Max still stood at the window. "You can take the woman. Aaron will be twice as affected seeing you bring his wife to the altar of sacrifice." Max turned and nodded, his voice smooth as he answered.

"Of course, Master. Nothing would please me more."

"Good. We leave immediately." Jack turned towards the other dragons. "Let's go declare a new Master."

"Hear, hear," said one of the dragons, raising the cup of wine he held. He looked about the same age as Aaron, with long blond hair tied at the nape of his neck. His green eyes turned on Keira, and he grinned at her mockingly. "I have been waiting for the day when Aaron Drake is cut down to size, and his rage when he sees you killed will be priceless." He rose to his feet. "What about your humans, Jack?"

"They stay here. They've served their purpose for now. We may have need of them later on, and if not..." Jack shrugged as the other dragons laughed. "Stay close, Uesli. We have the advantage of surprise, but we must not underestimate Aaron."

Uesli, the green-eyed dragon, nodded. "Of course."

It was a gray and misty day, with the clouds hanging low, and the dampness clung to Keira's skin as Max swung her onto his back. A steady cloud of vapor rose from his scales as the moist air flowed over him, steaming like a kettle of water hung over a fire. Keira could see the vague outlines of the dragons ahead of them through the thick mist, but even without the benefit of sight, Keira knew Max could have followed by scent alone. Keira wrapped her arms tighter around Max's neck and leaned forward.

"Where's Anna?" she asked.

"I left her in my chamber. Jack has all but forgotten her, and I took steps to ensure her safety while we are gone. As soon as this is over, I'll return for her."

"You're sure that you will be able to return for her?"

"Of course." Keira could hear the confidence in his tone, and smiled to herself.

They had been flying a few hours when Max dropped through the clouds. Keira could see Jack and the other dragons flying ahead, while not too much further an open area stretched out before them. It was bordered on one side by a wide swath of trees and on the other by a narrow stream. Jack was the first to land in the empty clearing, circling above a few times before landing. Keira could see Jack looking around as she and Max landed, his head cocked slightly as he sniffed the air. He turned as if to say something, but just at that moment, three more dragons dropped down from the sky and landed on the ground. The one in the center was Aaron, his golden scales dull in the gray light, with the other two dragons flanking him closely on either side.

"Well, well, look who's arrived to join the party," Jack said. Keira had slid off Max's back and was standing at his side as Aaron landed. She ran towards him, only to be caught up short when Max wrapped his claws around her chest and pulled her hard against him.

"Not so fast, Keira."

"Take your hands off my wife," Aaron snarled, but Max kept his claws around her as Jack laughed.

"Ah, Aaron," Jack said. "Isn't this wonderful? Do you see that I have both Max and your pretty little wife on my side,

although I must admit only one of them is here willingly."
Aaron pulled his lips back in a snarl as sparks flew from his
mouth.

"Let my wife go," he said through bared teeth. His tail
was swishing against the ground as he spoke, stirring up bits
of dried grass and twigs, while flames seeped from his mouth.

"Or what, Aaron?" Jack said. "What will you do? As you
can see, you are sorely outnumbered."

"I will kill you," Aaron growled. "I might have killed you
quickly before, but you took my wife and locked her in a
stone dungeon. For that, I will rip you apart limb by limb."

Jack started slightly, Aaron's knowledge of Keira's prison
clearly surprising him, but after a moment he laughed. "As I
have already pointed out, Aaron, you are quite
outnumbered."

"Stop!"

The word rang out across the clearing, and Keira turned
to see a group of men marching out from the trees where the
forest bordered the clearing. The man in front was Owain,
while behind him strode Favian and five other men whom
Keira recognized as dragon elders. At the sight of the elders,
all the dragons in the clearing fell back a few steps, except
Jack and Aaron. The men seemed unconcerned about the
fact that they wore not a stitch of clothing, and when they
came to a stop, they stood with feet firmly planted and their
arms folded across their chests. Despite their ages – Favian
was the only one younger than two hundred years – they
looked like men in their prime, strong and menacing. Jack
threw a quick, considering look at Max before turning back
to the elders.

"Jack," Owain said, "you have broken numerous dragon
laws, and we are here to hold you to account."

"Really?" Jack said. "And tell me what these laws are."

"You have made our ability to change form known to
humans, you have hunted humans indiscriminately and at
will, you have given humans your blood with the sole

purpose of bonding them to you, and you have abducted the mate of a fellow dragon. Furthermore, you have attempted to use subversive methods to defeat Aaron as Master, instead of challenging him to a fight, as is your prerogative."

"My, my, I am impressed. You have been thorough in your investigations. Clearly I was too trusting of those who swore their fealty to me." He glanced at Max as he said this. "But as for your charges, let me respond that our Dragon Master should also be held to account for his actions, for he too has shown himself to humans, and has created a blood bond with one who is not his mate."

Owain turned to Aaron. "Master? How do you answer these accusations?"

Aaron growled, long and low, before replying. "I have not hidden my actions from you or anyone else. I am guilty of the charges, but I have not done them to gain further power and control. Anyone who chooses to challenge me to a fight for Mastership is entitled within our laws to do so. But this traitor has not challenged me to an honorable fight, instead attempting to lure me into a trap by using my mate. So I will kill him, and any other who will challenge me. Also, any dragon who has given Jack support against me in these dishonorable actions will also forfeit his life."

Owain nodded. "It will be as you say, Master," he said.

Aaron turned to look at Jack, his eyes flaming as he lifted his fiercely armed tail into the air and whacked it against the ground with an ear-splitting crash. He lifted his head and roared, a terrifying, blood-curdling sound that sent a shiver down Keira's back. As swift as an arrow leaping from a bow, he launched himself into the air and streamlined his body towards Jack. He was traveling so fast, Keira couldn't even trace his movement, and when he slammed into the other dragon, the force of the impact sent him flying through the air.

Spinning around with a snarl, Jack turned to face Aaron, but Aaron was already upon him, his talons sinking into

Jack's belly. Jack wrenched himself free and launched himself into the air, circling heavenward as Aaron followed close on his tail. Massive wings spread through the sky, holding the two mighty beasts aloft, as flames spewed through the air. Keira gasped when she saw Jack swing his tail, his sharp spikes catching the front of Aaron's neck as blood spurted to the ground; but when Jack tried to clamp his jaw into Aaron's hide, his mouth found nothing but flames as Aaron pulled away in a fiery blaze, reforming a moment later and once more slamming his weight into Jack. A loud crash rang through the air as the hard, iron-like scales collided, while flashes of flame lit the low-lying clouds. The huge bodies twisted around each other, partially hidden by massive wings, but when they swung back into view, Aaron had his jaws clamped around Jack's neck. He was pushing Jack toward the ground, forcing him down with his weight. Flames trailed out behind Aaron, his tail like a burning whip that lit the sky behind him, while his form wavered between physical and hazy as he dragged Jack down.

The two dragons slammed into the ground, their impact making the earth shake as Jack tried to roll away from Aaron's grip. He shoved his claws into Aaron, drawing blood, but Aaron's jaws remained clamped on Jack's neck for another moment before he pulled away again, his body blazing brightly as he sunk flaming talons into Jack's chest. Jack's snarl was quickly cut short as Aaron ripped open his chest and buried his jaws in the steaming, bloody flesh. He lifted his head a moment later, his teeth dripping red, and throwing his head back, roared as flames rushed from his mouth and filled the air around him. The roar was wild and primal, and Keira shuddered. At the sound, the dragons who had been with Jack launched themselves into the air, seeking escape.

Favian and Owain and the other dragons standing with them transformed, filling the sky with a dazzling light that burned Keira's eyes, forcing her to look away. They threw themselves into the air, hurtling after the escaping dragons, creating a vast battlefield in the sky as they chased them down, crashing into them with talons extended. Keira, still held in Max's grasp, could not bear to watch, but as she glanced away she saw another dragon hurtling towards them. It was Uesli, the dragon who had taunted Keira, and his talons were outstretched as he headed straight towards her. She shouted at Max, but he had already seen the danger and his grasp on her tightened as he launched himself into the air – but he was not quick enough to avoid Uesli's flaming breath. Keira screamed as the blaze seared across her skin, setting her gown alight around her legs. Max twisted himself in the air, and using his tail knocked Uesli off course, but he only gained a few seconds before Uesli was once more chasing them.

The flames around Keira's legs were growing, reaching her waist, stoked by the wind rushing past them. Through the pain she heard Aaron roar, and then Max was dropping her into the icy water of the stream, where she fell onto her knees against the sharp rocks. She screamed again as the pain intensified, her cries turning to sobs as it was finally eased by the cool water. Above her Uesli plowed into Max, sending him hurtling through the air. She could see Aaron flaming towards her, followed by a red dragon on his tail. She rose to her knees in the water, but Uesli had already turned from Max and was bearing down on her, talons outstretched. She dropped down again, wrapping her arms around her stomach as his talons connected with her side, ripping through her skin and tearing through her belly. Something slammed into Uesli, and Keira was lifted out of the water as his talons continued to rip through her – before he was gone and she fell back into the water and darkness overtook her vision.

CHAPTER FORTY-TWO

Anna paced around the chamber in frustration. She could not believe she had been left behind while Max went off to fight his battle with Jack. At least if he had taken her, she might have found a way to warn Aaron of Max's deception.

Max had brought some food and wine to the chamber before leaving, and had given her a key to lock the door from within, removing the outside bar. He had admonished her to remain in the room while he was gone, telling her he would be back when all was over. And then he had gone. Flying away across the ocean, leaving her on her own. She had seen Jack's dragons from the window as they flew away. There had been seven of them, but Max's bronze scales caught her eye immediately as he flew within the middle of the pack. There was someone on his back, and as Anna screwed her eyes up against the light glittering on the ocean, she could see that it was Keira. She was holding Max's neck tightly, her head lowered as she said something to him. He turned to answer her, and his gaze caught Anna standing at the window. Something had clenched in her gut, but she refused to name it, instead turning away with a huff.

She wondered how many hours had passed since Max

left. It was morning when he had gone, and judging by the sun, it was now already late afternoon. She glanced down at the key lying next to the bed. Max had told her to remain in the chamber, but she was tired of being locked away. With Jack and the other dragons gone, what harm could she possibly come to? Picking up the key, she walked over to the door and unlocked it, pausing at the threshold to listen for sounds coming from the building, but all was quiet. She tucked the key into the bodice of her gown and stepped into the cold, dingy passage. She paused when she reached the top of the stairs, listening for sounds of activity, then slowly made her way down the narrow, circling staircase. The first flight of stairs brought her to the place where Max had taken her to see Jack, and she walked towards the door, pausing when she heard the soft murmuring of voices. For a moment she wondered at the wisdom of entering the room, but she pushed the thought aside as she opened the heavy, wooden door.

Everything in the room was exactly as she had seen it before – the table, the chairs, the fireplace with a fire burning low in the grate. However, there were no dragons, and the men who had previously been standing around the room at attention were now gathered in a tight circle in the corner of the room. There were eight of them, one of whom was Francis, and at her approach he looked up.

"Oh, they left you here, too," he said. "You've served your purpose to that dragon, have you? What was his name again? Mark?"

"Max," Anna said. "What are you all doing here?"

"It would appear we are no longer necessary, either," he said, his tone bitter.

"What are you talking about?" Anna glanced at the other men, but they looked away, refusing to meet her gaze. "I thought Jack was your Master. Didn't you choose to serve him?"

"Jack promised us strength and power beyond our wildest

dreams if we drank his blood. But he deceived us."

"But ..." Anna looked at them in confusion. "Why are you only realizing this now?"

Francis looked away, his gaze wandering over the other men in the group as they looked at him.

"We think something has happened," said a man with thin, lank hair that dragged onto his shoulders in greasy strands. A couple of the men nodded in agreement. "This morning we would have died for that monster, but now, we are wondering what we're doing here."

"You drank his blood?" Anna said. Francis and the other men nodded.

"That must be it. I remember Keira saying something about dragon blood binding you to the dragon."

"Keira? The woman in the dungeon?"

"Yes, she's my sister."

"And why exactly did Jack bring you and your sister here?"

"Keira is married to the Dragon Master. And I think Jack wants to kill him."

"Your sister is married to one of these monsters?" Francis's tone was horrified.

"Well," Anna said, "Aaron isn't a monster."

"But he's a dragon? Like the dragon who was using you?"

"Yes, Aaron is a dragon. And actually, Max wasn't using me." The men stared at her incredulously.

"You gave yourself willingly to that beast?" said Francis.

"No." Anna sighed. "Max didn't touch me. He and I were ... we knew each other ... before he betrayed Aaron and joined Jack."

"You were friends with a dragon?" Francis looked at her as though she had lost her mind. "Have *you* been drinking dragon's blood?"

"What? No! Of course not!"

Francis gazed at her for a moment, then turned to the others.

"Are we decided?"

"Wait. What are you deciding?" Anna asked. Francis turned back to her.

"We're leaving this place. Tom saw a boat pulled up below the rocks. We can use it to get away from this place and reach the mainland."

"Take me with you."

One of the men leaned towards her with a sneer. "Oh, we could take you, if you want, but it won't be to the boat." Anna glanced at the other men in the group. They were watching her impassively, and she suddenly realized the precariousness of her situation. She took a step back, then turned and ran out the room, the sound of laughter trailing behind her as she quickly headed back the way she had come, up the stairs to her room. No footsteps sounded behind her, but still she slammed the door shut and fumbled for the key. It dropped from her grasp onto the floor, ringing against the stone, but a moment later she was thrusting it with trembling fingers into the key hold and sending the bolt home. She fell back against the door with a sigh of relief, not moving.

The sound of voices drifting through her window finally had her back on her feet, and she moved over to the window to see the group of men scrambling down the rocky cliff towards the beach. Bulging sacks bumped against their backs as they clambered over the rocks. They reached the boat, and throwing the sacks into the bottom, climbed in and pushed themselves out onto the heaving ocean.

Anna watched until she could see them no longer, before leaving the room once more, creeping through the passages in case some of the men had remained. She reached the ground floor without encountering anyone, and pushing open a small wooden door, stepped outside. The only sounds were the cry of birds as they wheeled over the cliffs, and the roar of the ocean, crashing on the rocks below. It was late afternoon, but the heavy clouds allowed no sunlight through, and the landscape was drained of color. She looked out over the gray ocean, and a dark smudge on the horizon caught her eye. It grew larger as she watched and she realized with relief that it was Max, come to rescue her. He landed on the grass at the edge of the cliff.

"Anna," Max said as she walked towards him, and she could hear the relief in his voice. "Are you all right? I saw Jack's minions in the boat, attempting to escape."

"Yes," Anna said. "It appears they no longer want to serve Jack."

"That's because the bond is broken," Max said. "Jack is dead. Did they hurt you?"

"Jack is dead? Oh, I'm sorry," she said, her tone dripping with sarcasm, but Max responded in all seriousness.

"I don't know why. I wanted him dead as much as you."

"Oh! So that is why you pledged your allegiance to him."

"It was a ruse, Anna. I was serving Aaron all along."

"Really? How convenient! Now that Jack is dead, you quickly change your allegiance to the victor."

"That is not what I am doing," Max replied. "Please Anna, you must listen to me. Aaron and I hatched the plan together." He took a step closer as she took a step back.

"Don't come near me," she shouted. "For all I know, it is Aaron who is dead, and this is just a ploy to get me to come with you."

"You think I would lie to you?" he demanded. "Aaron was well aware of what I was doing. It was the best way for me to gain information, as well as to watch over you."

"Watch over me?" Anna shouted. "I was locked in a chamber."

"For your own safety!"

"If this was a ruse, why didn't you tell me?"

"I wasn't sure if I could trust you, at first, and then when I wanted to tell you, you refused to listen to anything I said!"

"You didn't know if you could trust me? What does that mean?"

"It means, Anna, that you could have given up the game

to Jack, either advertently, in an effort to hurt me, or inadvertently. Either way, I wasn't prepared to take the risk until I was sure you wouldn't give the plan away." Anna stared at him, hurt making her shout her next words.

"I don't believe you!" She spun around, placing her back to him. "Either way you're a liar. Just leave me alone."

"Fine!" Max ground out between clenched teeth. "If that is what you want, then that is what you shall have." She turned as she heard the rustle of his wings, gasping when he launched himself into the air. He headed out over the open water, disappearing into the darkening sky. She watched as he flew further away, waiting for him to turn around and come back, and when the sky grew too dark to see anything, she sat down on the ground against the fortress wall.

She had drifted off to sleep, her shoulder against the cold stone, when the sound of her voice being called brought her to attention. She rose to her feet, unsteady at first, and peered into the darkness to see a dragon walking towards her. As he drew closer, she could see his red coloring.

"Favian? What are you doing here? Where's Max?"

"Max asked me to get you," Favian said gently. "Come, I'll lift you onto my back." He swept his tail around her and lifted her up. "Did Max tell you what happened?" Favian asked as he launched himself into the air.

"He said Jack was dead," Anna replied.

"Yes. Jack is dead. But Keira was badly injured."

"Injured? How?"

"One of Jack's dragons was trying to kill her. She's alive, but her injuries are extensive."

"No," whispered Anna with a sudden rush of guilt. She had barely spared Keira a thought. "Will she live?"

"It is too soon to tell. Aaron took her to Drake Manor, and my mother is tending her. Fortunately, Aaron had made Keira drink his blood when he was here. If not for that, she would not even have survived this long."

"Aaron was here? When?"

"He managed to sneak in a few days ago and rendezvous with Max. Max told him what Jack was planning, which gave Aaron quite an advantage."

"So Max wasn't working for Jack? He really didn't betray Aaron?"

"No, of course not. Max would no more betray Aaron than I would." Favian turned to look at her. "Surely you knew that?"

Anna turned her face away as shame wound its way through her belly. She could feel the tears collecting in her eyes, and she turned into the wind, allowing it to whip at her face, burning away the tears.

CHAPTER FORTY-THREE

Keira lay on a bed, tossing and turning as she mumbled in her sleep. Dragons chased her through her dreams, and she cried out as talons reached for her, then gasped as she was overcome with cold. Someone called to her, his voice desperate, and the monsters fled as she was pulled back to the light, wrapped in warmth.

Days passed, and troubling memories haunted Keira's unconscious mind. She screamed when flames licked at her legs, burning through the fabric of the gown. She tried to run, but her feet could find no purchase against the soft ground that was slowly pulling her under. She could feel the cold hand of death, and she let it wash over her, before she was snatched away once again, back into the land of the living.

A spark of light penetrated Keira's eyelids, and she opened them to see glowing tawny eyes staring down at her. Someone squeezed her hand as she closed her eyes once more. The soft *shh, shh* of voices flowed around her, the sounds carrying no meaning as darkness rushed over her again.

Keira awoke to the light streaming through the window. The room was empty, but a fire was burning in the grate. She watched the dancing flames for a moment, as the memories slowly returned. The last thing she recalled was being ripped apart by a dragon. She pushed back the sheet, and lifting her chemise, looked at her stomach. There was a thin line of red scarring, but the skin had already knit together. Moving slowly, she slid her hands over her belly, probing cautiously. There was a slight twinge of pain, but nothing more, and she dropped her hands back to the mattress. She felt hollow and empty, and she stared at the ceiling, looking at the cracks with unseeing eyes. A sound outside the door had her pushing down her chemise and yanking up the quilt as the door opened. Margaret walked into the room, a bowl of water in her hands and a pile of fresh linens over her arm. She glanced at her patient, smiling when she saw Keira watching her. Carefully placing the water on the table, she went to the side of the bed, gently taking Keira's hand in her own.

"How are you feeling, my dear?" She touched a cool hand to Keira's forehead and nodded. "You sustained a very serious injury, and if Aaron had not given you his blood just days before, you would not have survived. As it is, you have been unwell for nigh on a week."

"A week?" Keira whispered. Margaret nodded, gently restraining Keira when she struggled to rise.

"You need to lie still, my dear. Your body is still healing. I will go and let Aaron know you are awake. He has been pacing the halls, unwilling to stray too far from your side. He will be very relieved to know that the worst is behind us." She patted the younger woman's hand and left the room, closing the door quietly behind her. It opened a few moments later as Aaron walked into the room.

He stopped at the threshold, gazing at Keira as she stared back at him. Although he smiled, Keira could see the worry creased into his brow, and the shadows under his eyes.

"Keira," he said softly, his voice reverent. He went to the bed and dropped down on his knees at her side, gently taking her hand between his own. Lifting it to his mouth, he brushed his lips over her skin. "I'm so sorry," he whispered. "This should not have happened. You nearly lost your life because of me, and I was unable to save you."

"You did save me," Keira said, her tone just as low. "You gave me your blood."

At her words, Aaron dropped her hand and pushing himself up, gathered her into his arms. He buried his face in her hair as tears spilled unheeded down his cheeks. Keira wrapped her hands around his neck, and they clung to each other in silence until Aaron finally pulled away. He trailed his fingers down her cheeks as he gazed into her eyes.

"I thought I had lost you," he whispered. "I heard you scream, and turned to see Uesli chasing you down." Aaron's voice cracked as he continued. "I couldn't get to you in time. He ripped his claws through your stomach, and I couldn't stop him until it was too late. You lost so much blood. I pulled you from the water and let my blood cover you. I forced it down your throat, and poured it over your wounds. You were just barely alive, but I knew if I could get enough into you, you would live. But I couldn't save the baby."

"The baby," Keira whispered. Of course. It had been too soon to be sure, but the knowledge had still been there. She turned to look out the window as tears slipped down her cheeks.

"I'm sorry," Aaron said, his voice breaking. Keira felt him cover her hand with his own as he dropped back to his knees beside the bed. She could hear the remorse in his voice, and had seen the sadness in his eyes, but it seemed meaningless. How could he possibly understand the sense of loss she felt for a child she barely knew she was carrying? She gazed out the window, thinking about the child she would now never hold in her arms. Never sing to, or take for walks in the woods. For a brief moment, the world's axis shifted. It didn't matter whether Jack was dead or alive, that people had died because of a dragon. It didn't even matter if Aaron decided he could no longer love her. She could feel the darkness closing in around her, suffocating her. But then a spark, just the slightest flicker, broke through the darkness. She was not alone. She had Aaron, and she loved him. Slowly the world righted itself again, the darkness pulling back as the spark grew to a flame. She would mourn the life that had been lost, but she would not lose the life she had. She turned back to Aaron, and lifting the hand that held hers, kissed it. She watched as Aaron lifted his head, and read the understanding in his eyes. She wasn't offering absolution, just forgiveness.

The door opened, and Aaron rose from his knees, still holding her hand, and sat down on the edge of the bed as Anna entered the room.

"Keira! I heard you were awake."

"Anna," Keira smiled at her sister. "I see you made it from that horrible place in one piece."

"Yes." Anna glanced away. "Favian brought me back." Keira flashed a look of confusion at Aaron, but he gave a slight shake of his head.

"Good. And are you ... all right?"

Anna returned her gaze to Keira's. "Yes. Max ..." She paused. "My quarters were more comfortable than yours." She smiled slightly at Aaron. "I think Aaron is anxious to spend time with you, so I'm not going to stay. I just wanted to see for myself that you are all right." She turned towards the door. "I will visit later when you're better recovered."

As the door closed, Keira turned with a questioning look to Aaron.

"Max has gone," he said.

"What do you mean? Gone where?"

Aaron sighed. "He came to see me a few days ago. He requested my permission to travel to our more distant territories for a while."

"Why?"

"I can only speculate. After the battle he returned to Jack's lair to fetch Anna, but came back alone. Favian returned in his stead and brought her back to Drake Manor."

Keira lifted her eyebrows in surprise. "How long will he be gone?"

"A while. He will return when he is ready."

"Did he see Anna while he was here?"

"No. Anna had taken the children for a walk to the pond. I suspect Max was watching to see when she was away, coming when he knew he wouldn't see her."

"But she knows Max is gone?"

"Yes. Cathryn told her." Aaron paused a moment. "Max may not have wanted to see Anna, but he did want to see you. Even though you could not hear him, he gave you his formal oath of loyalty and protection. Should anything ever happen again while you are in his care, he will forfeit his life. Favian and I were here to bear witness to his oath."

"What? Why?"

"He feels responsible for your injuries."

"That's ridiculous. He saved me."

Aaron shrugged. "Perhaps. But you were under his protection, and he has done what any honorable dragon would do." Aaron brought his head close, his gaze meeting hers. "But I will kill any dragon that does not do all he can to protect you, so his oath was merely for form."

The door opened again and Margaret entered the room, holding a bowl of steaming broth. She gave Aaron a glare as he drew back.

"My patient needs her food and rest, so shoo with you." Aaron grinned at her, then turned back to Keira.

"I'll be back soon, my sweet, as soon as that dragon lady leaves." He dropped a kiss on her forehead and rose to his feet.

"I can hear you perfectly well, Aaron Drake," Margaret said with a playful scowl. "Who is the dragon around here?"

"That would be me," Aaron said with a laugh as he skirted past his aunt and out the door.

Keira fell asleep again soon after, awakening when the sun was low in the sky. Aaron sat on a chair watching her, but he crossed over to the bed when he saw her eyes flutter open. He lay down beside her, pulling her gently against his chest.

"Margaret said I have been ill for a week."

"The worst week of my life," Aaron said. "I thought I understood loss when Jack abducted you, but then you nearly died. For the first time I could understand the sense of despair my father felt when my mother was killed." Aaron raised himself up on an elbow and looked down at her. "But I am not my father. When I saw you lying there, thinking you may be dead, I didn't want to die myself. I wanted to live so I could exact revenge on everyone who had helped Jack. I was filled with anger, but never for a moment did I lose control." Aaron ran a hand through Keira's hair. "I thought that I was weak like my father, but I now understand what Owain has been saying all along. I can adopt my father's legacy as my own, or I can forge my own path. And it wasn't until I saw your lifeblood draining away that I fully realized that. I would have been filled with misery and all the joy would have been stolen from my life, but I would not have given up, Keira. I would have stood my ground and fought my battles. And I would have cherished the love we shared for the remainder of my days." His eyes started to glow as he gazed at her, and she lifted a hand to his cheek, feeling the warmth just beneath his skin.

"You may have doubted yourself, but I never doubted you, Aaron Drake. Not only are you a strong and powerful dragon, more powerful than any other, but you are also a man of wisdom, courage, and honor. I always knew that life was the only choice you could ever make."

"Thank you for your faith in me," Aaron whispered as his lips covered hers. His kiss was sweet and tender, and he pulled away after a moment, his hand lingering on her cheek.

"There are a few matters I need to take care of now that you are on the road to recovery, but as soon as they are sorted, I want to quit this place."

"Go back to Storbrook?"

"Eventually. But first, I want to take you to Dracomere, and spend some time alone with you."

"Dracomere?"

"Yes, it's a small manor house a few hours west of here. It was built on a small island in the middle of the lake. It is surrounded by trees, and with spring just around the corner, we can watch the buds blooming and the birds courting."

"Is it yours?"

"It is ours," Aaron said with a smile.

"What about Anna?"

"Cathryn and Favian have already said she can remain here. From what I understand, Anna has made herself quite indispensable to Will and Bronwyn."

Keira smiled. "How soon can we leave?"

CHAPTER FORTY-FOUR

Anna closed the door quietly behind her as she left Keira's room, unable to suppress her smile. Keira was going to live. Those first few days had been terrible, with everyone wondering whether she was going to recover from her wounds, but now that Keira was awake, Margaret said she would make a full recovery. Aaron had suffered almost as much as Keira, Anna knew, and had stayed by his wife's side as much as possible. He had only left when Margaret chased him from the room, but then spent the time pacing the halls and passages of the manor. Once he and Favian had gone out hunting, but they had returned within an hour and he didn't leave again.

Margaret had been the one to shoulder the burden of Keira's care, refusing to allow anyone else to do more than sit with Keira. Even the servants weren't allowed to do more than fetch and carry. Margaret said that the only reason Keira had survived the attack at all was because of the blood Aaron gave her before the battle, when he had sneaked into her prison on the island. He had already known where they were, before Anna even attempted her escape, and Max had been working with him, just as he had said.

At the thought of Max, Anna dropped her head, running her hand over her forehead. She had been so sure he would come to see her once his anger had cooled. She could see now how churlish she had been, how childish and ungrateful. She longed to apologize, wanted to tell him that she had been silly, but she hadn't been given the chance. She had played her cards all wrong, and she wished desperately that she could go back and change things, but there were no second chances.

Her mind flew back to the only time she had seen Max since returning from her prison. Keira still lay unconscious, but it had been a lovely day, one of the first days of spring, with birds singing outside the window and new buds appearing on the trees. A perfect day to escape the confines of the house, and all the misery contained within it. The children had needed no encouragement to go outside, and within minutes Anna had been crossing the courtyard while the children ran up ahead. The lake lay beyond an expanse of wilderness, and it had taken them about twenty minutes to reach it. The children had arrived ahead of Anna, and by the time she reached the edge, they had already stripped off their shoes and stockings and were wading in the shallow waters.

"Come, Anna," Will had shouted. "It feels lovely."

Anna had looked at the cool water longingly, thinking of the lake back home. Before a moment had passed she was sitting on the ground, lifting her foot to pull off her boot. A glint of light in the sky caught her eye and she looked up, shielding her eyes against the sun as she stared at the growing patch of shining bronze. Her heart had started to race, and she'd leapt to her feet, shouting to the children to get out the water. They had complained, of course, but Anna had insisted.

"Uncle Max is here," she'd shouted. "Don't you want to see him?"

She hadn't even waited to see if the children were following when she started towards the house, her walk quickly becoming a run. But she hadn't been fast enough. Before they had reached the house a large shadow passed over her, and she had looked up to see Max circling in the air, heading towards the distant mountains.

"No," she whispered. He had glanced back, and his fiery gaze met hers for a moment before he turned his head away and thrust himself upwards into the clouds. "Come back," she said, but he disappeared into the distance, and she watched until she could no longer see him.

"Was that Uncle Max?" Will demanded, panting as he ran up beside her. "He didn't even wait to see us."

"No, he didn't," Anna said.

She walked towards the door, looking up when Cathryn approached.

"Oh, I thought you were at the pond," she said.

"We were," Anna said. "Was Max just here?"

"He was," Cathryn said, meeting Anna's gaze. "He came to ask Aaron's permission to travel abroad for a while."

"Abroad? For how long?"

"Anna." Cathryn took a step forward and gently took Anna's hands within her own. "Max isn't coming back." It had taken a moment for Cathryn's words to sink in as Anna stared at the older woman. Pulling her hands out of Cathryn's she took a step back and turned away.

"No," she had whispered. "Of course not. Not that it matters to me, anyway. Max means nothing to me." She pulled in a deep breath. "Nothing."

CHAPTER FORTY-FIVE

Keira found her strength returning with each day, and soon she was venturing beyond the room under Margaret's watchful eye. The weather was warming as spring started to arrive, and Keira sat in the sun with a quilt wrapped around her shoulders, talking to Anna or Cathryn. In the evenings she rested on the bed, with Aaron lying beside her, or seated on a chair opposite.

"What happened to the humans who were serving Jack?" she asked one evening.

"Max killed them when he went back for Anna. Jack had given them blood with the intent of creating a bond, but when he died, the bond was broken."

"They are all dead?"

"Keira, we could not leave them alive. They knew too much, for one thing, and their minds were damaged by the bond."

"But they didn't choose to bond with Jack. It was forced on them against their will."

"Perhaps they didn't choose a bond, but those men took Jack's blood willingly. Jack may have made false promises, but the men were looking to gain rewards they did not earn.

They chose to overlook the question of why a dragon would want to give them his blood, and what he would gain from the transaction."

"But what about my father? He did not have an opportunity to ask those questions."

"No, he didn't. I made the choice for him. But no one can take another's free will. It has to be given. So although your father feels a bond with me that he does not share with another, I cannot make him do something he does not wish to do. I would have to use more human tactics to achieve that!"

"So the humans are all dead." Aaron nodded. "What about the dragons who sided with Jack?"

"All the dragons who were with Jack at the battle are dead. We are hunting down any others who gave Jack their support, and they will be killed too."

"Is that necessary?"

"Absolutely! A dragon can choose to challenge the Master at any time, but must do so in the open, without subversion. Jack and his supporters planned to wrest Mastership from me using means we consider abhorrent, and as such they are traitors not just to me, but to all dragons. They knew death would be the penalty, should they fail."

Keira nodded. "I saw you kill Jack."

"I ripped out his heart and ate it."

Keira grimaced. "That is ... disgusting."

"It was the tastiest morsel I have had in a long time. If there had been time, I would have savored every ounce of his flesh." Aaron smiled wryly as Keira shuddered. "Dragons aren't the only ones who eat the heart of their enemy," Aaron said. "Many human tribes do that, too."

"Lowering yourself to human standards, are you?"

"No," Aaron replied, "humans learnt that from dragons."

Keira was silent for a moment. "Jack said something about a dragon that will break the curse."

"For a long time dragons believed in a savior that would

free us from the curse. But it's just a story."

"Like the story about dragons being able to turn into living flames?"

Aaron grinned. "Yes, a story like that." His expression grew solemn. "The story goes that one will be born more powerful than any other dragon, and with his power he will break the curse that makes us need human flesh to survive."

"But you don't believe it?"

Aaron shrugged. "Who am I to say? It hasn't happened yet, but perhaps it still will."

Keira was recovering well enough for Aaron to make plans to leave Drake Manor and travel to Dracomere, but a few days before they were to leave, Aaron came to find Keira as she sat in the warm sunshine just beyond the courtyard.

"The prince has asked me to call on him," Aaron said. "He has heard that the dragon was killed and wants to thank me in person."

"Then you must go," Keira said.

"He wants to see you, too."

"He's not inviting us to another ball, is he?"

"No. He demands our presence at court in the morning." Aaron frowned.

"He's the prince," Keira said. "He can do what he wants."

"He may be a prince, but I am not his subject."

"But he doesn't know that. I am happy to go with you, Aaron."

Aaron growled under his breath. "Very well."

The next morning Aaron flew himself and Keira to the palace, landing as close as he dared without taking the risk of being seen. Once suitably attired, he led Keira towards the palace and into the courtyard. Entering the door, they headed up the stairs and into the antechamber, where they took a seat. There was no-one else in the room, and Aaron curled his fingers around Keira's as they waited. A few minutes passed before the door was opened, but it was clear that

Aaron and Keira were expected.

"Master Drake, Milady, please, His Highness is waiting," said the chamberlain. They followed the man into the room beyond.

"Ah! Aaron Drake and his lovely wife." The prince rose to his feet as Aaron and Keira made their way across the floor, stopping to bow to His Royal Highness in proper courtly fashion. As before, men stood around the room, engaged in private conversations as they watched Aaron. The prince turned towards the others with a flick of his hand.

"Everyone, out. I wish to have a few private words with Master Drake." A few of the men cast curious glances at Aaron as they filed past him, and within moments the room was empty.

Unlike the other times Keira had seen the prince, he was dressed in a simple tunic of dark green that hung below his waist, and brown breeches. The effect was somber, making Keira wonder what all this was about. He stood a few feet away from Aaron, gazing at him with eyes narrowed. Aaron looked down at the him, meeting his gaze calmly as he waited for the prince to speak. After a long moment, Alfred turned away and started to pace the length of the room, his hands clasped behind his back.

"Aaron Drake." He spoke the words slowly, as though his very name contained a coded message. "The last time I saw you was under this very roof. However, you left without my permission, taking your lovely lady with you. A few of my other guests were also noticed as missing."

"Indeed?" Aaron said. Keira glanced at Aaron to see a slight frown furrowing his forehead. "For myself, I can only say that urgent business called me and my wife away, but please accept my belated apologies."

"Of course, Aaron. Urgent business, you say? Something to do with a certain dragon?"

"Yes, it was, actually."

"Ah!" Alfred paused in his pacing and turned to look at

Aaron. "And I understand that the threat from the dragon has been removed."

"You understand correctly."

The prince nodded, resuming his pacing before speaking again. "I am most curious to know, Aaron, how this was accomplished."

Aaron's finger tapped the side of the leg, but his tone was even. "The dragon was killed by another dragon."

"Really? Fascinating!" Alfred said.

Keira shot Aaron a puzzled look, but he was staring at the prince. She saw his nostrils flare as he breathed in deeply.

"Were you there?" the prince continued.

"I was."

"So you saw the dragon being killed?"

"I did."

Alfred had reached the end of the room and turned back, stopping when he came abreast of Aaron. "You know, Aaron, I heard the most fantastic story recently. Would you like me to share it with you?"

"If it so pleases Your Majesty, I would be delighted," Aaron replied.

"Good!" Prince Alfred rubbed his hands together. "A man came to court the other day, requesting an audience with me. Usually I would have someone else deal with a man like this, but he said he had information about a dragon. Or, I should say, dragons." The prince took a few steps closer. "He said he had been forced to drink dragon's blood." The prince stared at Aaron as he spoke, their gazes locking.

"Interesting," Aaron said, his tone bland. "I have heard of humans drinking dragon blood, but it doesn't usually turn out well for the human."

"No, it didn't seem to turn out too well for this human, either, although he fared better than his fellows. He said he was one of eight men who drank dragon blood, but was the only one to escape with his life. The others were killed by another dragon as they traveled from some small island by means of a rowboat. When the dragon attacked, the boat flipped over in the water, trapping the man beneath the hull, thereby saving his life. He said the dragon who gave them his blood controlled them and forced them to do things they did not wish to do." Alfred paused for a moment, his gaze intent. "But the story gets even more interesting," he continued. "He also said that dragons can take on the form and manners of man." Keira saw Aaron's hand tighten into a fist, but his expression gave nothing away. "They even had a name for the dragon," the prince continued. "Jack."

"Jack? Well, that is a fairly common name."

"Yes, indeed." The prince turned away again. "He spoke about Jack wanting revenge on another dragon – and planning to use that dragon's wife to exact that revenge." A small gasp escaped Keira, and Aaron turned to her, his gaze meeting hers as he shook his head.

"That is an interesting story."

"Isn't it? There is more, however," the prince continued. "He also mentioned a girl. The girl and her sister, the other dragon's wife, had been abducted by Jack and taken to some rocky hideout, where they had been locked away. The girl mentioned that her sister was married to the Dragon Master. She also gave the Master a name. What do you suppose it was?"

"I cannot imagine, Your Highness," Aaron said tightly.

The prince smiled. "Can you not? Well it is quite a coincidence, since the Dragon Master apparently shares the same name as you, Aaron."

"Indeed?"

"Yes. And the coincidences continue." The prince turned to Keira. "Tell me, Lady Drake, what is your sister's name?"

Keira drew in a deep breath. "Anna, Your Highness."

"Anna! Imagine that! That is the same name as the girl." The prince took a step towards Aaron, his eyes watching him intently. "Tell me, Aaron Drake, what exactly are you?"

Aaron returned the prince's gaze, but remained silent.

"Do you consider yourself a loyal subject?" the prince asked softly.

"I believe I have proven my loyalty to you many times over, Alfred," Aaron replied, his voice just as low. The prince's brows rose slightly at the informal use of his name.

"Yes, I cannot doubt your loyalty. It is your subjugation I am wondering about."

Aaron gazed down at the prince. "I am subject only to God," he replied.

"I am a prince of this realm, and will be king when my father dies. Everything in this land will be under my dominion. Do you consider yourself to be above my rule?"

"Your rule extends only to the human realm. As you have rightly surmised, that is a realm of which I am not a part."

"You are not human?"

"I am not."

"You are a dragon?"

"I am."

"Are you this Dragon Master that the man was talking about?"

"I am."

The prince looked at Aaron speculatively. "You are aware that by knowing your secret, I hold the means to destroy you?"

Aaron's eyes flared slightly, and the prince took a hasty step back. Lifting his fist, Aaron opened his hand to show a flame burning in his palm. "I am the most powerful creature on this earth, Your Highness," Aaron said softly. "I can kill you in a single instant, and burn this fortress to the ground. If humans choose to wage a war against dragons, the earth will soon be emptied of humans. There is very little you can do to kill me." He closed his fist, extinguishing the flame. "But I have not once tried to harm you, and instead have chosen to help you. I have not placed myself above you, but instead have offered you my loyalty. I will never be subject to you, Alfred, but I do call you my friend. But remember, dragons live very long lives, and we have very long memories. If you reveal to anyone what you know about me or any of my kin, I will destroy you."

The prince's face paled, and Keira saw him swallow hard.

"Of course, Aaron, I would never seek to harm you. As you say, you have already shown me your loyalty."

"Of course," Aaron replied smoothly.

The prince glanced over at Keira. "The Lady Drake," he said to Aaron, "she is ... er ... is she human?"

"I am," Keira replied tightly.

"She is," reiterated Aaron, throwing Keira a wry smile. "But do not, for one moment, think she is weak because of that. Apart from the fact that my blood courses through her veins" – the prince paled even more as Keira smiled – "she has the protection of every dragon in this land."

"I'm sure she does," the prince said weakly. "I was just curious." He walked over to his throne, and sank down on the seat.

"Quite understandable," Aaron said. "Is there anything further you wish to discuss?"

"No, thank you for responding to my summons, Master Drake."

"Of course. And I will do so again should the need arise. I remain your friend, Alfred."

"Thank you, Aaron."

Aaron nodded, and taking Keira by the hand, turned his back on the prince and started towards the door.

"Wait!"

Aaron stopped and turned a questioning glance on the prince.

"How old are you, exactly?"

Aaron grinned as he responded. "Let's just say, I remember the birth of your great-grandfather."

The prince's mouth dropped open as Aaron turned and pulled Keira from the room.

"That went well," Keira said with a laugh, but Aaron's

expression was solemn.

"That depends on your definition of 'well.' The prince now knows not only that dragons can appear as humans, but that I am their Master. If he gives this knowledge to anyone, the consequences could be dire."

"Do you think he will?"

"He may feel that he should share this knowledge with his advisors. It is regrettable that Max missed that one human; however, there is nothing more to be done. Let's get away from here."

They were nearing the staircase when someone behind them called Aaron's name. Aaron's hand tightened around Keira's as he slowly turned to look at the caller.

"Elise."

Tugging her hand free, Keira stared at the beautiful woman whom she had last seen at the ball as she walked towards them.

"Aaron, I was told you and your wife were here." She turned with a smile to Keira. "I had to meet the woman who has made Aaron so happy. He told me he never knew it was possible for him to love anyone the way he loves you." She glanced at Aaron. "Aaron knows that I care for him, and knowing that he has found someone pleases me a great deal." She looked back to Keira. "I wish you all the happiness in the world, Mistress."

"Thank you," Keira said with smile. The woman nodded, and turning around with a swish of her gown, walked away without a backward glance. Keira looked at Aaron, who raised his eyebrows at her with a smile. She smiled back, and taking his hand in hers, allowed him to lead her away.

CHAPTER FORTY-SIX

Anna remained at Drake Manor when Aaron and Keira left for Dracomere. Spring gave way to summer, and she spent the days with the children, sometimes teaching them their letters, and sometimes exploring the great estate with them in the warm summer sun. Owain had a splendid library, and Anna would pass the evenings reading, or playing games with the others. Once Cathryn and Favian had invited Anna to travel with them into the city, and she rode with Cathryn on Favian's broad back. They had stayed the night, and in the evening they went to a play at the newly built theater near the river. It was exciting to watch the players act out the story on a stage built just for them, with benches for the audience to sit upon, and Anna had felt sorry for the actors when a few people in the audience threw rotten vegetables at them because they did not approve of the performance.

Midsummer came and went, and the days were already growing shorter before they received news that Aaron and Keira would be back at Drake Manor in another week.

Anna sat in the grass watching Bronwyn as she twirled around.

"Aunty Anna! Look at me!"

"I see you," Anna replied with a laugh.

"Aunty Anna? When is Uncle Aaron coming back? And Aunty Keira?"

"Uncle Aaron and Aunty Keira will be back in two days. Do you know what day that is?"

Bronwyn thought for a while.

"Friday," she finally said.

"Correct!"

"Aunty Anna?"

"Hmm?"

"Will you stay here when Aunty Keira goes to Storbrook?"

"No, Bron, I need to go home too."

"But why? Why can't you stay here?"

Anna wrapped her arms around the little girl and pulled her close.

"Because Storbrook is my home."

"But this could be your home."

"I wish I didn't have to leave you and your brother, but I will visit whenever I can. All right?"

Anna could see the 'no' forming on Bronwyn's lips, and she placed her finger over her mouth.

"I won't forget about you, I promise. But I do have to go."

Bronwyn stared at her for a moment, then dropped her head.

"All right," she whispered.

Anna hugged her tightly, before gently pushing her to arm's length. "Let's get the grass out of your hair before your mother sees what a ragamuffin you have become!" Bronwyn giggled as Anna bent to her task.

It was high noon when Aaron and Keira arrived on Friday, the sun glinting off Aaron's back as he glided down to the wide swath of lawn before the house. More than six months had passed since Anna had last seen Keira, and she rushed over to her sister with outstretched arms.

"I'm so glad to see you," Anna said. "How are you?"

"Very well. Dracomere is the most wonderful place, and Aaron took such great care of me." Keira threw a quick look at Aaron, whose fiery gaze seemed to burn even brighter. "I have much to tell you, but the first thing is, I'm with child."

"With child?" Anna threw her arms around Keira once more. "That's wonderful!"

"It is very early yet, but I'm confident that all will be well. Aaron has been forcing me to drink his blood every day. He thinks it may be twins."

"Twins?" Anna turned to look at the dragon once more. "How does he know?"

"He can hear the heartbeats, and he's certain there are two." Keira turned a loving smile on the dragon. "Time will tell if he is right." She returned her gaze to Anna. "It is lovely to be back at Drake Manor, but I am looking forward to returning to Storbrook. Are you ready to go back?"

"Yes," Anna said, nodding. She glanced around, taking in the house, the gardens, and the woods in the distance. She saw the children chasing after a duck, and watched them fondly for a moment, before turning her gaze back to Keira. "I'm ready," she said. "Let's go home."

GLOSSARY OF TERMS

The setting for this story is the Medieval period or the High Middle Ages, which covers roughly the time period from AD 1000 to 1300. In the course of the story I have used terms that not everyone is familiar with. Below is an explanation of these terms.

Bower – a private study or sitting room for the lady of the house.

Cabinet – a study or library.

Carol – a dance (not a song) where everyone holds hands and dances in a circle.

Doublet – a tight-fitting jacket that buttons up the front.

Great Hall – a multi-purpose room for receiving guests, conducting business, eating meals, and when necessary, sleeping.

Kirtle – a gown worn over a chemise and laced across the front, side or back.

Reeve – an overseer of a town, reporting to the local lord. (In this story, Aaron Drake is referred to as 'milord', a title used for someone of superior social standing. However, he is not the lord of the district, and the reeve does not report to him.) The word 'sheriff' comes from the word reeve. The reeve carries a white stick as a symbol of his authority.

Solar – a private sitting room used by family and close friends. The word solar does not refer to the sun, but rather to the fact that the room has sole or private use.

Tunic – a garment pulled over the head that reaches around mid-thigh. It is worn over a shirt and cinched at the waist with a belt.

A note about meals. During the Early and High Middle Ages, the entire household typically ate meals together. There were only two meals a day, although the working classes would usually eat something small, such as a piece of bread, when they first arose and before they started working. The first meal, called dinner, was served at around 11 a.m. and was the larger meal, with numerous courses. A second meal was served in the late afternoon.

If you are interested in learning more about the Medieval period, head over to the author's website, www.lindakhopkins.com.

CONTINUE READING FOR A PREVIEW OF THE NEXT
BOOK IN *THE DRAGON ARCHIVES*,
DANCE WITH A DRAGON

CHAPTER ONE

"Mistress Anna!"

Anna turned to watch Peggy as she rushed along the stone passage.

"I've lost the twins again," Peggy said. She clutched her skirts as she tittered nervously. "They are always escaping me."

Anna sighed. It was true that Zachary and Lydia were quick on their feet, but this was the third time *today*. "Have you searched the gardens?"

"Yes. They aren't anywhere!" The last word ended on a wail, and Peggy quickly covered her mouth with her hand, her gaze searching the walls and ceiling as if expecting to find a monster lurking between the stones. Or maybe she was just looking for a pair of four-year-olds. Her voice dropped to a whisper. "Do you think they are …?" She nodded at the ceiling, indicating the floor above, where the master's chambers were situated.

Anna shrugged. "Probably. Why don't you go and check?"

Peggy's face paled slightly. "I couldn't possibly," she whispered. "What if *it* is there?" *It* was the dragon of Storbrook Castle, a huge, winged beast that came and went as it pleased. It was well-known amongst the servants of Storbrook that Master Aaron Drake had no fear of the dragon, and allowed it free access into all the upper chambers, including those of his wife, the lady Keira. He even allowed his children to play with the monster, quite unconcerned about the danger it posed.

Anna knew it was pointless to try and convince Peggy that the dragon was harmless. "I'll go find them," she said. "Wait for us in the nursery."

"Oh, thank you," Peggy said. "It's just that their supper is growing cold and …" She trailed into silence as Anna turned away and headed towards the staircase.

Anna's shoes rang against the hard stone as she mounted the wide staircase that led to the upper floors. A low growl reached her as she walked along the dingy passage, followed by childish shrieks. The sounds came from the direction of the master's chambers, and the growl was definitely not human. Pushing open the heavy wooden door, Anna stepped across the threshold, taking in the scene before her.

The room she'd stepped into was huge, stretching thirty feet from one side to the other. The ceilings soared high above her, while overlooking the range of mountains was a series of large, arched windows that reached almost as high as the ceiling. The center of the room was bare of all furnishings, and lying in the middle of the stone floor was an enormous, golden dragon. Anna paused, staring at the magnificent creature. She never failed to feel a sense of awe at the beast who was now a member of her family. He had a long neck, which, when raised, stretched taller than her, while golden horns curved from the top of his skull. Sharp rows of teeth lined his long snout, from which blazing flames sometimes spewed. His cat-like eyes gleamed yellow, but when aroused by emotion, they were windows into the flaming furnace that burned within him, revealing leaping flames. Huge wings lay folded over his scaly back, and a long tail armed with sharp spikes curved around his body. Keira, Anna's sister, was leaning against his side, her feet drawn up beneath her, a book resting against her knees. She looked up as Anna entered the room.

"We've been reading a story," she said.

"I can see you have a rapt audience," Anna replied in amusement. The children Anna had come to retrieve were clambering over the huge back of the dragon, clutching the folded wings in tight fists.

"They're still listening!" Keira said, frowning when Anna laughed.

"I'm sure they are," Anna said.

The dragon, who was watching the children on his back, looked up at Anna with a grin. "They've heard the story so many times, they know it by heart," he said.

Anna laughed, then nodded at the children. "Peggy is looking for them," she said. "Again!"

"Oh dear," Keira said with a sigh. "They do seem to frequently escape her attention."

"And she is far too scared to come here to look for them," Anna added.

"So she should be," said the dragon. He turned to look at Keira. "Perhaps it is time to hire a tutor for them."

"They are only four," Keira protested.

"Ah, yes, but they are dragons, so they will learn very quickly."

Keira laughed. "Of course! How dull of me to forget that the children of the Dragon Master will be superior in every possible way to any other children." She rose to her feet and turned to face the creature. "But maybe they inherited their intelligence from their mother."

Aaron brought his face close to hers. "Then they are doubly blessed, my sweet," he said. She smiled and ran her hand down his snout, before turning to look at her offspring.

"Zachary! Lydia! Nurse Peggy has been looking for you."

Neither of the children paid their mother the slightest attention, but were instead intent on the task of walking bravely along the length of their father's back towards his tail. Opening his wings, he gave a gentle shake and they fell onto the outstretched appendages, sliding onto the stone with a thump when he lowered them. Anna winced, but the children rose to their feet unhurt. Lydia looked at her mother, then dropped her gaze to the ground, but Zachary placed his hands on his waist and gave his father a defiant stare.

"I don't want to play with Nurse Peggy. I want to play with you."

"I want to play with you, too, son," said the dragon, "but you should never have run away from Nurse." Zachary glared for another moment, but at his father's upraised eyebrows, his expression crumpled.

"But I want to be with you," he said. "Make Nursey go away."

"No. You need to learn to listen to her and be more obedient. But if you go with Aunty Anna now, then I will come see you in the nursery after supper." Zach smiled.

"Like this?" he said.

"No, silly," Lydia said with a giggle. "Nursey's scared of Papa when he's a dragon." Zach's expression went from incredulity to outright disbelief.

"Papa's *not* scary," he said, with a stomp of a foot.

"Off you go with your Aunty," Keira said. "You have kept Nurse waiting long enough, and your father has said he will come find you later."

"Will you take us for a ride?" Zach asked the dragon as

Anna took him by the hand.

"We'll see, son. Perhaps if you behave yourselves." The dragon pushed himself to his full height, and looked down at them with his bony eyebrows raised.

"Yes, Father," said the boy with a sigh, allowing Anna to finally take him by the hand and lead him and his sister from the room.

Anna marched the children down the stairs and delivered them to their relieved nurse, waiting in the nursery. She watched for a while as they dutifully sat down at the table and waited for Peggy to serve them their food. Peggy had been hired at Storbrook when the children were toddlers. Only a few years older than Keira, she had spent the years of her youth caring for an elderly parent. Shy and slightly awkward, she was never completely comfortable around other adults, but she loved being with the children. Her biggest fear, however, was for the dragon who was a regular feature of the Storbrook landscape. Although the creature never came near her, she trembled when it circled the skies, or when its roar rang through the stone mountain-top castle, certain that the beast was about to eat them all. Zach watched Peggy as she bustled around the room, giving her a penetrating stare.

"What is it, Zach?" she finally asked.

"Are you scared of Papa?" he asked.

Peggy looked at him in surprise. "Scared of your Papa? Why would you think that?"

"Well, because he's —"

At his words, Lydia, with an insight that went beyond her years, smacked her brother on the arm.

"Shh," she said loudly, her finger over her lips as she glared at Zach. She turned to Peggy. "Papa can be scary looking sometimes."

Peggy stared at Lydia for a moment as the color rose in her cheeks, before turning and brushing nonexistent crumbs from the table.

"I'm not scared of your father," Peggy whispered,

"although he can be quite, er, stern at times. I do wish he wouldn't let the dragon near the castle, though."

"But the dragon is ..." Zach began, and Anna quickly intervened.

"Zach," she said, "I have a surprise for you." The boy looked at his aunt eagerly.

"What su'p'ise?" he said.

"If you are very good, I will ask Cook to bake you a honeyed apple."

"Me too?" Lydia asked.

"Yes, you too," Anna said with a smile. She knelt down between the two chairs, watching for a moment until Peggy's back was turned before speaking again, her voice low.

"Do you remember what your Papa said about keeping secrets?" she said. Zach and Lydia both nodded. "Nurse must never know that your Papa is a dragon. All right?" Lydia stared at her in silence as Zach nodded. "You can only have a baked apple if you keep the secret." Again both children nodded. "Good," Anna said with a smile. She rose to her feet, and watched as Peggy poured warm milk into wooden cups and placed them on the table, before turning and leaving the room, confident that the importance of keeping the family secret had been impressed on Zach, at least for now.

Descending the stairs, Anna crossed the low hall, where the servants slept, and exited the castle into the warmth of a late spring day. She skirted the courtyard and headed into the gardens, pausing at a large spreading oak. They had celebrated the twins' fourth birthday beneath the shade of the tree just a few days before. A quilt had been spread over the new grass, and Cook had made honeyed cakes and sticky buns, served with warm milk, straight from the cowshed. The twins had polished off the treats, complaining later that their stomachs ached.

Anna smiled at the memory. It was hard to believe four years had passed since the twins were born – and more than five since she and Keira had been abducted by Jack, a rogue dragon seeking vengeance against Aaron, the Dragon Master. Jack had been killed in the resulting fray, and Keira had been grievously injured, saved only because Aaron had insisted she drink his blood a few days before. And then there had been Max. Anna closed her eyes, and pushed the memory away. She had not seen Max since the day he left the dragon domain, and although he often crept into her thoughts, bringing with him a tangle of yearning, regret and shame, she was determined to put him from her mind and get on with her life.

Anna leaned back against the tree and lifted her face to the sunlight, the new leaves painting a pattern of shadows against her skin. The sounds of the castle rose in a hum behind her, while closer at hand, birds twittered in the trees. It was calm and serene, but her soul was anything but serene. She took a deep breath, then pushed herself away from the knobbly trunk, annoyed at the disquiet she felt. She loved living at Storbrook, being with her sister, and helping with her young niece and nephew, but there were times when she felt like Storbrook was a cord wrapped around her neck, slowly choking her. It wasn't Aaron and Keira's fault, of course, but there were times when all she wanted was a life of her own. She sighed and turned back towards the castle, waving at Garrick, the castle groundsman, as he led a horse across the courtyard. He waved back with a smile, his eyes lifting to watch her as she walked. The smile turned to a grimace when he stepped into a pile of muck that had not been cleaned away, and Anna snorted back a laugh as she continued towards the doorway. She had friends and family – surely that should be enough?

CHAPTER TWO

Anna adjusted herself in her saddle, leaning back as the horse picked its way down the steep path that led through the mountains to the village where she had grown up. Garrick rode a few feet ahead of her, and she watched his back as he rolled easily with the movement of his mount. A year younger than her, he had filled out from the gangly youth she first met almost six years ago when she moved to Storbrook. His sandy-colored hair had darkened to brown, and his blue eyes creased at the corners when he smiled.

He was a man of few words, and did not seem to notice the glances that were frequently thrown his way by the young maids at Storbrook or in the village. When Anna had returned with Keira and Aaron after the troubles with Jack, it was Garrick who teased her out of her doldrums, dragging her through the forest while he trapped rabbits and hunted deer. He was an excellent marksman, and often it was his skill that placed meat on the tables at Storbrook. He had taught her about birds, pointing out the secret places where the hidden nests of robins and sparrows could be found, then dragging her away so the birds would not be anxious. He made her lie still for hours on end as they watched a spider spin her web, until finally Anna's fidgeting grew too much for even him to ignore. They swam in the river, and lay on the rocks in the sun afterwards, and once, he had kissed her on the forehead, then turned away in embarrassment. There had been a few moments of awkward silence, before he jumped into the deep pool formed by the river, drenching her from head to toe, and she had yelled at him while he laughed. Later, when she thought about it, she decided that it had been a brotherly kiss, and meant nothing more. She was relieved at this conclusion, although she did not think to wonder why. As the years went by, she sought him out while he mucked in the stables or chopped wood behind the shed. He would stop and smile at her, and occasionally tease her into helping him. She smiled now at the memories. Garrick was a good friend – probably better than she deserved.

It was over thirty miles to the village from Storbrook, but they made it in good time, reaching the outskirts of the village before noon. Garrick turned to face Anna. "I'll fetch you from your parents, shall I?" he asked.

She shook her head. "No, I'll meet you at the churchyard. I don't plan to visit for long, since I have a list of purchases I want to make in the village." Garrick nodded, then turned away, taking the path to the village smith, while Anna took the path that led to her old home. She made this trip every few weeks, sometimes with Garrick, other times with Thomas, Aaron's steward. Keira would often accompany her as well, bringing the children along, and then Aaron would carry them all on his back. But Aaron had urgent matters to attend to this day, and it was too far for the children to travel the distance on horseback in one day, so they had remained behind. Anna did not mind. She knew she was quite safe with Garrick, and his silence gave her time alone with her thoughts as they rode down the mountain.

Richard and Jenny Carver lived in a small house at the edge of the village. Richard was a Master Craftsman, and his wooden wares were sold in many of the surrounding towns and villages, gracing the tables of poor and wealthy alike. He was also the village reeve, employed in the service of Lord Warren to represent the people of the village as well as serve the lord's interests. The previous reeve, Matthew Hobbes, had been intent on killing the Storbrook dragon, a foolish mistake which had almost cost him his life, and left him with a serious injury. Richard had also been injured – not by the dragon, but by another villager who had accidentally impaled him with a pitchfork. It was the dragon's blood, spilt over his wounds, that saved Richard's life, an action that had won Richard's undying gratitude. He looked up through the doorway of his workshop as Anna approached, and with a wide smile hurried out to greet her.

"Are you here alone?" he asked, glancing behind her, and Anna could hear the slight regret in his tone. He loved his daughters, but it was Aaron that he revered.

"Yes, just me," she replied lightly. She hooked her arm around Richard's and led him towards the house. "Aaron and Keira send their regards, of course," she said as they crossed over the threshold. Jenny was sitting near the fire when Anna entered the small parlor at the front of the house. The passing years had not been kind to Jenny, and she looked far older than her forty-eight years. She smiled at Anna, but her eyes were dull, lined with black rings, while the skin sagged around her cheekbones.

"Anna, you have come to visit. How lovely."

"Yes, Mother," Anna said, dragging a stool towards her parent and taking her frail hands. "How are you doing today?"

"Not well, Anna, not well. I believe I'm not long for this world." Anna glanced at Richard, and he smiled sadly.

"Dame Lamb came to see your mother this morning," he explained. "She says there is nothing more to be done."

Anna turned back to Jenny, who was already patting her hand. "We are all marked for death, daughter," she said. "I have many regrets in life, but at least I know one daughter has a secure future, even if he is not the man I would have chosen. Now if I can just see *you* married, I could be at peace, ready to meet my Maker."

"Well, Mother," she replied, "it may be that God has seen fit to leave me a spinster. There are few men as worthy as Father, or Aaron, so I am quite content to remain in the unmarried state." She saw the dismay in Jenny's face, but was saved from reproach by the announcement that dinner was served.

"Come Mother," Anna said, helping Jenny to her feet. "Let me help you to the table."

Anna did not stay long after the meal was finished. She led Jenny to her room and helped her lie down on the bed. The fire had died down a little, and she stoked it back into flames before shutting the light from the windows and closing the door behind her. Richard had already returned to his workshop, but he lifted his head to give a distracted wave goodbye as she walked past.

Nothing in the village was a great distance apart, and it took Anna only a few minutes to reach the high street, with its collection of shops and services. It ran perpendicular to the churchyard, and Anna paused to tie her horse next to Garrick's before continuing on her way. Someone called her name, and she turned, her heart sinking when she saw Sarah Draper hurrying towards her.

"Anna! How lovely to see you! You have become quite the stranger!" She hooked her arm around Anna's, dragging her along the street. "I must confess, I am surprised to see that you are still alive and well."

Anna pulled her arm free. "Why?"

Sarah laughed shrilly. "Well, you do live in the mountains with a dragon."

"The dragon would never harm me."

"It would if Aaron Drake allowed it to," Sarah responded knowingly. "But I'm not really interested in hideous monsters. It is Garrick Flynn I want to hear about. Did I see him at the smith?" Anna shrugged. "He is so handsome," Sarah continued. "I'm sure he would kiss a girl very prettily."

"I wouldn't know," Anna said.

"He wouldn't be able to resist *me*," Sarah said, slyly. "I'm going to tell him you are delayed, and that you sent me to tell him."

"No." Anna was aghast. "Do what you will, but do not drag me into your affairs."

"Oh, la," Sarah said with a wave of her hand, before running lightly down the road, and disappearing around the corner. Anna watched her for a moment, then with a slight shrug of her shoulders, turned in the direction of the shops.

Anna took her time completing her purchases. She ordered new boots from the shoemaker, selecting the softest and most supple leather; she stopped by the parchmenter to pick up a roll of parchment; and she spent twenty minutes selecting a fine woolen worsted at the milliner to make a new gown. It had been dyed a soft blue, and Anna was sure the color would become her. She reached the end of the high street, where the cobbled paving petered into a muddy lane, before she turned around and headed back in the direction she had come. She had forgotten Sarah Draper and her plans to trap Garrick, but as she neared the end of the street, she was startled to see Sarah stomping towards her, scowling furiously. She glared at Anna as she walked past, but said nothing. Anna glanced towards the trees where the horses had been tied, and saw Garrick staring angrily after Sarah, arms crossed and eyes narrowed.

"That woman is entirely lacking in propriety," he growled as Anna drew near, "and refuses to even consider that her advances may not be welcome. She would have thrown me to the ground if given half a chance. Even so, I had to endure her touching and stroking me until I was forced to give the harshest putdown."

"Am I correct in understanding," Anna said with a grin, "that Sarah Draper is not the kind of woman you admire?"

Garrick's angry gaze swung to Anna, until a reluctant grin tugged at his mouth. "No, Sarah Draper is not the kind of woman I admire."

"Tell me, then," Anna said playfully, "what kind of woman *do* you admire?"

The smile dropped from Garrick's face, and he turned away to check the straps on Anna's horse. "A woman who can engage in a good conversation without being coy. A woman with spirit and fortitude. A woman who knows how to endure trials and still be cheerful."

Anna was silent, taken aback at the directness of his response, and she wished she hadn't posed the question. Garrick moved to the horse's head and checked the bit, before turning towards Anna, cupping his hands to boost her into the saddle. He did not meet her gaze, but when he placed his hand on her back to steady her, it lingered a moment longer than necessary. She saw a frown crease his brow before he turned away and mounted his own horse. He turned onto the path that wound behind the church and towards the forest at the foothills of the mountains. He did not speak as they crossed the open fields, but when they gained the shade of the trees, he drew his horse to a halt, forcing Anna, who was a step behind, to stop as well.

"Anna." He paused.

"Do you think we will reach Storbrook before nightfall?" she said.

Garrick shook his head. "Probably not." He was staring at her, and she looked away, suddenly uncomfortable.

"Well, I hope it won't get too cold. My cloak is not very warm," she said. "Perhaps if we –"

"Anna." Garrick's voice was firm. "There is something I would say."

She glanced back at him, and shook her head. "No."

"I cannot keep silent any longer. It is destroying me to see you every day, and not speak of how I feel. I have waited for some sign from you – anything that I could take as an encouragement, but my patience is wearing thin."

"Please, Garrick –"

"Tell me, Anna, do you feel anything for me?" he said.

Anna turned away and stared into the trees. "Garrick," she finally said, "I like you very much. You are a good man, and I consider you a great friend."

"A good man. A great friend." Garrick laughed dryly. "Words of the damned. You're still hankering after that dragon, aren't you?"

Anna turned to him with a look of surprise as her heart skittered within her chest. "What are you talking about?"

"Don't take me for a fool, Anna. I have lived at Storbrook most of my life, and like everyone else who lives there, I know exactly what Master Drake is. Don't worry," he added as she pulled in a startled breath, "we all know that there are some secrets that must be kept. But that does not change what Master Drake is, or the friends that arrive at the dead of night, through entrances other than the gate. Friends like Max Brant." The air was suddenly too heavy to breath. "You still have feelings for him," Garrick continued. "Even after all these years. But where is he now, Anna? He left you, didn't he? Probably without a backward glance."

Anna looked away as a pounding grew in her ears. "No," she whispered. "It wasn't like that."

"No? Then where is he now? He's not here, Anna." Garrick paused, then added gently, "But I am." Anna glanced down at the ground. A small, brown beetle was clinging to the edge of a leaf, dry and speckled with spots, and she watched as it fell on its back, its little legs waving furiously in the air, before it righted itself. Garrick leaned closer. "Anna," he said, "I love you. I know your feelings for me are not the same, but I love you enough for both of us. I want you to become my wife." She glanced up at him in dismay. "We could be happy," he continued quickly. "We already have friendship, which is more than many couples start with, and in time you will learn to love me." She opened her mouth to respond, but he covered her lips with his fingers. "Think about it, please," he said. "At least give me that much." She stared at him for a moment, then dropping her eyes, nodded slowly. "Thank you," he said, pulling his fingers away. He stared at her for another long moment, then turning away, nudged his horse down the path, as Anna did the same.

The rest of the journey was traversed in silence. Anna's first thoughts had been of bewilderment, dismay, and wild refusal, but as the initial shock wore off, she was able to consider Garrick's words with more composure. She didn't love him, it was true, but she had been honest when she said he was a good man, and she knew he would treat her well. And she could learn to love him. It wouldn't be wild or passionate, but steady and enduring. She would have a husband who loved her, and a home of her own, filled with children. She would have a life that did not depend on Keira or Aaron. A life that was hers alone. That was what she wanted, wasn't it?

I am thrilled to offer my readers free short stories from *The Dragon Archives*. Head over to my website, www.lindakhopkins.com and click on the tab, Short Stories, to learn more.

ACKNOWLEDGMENTS

Thank you to my friends and family for your support and encouragement. Special thanks goes to Belinda, Tara and Vickie for reading my draft and providing such valuable feedback.

And, as always, thank you Claye, Kristin and Bethany for giving me time and space to pursue my dreams. Love you guys!

ABOUT THE AUTHOR

Linda K. Hopkins is originally from South Africa, but now lives in Calgary, Canada with her husband and two daughters. Head over to her website, www.lindakhopkins.com, to learn more about the author.

BOOKS BY LINDA K. HOPKINS

Books in *The Dragon Archives* Series
Bound by a Dragon
Pursued by a Dragon
Loved by a Dragon
Dance with a Dragon
Forever a Dragon

Other Books
Moondance